SERIAL KILLER

A. S. FRENCH

NEONOIR BOOKS

ALSO BY A. S. FRENCH

Crime Fiction and Thrillers

The Astrid Snow series

Book one: Don't Fear the Reaper

Book two: The Killing Moon

Book three: Lost in America

Book four: Gone to Texas

Book five: The Final Girl

The Ophelia Red series

Book one: Ophelia Red

The Detective Jen Flowers series

Book one: The Hashtag Killer

Book two: Serial Killer

Book three: Night Killer

Book four: The Killer Inside Them

Northern Crime Fiction

Where The Bodies Are Buried

Crime Short Stories

Call Me: An Astrid Snow Short Story

Dark Snow: An Astrid Snow Short Story

Bette Davis Eyes: Detective Flowers Short Story

Writing as Andrew. S. French

Science Fiction

The Time Traveller's Murder

The Mercy Sleep

Bodies

The Arcane Supernatural Thriller Series

Book one: The Arcane

Book two: The Arcane Identity

Book three: The Arcane Quest

Book four: The Arcane Ultimatum

The Ella Finn Fantasy Novella Series

Ella and the Elementals

Ella and the Multiverse

Ella and the Monsters

Ella and the Dreamers

Supernatural Short Stories

Dead Souls

The Shadow

Go to www.andrewsfrench.com for more information.

1 EXERCISE ONE

Eddie Blair had been born in the same room his mother died. He learnt this on his sixth birthday, discovering how his introduction into the world robbed his father of the love of his life. His mother's death left an invisible burden which dragged them into a relationship neither understood. There were other things about Eddie his father never recognised, obstacles adding to the wall between them. He tried to crack the barrier, but to no avail. His mother was gone and his father distant, so he sought a connection elsewhere.

It started with running. First, at school, but he continued outside when he could. Once he was away from the other kids, beyond the insults hurled at him, he'd go home to get changed, and then run out again. His father was never around, so it didn't matter what he did. He kept on running, jogging and sprinting dependent upon his mood. It focused his mind and calmed the noise behind his eyes. Eddie knew the running would help him someday, and it did; all that time and effort, pushing his body to the limit, sent him towards a better existence.

He never forgot when his life improved. It was the day

he left school with no qualifications and told his father he wouldn't follow in the old man's footsteps. His father's face crumpling into utter disgust was all Eddie needed to understand he had to make his own way in life. A decade later, he knew some would say he'd wasted his life, but he didn't care. He was fit, healthy, and never short of female company. Why would any bloke his age be disappointed with that?

Eddie had a lot to thank the running for, which was why he'd never stopped. Five times a week, he hit the streets in his continuous pursuit of a greater connection. Thirty minutes into his morning run, he paused against the nearest tree; sweat streamed down his head as his legs ached, and he forced oxygen into his lungs. The haze of last night's partying played havoc with his head, but he felt great to be alive. He scanned the surrounding area, taking in the trees' aroma and the fresh grass nibbling at his new running shoes. Birds flew and sang above him, an idyllic sight which lifted his spirits. It still amazed him so few people had discovered this part of London, this uncorrupted woodland which presented the perfect path for joggers and nature lovers alike. In all the time he'd taken this route, he'd only seen other people on one occasion when he caught a couple getting down and dirty in the bushes. The memory of it made him smile as the sun caressed his face and he reached for the bottle. He only drank one mineral water brand and had been lucky to get the last one from the shop before entering the woods.

He sipped at the drink as a squirrel scampered across the leaves, the liquid chilling his throat. His heart was thumping against his chest and inside his head, but he heard the crunch of branches behind him. He glanced over his shoulder and gazed into the trees. He peered into the greenery, but it was empty.

Water dribbled over his lips as he admired the view; he loved the contrast between his life working at the bar and this regular excursion into a healthier existence. His alcohol-fuelled sweat only made him seem more alive. He wondered what his father would think if he saw him now. He stared at the label at the bottom of the bottle, unconcerned about the letters swirling before his eyes.

Eddie downed half the drink, ready to continue his run but finding lead in his legs. Perhaps he'd overdone it last night with the new girl at the club. She was ten years younger than him and liked to party, but he hadn't drunk enough for it to make his head swoon now. Perhaps it was payback for being such a cradle snatcher. He'd seen some of his older conquests glaring at him when he'd left with the girl, but he didn't care.

He lifted one hand to his face, his fingers appearing to shimmer in the glimmering sun. His toes tingled as he tried to move his feet. Perhaps he was ill, coming down with a bug. He'd noticed customers coughing in the club last night. Jesus, he might have caught something from that girl. He grabbed at his side and swore he'd be more careful as the trees whispered behind him.

It sounded as if the branches were moving, his mind a haze of strange ideas of the trees reaching out for his shaking legs and lifting him. Then nature would cradle him in its arms and he'd find love. The noises came again. Did he imagine it? He turned his head as his vision blurred. There was someone with him; he was sure of it.

'Who's there?' He slurred the words, his voice sounding drunk.

Eddie struggled to move his hand, wiping at his eyes.

But it didn't work. The twigs cracked as the shadowy figure walked towards him. Then it vanished as he blinked so hard he thought his eyes would fall out.

He leant against the tree for support, his fingers clutching at the bark, dirt sticking to his nails. The pain in his legs increased as an early morning mist settled on his face; his breathing came in slow, short bursts. Perhaps this was only a dizzy spell. He might have been overdoing the exercise and mixing it with too many late nights.

The tree nipped at his skin as he pushed away from it. Eddie's legs quivered, his body ready to collapse into the surrounding leaves. The only thing stopping him from collapsing was the rope that had dropped over his head. Before he could react, it snapped tight against his throat. As his breath vanished, he raised one hand and clawed at the thing killing him. His nails broke as he tore at the rope, blood seeping from his flesh as his eyes bulged. His legs shook as his feet lifted from the ground.

Eddie Blair's vision returned for a brief instant, the yellow of the sun hurting his eyes before the life seeped from him. As he dangled there, his final thought was what his father would think of him now.

2 HEART AND SOUL

A middle-aged man with a Victorian moustache slipped into the seat opposite me.

'Tell me something interesting about you.' I hit the timer on the clock.

He twirled one end of his extravagant facial hair between his fingers.

'I work in financial services.' Imagine believing that was something anyone would find interesting, let alone a potential romantic partner. He grinned at me through teeth brighter than the sun. 'Now it's your turn,' he stared at the label pinned to my chest, 'Jen.'

His eyes lingered there longer than they should, and I considered sticking one of my freshly manicured nails into those obtrusive orbs. Then I thought what a terrible example that would be to my teenage daughter. So I told him what I'd said to the others who'd sat opposite me the previous two weeks. And my words had the same result. He was out of the seat and onto someone else quicker than you could say 'This is worse than Tinder.'

I sucked stale orange juice through a paper straw as

desperate men and women shuffled around the room like the last sweets nobody wanted in a chocolate box. This was all Abbey's fault since she'd convinced me to go to these speed dating events on my rare afternoons off work. At least if they'd been evening sessions, I'd have vodka with the terrible orange.

The thought of booze made my stomach flutter. Alcohol had never been a crutch for me like it was for my mother, but I couldn't deny I'd been drinking more than usual. I put it down to overwork and extra stress, pushing the guilt from my head as I glanced across the room. My next potential suitor waddled towards me and slipped into the seat. He looked like someone about to open a new wing of an abattoir, with more gold on his fingers than you'd find in a jewellery shop. He said his name was Gravy and he worked in a graveyard. As interesting as his job sounded, he was as bald as an egg, with as much personality as he had hair. Gravy was wavy with expectation when he finished talking, but scuttled away like the others once he heard my story.

It appeared I was on my own for the next burst of frenzied flirting, which suited me. I removed my phone and skimmed through the files on the latest murder case under investigation. Not that everyone at work believed they were murders. I moved the images across the screen and the bodies lined up together. Two homeless men found dead either side of the river, hands across their chests but with no signs of violence and no definite cause of death. Even my partner thought they had died of natural causes.

But if two bodies perfectly lined up on opposite sides of the Thames was not foul play, then it was time for me to give up being a copper. I scrutinised the images a police drone high above the river had snapped, checking every angle to find some clue. I was struggling to answer the puzzle when a tall man with sparkling blue eyes took the seat opposite, bending his long legs into the cramped space. A black suit enclosed his lean frame; a weathered face upon which stubble and short grey hair gave him a downmarket George Clooney appearance. He wasn't unattractive, and for the first time since I'd started attending these events, something trembled in my veins. But the big test would be when he opened his mouth.

'I'm Steve.' He started the timer, which showed we had two minutes to impress each other. 'And I once met Scarlett Johansson.'

Well, that impressed me. 'Tell me more, Steve.'

'I was a teacher for twenty years, but for the last eighteen months, I've followed my childhood dream, and I own a comic book store. The meeting with Scar Jo was a promotional gimmick for one of the Marvel movies.'

'Did you have a wonderful time?' I got goosebumps along my arms thinking about a night out with Thor, obviously too much thunderbolt and lightning seeping through my system.

'It was great. We talked about silent films and Raymond Chandler books.'

'I can't compete with that.'

He stopped the clock, then started it again.

'Tell me something interesting about you, Jen.'

So I repeated what I'd said to the others.

'A month ago, I was up to my elbows in blood and guts.'

I didn't want to lie to any potential suitors about my job, but also didn't want to blurt it out at the first opportunity. I studied his face, curious to know what was happening behind those piercing sea-blue eyes. Unlike the others, he didn't flee immediately, but narrowed his gaze and examined me as if I was a jigsaw waiting for completion. His voice was low and hypnotic.

'You don't look like a butcher.'

'I've been called worse.'

The others I'd tried this line on had moved onto another prospect within the first minute. But he stayed.

'You're a consultant for the government.'

I gulped at my drink to stop myself from laughing.

'Wrong again, but you're getting closer.' I scratched my nails against the glass. 'You've got one last try before I leave.'

He wiped at his brow and I noticed he had perfect fingernails.

'I didn't realise it was three strikes and you're out.'

'If you can't survive under pressure, you're no good to me.' I wanted it to sound like a joke, but it came out harsher than I expected. He clasped his hands to his cheeks in mock horror and rolled his eyes.

'Last month, you say?'

'It was all over the news.'

He leant forward. 'I recall some media frenzy about a shoot-out in a warehouse in the East End, two rival crime gangs warring over drug territory. Yet you don't seem like a criminal.'

I shrugged. 'That's not for me to decide.'

'Don't tell me.' He paused for effect. 'You're a copper.'

'I'm a Detective Inspector.' The smile crept between my lips when I least expected it. 'And I can spot a liar at ten paces.'

'Should I sit further away then?'

The bell rang on our table; time to stick or twist.

'You're okay for now.'

He breathed out. 'So what happened with the shoot-out?'

'It was all done and dusted when we arrived. But I slipped over when I got inside and fell on top of a body, my arm covered in blood and fingers deep in blown-out brains. It took a week to get the smell from my clothes.'

'So, it's Scarlett Johansson versus dead criminals.' He contemplated it for a second. 'I declare you're the winner there.'

'I don't know about that. Tell me something else about you.'

He didn't hesitate.

'I was once on trial in Manchester.'

I leant forward and scrutinised him. 'That's the truth and a lie.'

Against my better judgement, he intrigued me. I'd only agreed to go to these speed dating events to keep Abbey happy and decided this would be the last one, but perhaps things were now out of my control. My fingers trembled as I placed them on my leg under the table. When was the last time I'd flirted with anyone? I peered at the bar behind him and wondered what the house wine tasted like.

'I can see your mind working overtime, Jen. You're trying to decipher what I did in Manchester.'

That and wondering how bad it would look if I had a glass of wine in the afternoon at a no-alcohol speed dating event.

'You didn't commit a crime?'

His laugh was loud enough for heads to turn in our direction.

'Some people might disagree with you.'

'Put me out of my misery then.'

He finished his drink and licked his lips.

'On my twelfth birthday, I had a trial with Manchester United. And I failed miserably. When I returned home, I shrank from my father's wrath and the humiliation heaped upon me at school and found solace in the world of comic books. And I've been there ever since.'

'Comic books?'

'You know, Batman, Superman and the Avengers. I run a shop which sells comics and related ephemera.'

'I thought they were just for kids?'

'We're all kids at heart, Jen.'

'Tell me more about this comic book store you own.'

'There's not much to say. My parents were in the military, so we moved around a lot. I read comics for some company, and as I got older, I started collecting them. Once, I even tried to write my own. When I left university, I gravitated towards teaching.' He puffed out his cheeks as if releasing a lifestyle of stress.

'What did you teach?'

'I travelled abroad and taught English as a Second Language. When I returned home, I worked in a secondary school as an English teacher.'

'It sounds like hard work.' Having dealt with Abbey's troubles at school, I knew it wasn't easy. Dealing with a single teenager was traumatic, so I couldn't imagine what it was like spending time with large groups of them in a classroom.

'It was rewarding in different ways. By the time I became a head teacher, I could afford all the rare comics beyond my reach as a kid. When I left teaching, I sold some of the more expensive issues to start my business. And that's where I am now.' He handed me a small card.

'Soapbox Comics?'

'It's a silly name, but I wanted something different for the shop.'

An address and phone number came with the name.

'Are you still collecting?'

He shook his head.

'Not comics. I only buy them for investment and resale now. And the shop is great for creating a community spirit with the regulars. I also use it to donate comics to schools, community centres and nursing homes. They help improve literacy, get kids to read, and assist older people in occupying their minds.'

As someone who felt like they were losing their mind daily, I was intrigued.

'How does that work in the nursing homes?'

He placed his elbows on the table, and I noticed how muscular his arms were.

'There's a guy who works in social services who is a regular customer in the shop, and he told me how some people with dementia can be helped by talking about things from their past. I suggested that perhaps using comics, where they can read and look through the images, might be a memory trigger, so it started from there.'

'That sounds great.' As he smiled at me, I wondered what comics would help me make something good from my pig's ear of a past. 'So what do you collect now?'

'First edition novels are my passion.' I waited for him to invite me to see them, but he didn't. 'So what's it like being a Detective Inspector?'

'It's hectic at the best of times.' And I felt guilty not working on those river murders. And I knew they were murders. But what was the motive? As I contemplated that, my phone rang. I ignored it. Everywhere else, punters rose and swapped places. We were the only ones unmoving.

Then the phone rang again.

'You should get that, Jen. It might be important.'

'It's probably my partner asking about shirts again.'

'Shirts?'

'He looked at some yesterday and texted me so I could tell him which one to buy, but I never replied.'

The phone continued to ring.

'Maybe you should put him out of his misery.'

I removed the phone from my jacket, and sure enough, it was Jack calling. I tapped on the screen.

'Buy the purple Paisley one. It goes with your new brogues.'

'There's been another murder, Jen.'

'By the river, a homeless person?' Damn it! The guilt grew in me.

'No. This is different.'

I relaxed a little.

'We've already got an investigation on the go, Jack. We don't need another.' I glanced up at the comic book man. His eyes were distractingly blue, like one of those warm Caribbean oceans you see in glamorous photographs. 'And this is my afternoon off.'

'I'm only passing on the message, partner. This is from on high.'

'God?'

'Even worse.'

'Chief Superintendent Cane?'

'She called me personally when she couldn't reach you.'

I'd turned my phone off for most of the morning.

'Why does she need us?'

'She wants the best. I guess she meant you rather than me.'

'What's so special about this body?'

'I'll tell you when you get here. I'm texting over the address now.' He finished the call and sent the message. I got up to leave, still fixed on those azure eyes, comic book man's business card between my fingers.

'Twenty per cent discount on anything in the shop for you, Jen.'

I looked at the opening hours.

'I might pop along at some point.'

'That's great. No fancy dress required.'

'I can't promise to be as exciting as Scar Jo.'

'But at least you're taller.'

As I left, I smiled at him, noticing the pneumatic blonde who took my place opposite as I stepped into the afternoon air. I tried to shove the image from my mind as I walked to the car, but it kept lingering there. It was a good five years since my last romantic entanglement, and I'd said after that disaster it would be a long time until the next one, but now, against my better judgement, there was a spring in my step as I headed to the car.

It was time to examine a corpse.

3 NEW DAWN FADES

It wasn't difficult to find the scene of the crime. Half a dozen police cars lined the woods' entrance, with uniformed officers keeping the public and media away. Leaves littered the path as I trudged through. None of the PCs looked me in the eye, more out of respect than fear, I hoped. Maybe it was a bit of both. Up ahead, my partner spoke to a constable. When he turned to me, I noticed he was wearing that Paisley shirt.

'Why are we here, Jack? What's Cane all hot and bothered about?'

Chief Superintendent Cassandra Cane was twenty years older than Jack and me and had a reputation for stating the bleeding obvious every time she opened her mouth. It was this, and her first name, which meant officers called her The Prophet behind her back. Some poor unfortunate DI said it to her face one day, and he'd never been seen since. She liked to rule by fear and intimidation, though she'd mellowed a bit in the last year after a brush with cancer gave her a greater appreciation of life. Even with that, praise and support were mythical creatures to her.

'All in good time, petal.'

He pointed at the leaves on the ground, his grin telling me he was enjoying the tired joke he'd used on me a thousand times before. I put up with it from him and no one else because he was my partner and we had an unspoken understanding I wouldn't punch him in the face when others were around. He'd pay for it later, though.

He moved from the path and into the trees, so I followed, our feet crunching through fallen leaves and broken branches. The place smelt of the countryside, all wet tree trunks and fresh flowers, which was strange considering London's polluted metropolis was not far away. It didn't take long before we reached the half-hidden corpse among nature's tears. Someone had brushed chunks of grass aside to expose the head.

'It wasn't well concealed; a kid on the way to school discovered him.'

Jack handed me a pair of plastic gloves. I snapped them over my hands and examined the dead man's neck.

'Strangulation?'

'It appears so.'

It wasn't only the harsh burn marks lining his throat which gave it away, but how his eyes had expanded and bulged from the sockets. They'd filled up with so much blood, they resembled the colour of Jack's new shirt.

'We can rule out suicide then. Where's the rope?'

'Good question. Forensics are scouring the area, but no luck yet.'

'They've finished with the victim?'

'Just about.'

I bent over and moved leaves from the rest of the corpse.

'He must have been jogging.'

I scanned the body for more injuries but discovered nothing unusual. Then I saw the marks on his palm when I lifted it; only they weren't marks but a tattoo or penguin stamp. The same design was on both hands. I touched the ink through the plastic. When I removed my finger, there was a light smudge. Whoever had stamped the victim's hands wasn't long gone.

My knees creaked as I scanned the area. I peered through the people working the scene, searching beyond my colleagues and visualising the killer, or killers, approaching this place and attacking the victim as he jogged. Surely they would have made sounds coming through the leaves and branches, creating too much noise to take him by surprise? I glanced at the body again; he was tall and muscular, so how could anyone overpower him as he ran?

Jack peered at the smear on my plastic covered finger.

'Those penguin stamps are fresh.'

I rechecked them; the penguins were both the same, with beaks staring forward and wings pointing out at either side. These were a message; I didn't understand what they meant, but knew it was likely to make things harder and not easier for the investigation. I stood to scrutinise the location.

'I suppose this is isolated enough to commit murder and then leave these penguin images with no interruptions.' Still, it was risky.

Jack glanced at the bushes and the trees.

'It doesn't seem random.'

'That's because it wasn't, Jack.' He peered at me. 'Who carries rope with them on the chance of a spontaneous killing? Have Forensics found anything?'

'Not yet.'

'Make sure they check all this foliage.' I pointed to the branches. 'They appear an excellent place to hang someone from.' I stepped from the body and back towards the path. As I reached it, my phone rang. It was The Prophet. I let it ring and turned to Jack. 'Any clues what she wants before I take this?'

'It's best if you hear it from her.'

I sighed and answered the call.

'Ma'am?'

'Are you deaf, Flowers? My office has been ringing you all afternoon.'

I resisted the urge to mention my speed dating with a comic book nerd.

'I'm sorry, ma'am. I'm at the scene now.'

'It's about time. I want you to drop everything and concentrate on this.'

I wouldn't step so easily away from my current investigation, even if the command did come from the top of the food chain.

'I'm working on the river murders, ma'am. I think our killer is sending a message and will strike again sooner rather than later.'

'I've already transferred that to another team, Detective Inspector, and I'm unconvinced they are murders. The new team has all your notes so you two will focus on this.' Her voice was liquid steel slithering down the line.

'Yes, ma'am.' I spoke through gritted teeth, unwilling to hide my disappointment.

'And I want regular updates from you personally, do you understand? In my office or over the phone; none of that electronic messaging nonsense.'

Listening to her, I assumed Chief Superintendent Cane

was astride a dinosaur somewhere. Then she hung up on me. I puffed out cold air.

'She didn't tell me anything important.'

I trudged through the leaves towards the victim. A white-suited forensic team looking like they'd stepped out of a 1970s science fiction film was preparing the body for transportation to the morgue.

'It's your turn to spill the beans, Jack.'

'Our victim is Edwin Blair, a twenty-eight-year-old barman at the Blitz club in the West End. Do you know it?'

The last time I visited a nightclub, my hair was naturally black and I didn't have suitcases under my eyes. I gazed into Edwin Blair's disfigured face, wondering, not for the first time, what goes through someone's head when they're having the life taken from them.

'I've never heard of it. Am I supposed to recognise his name?'

'I wouldn't have thought so. But you're aware of his father, Sir Oswald Blair.'

'Shit!'

'Shit indeed. Now you know why Cane wants us on this.'

Oswald Blair, once a high flying prosecution lawyer and more than likely old college chum with Cassandra Cane at Oxford or Cambridge. Sir Oswald Blair. The Home Secretary in Her Majesty's Government and, by default, my boss.

I watched my colleagues slip the Home Secretary's son into a body bag and wondered how he'd take this news. Informing friends and relatives of a loved one's death was one of the worst parts of the job. No matter how many times I'd done it, it never got easy. And now I had to tell a government minister about the murder of his child.

Squirrels scampered up the trees as we left the woods.

'Do we know where the Home Secretary and his wife are?'

Oswald Blair hadn't been out of the media for the last month, always in the press or on TV, urging both sides of Parliament to get the government's new Crime Bill into law. I thought of his dead son and considered if it had something to do with his father and that Bill.

Jack peered at his phone as we walked.

'Clementine Blair died in childbirth. I'd guess Oswald Blair is at Downing Street or in Westminster.'

'We only have one parent to break the unpleasant news to then.'

'The Home Secretary has been informed about his son's death. I think The Prophet wanted that privilege.'

My knees continued to creak as I moved.

'At least that's one less job for us.'

Jack ran his hand over his shirt and removed a stray piece of fluff.

'Shall we visit him first to get it out of the way?'

I stopped as we approached two uniformed officers guarding the entrance to the woods.

'What, so we can ask him awkward questions about his dead son? Best if we leave that for later, after he's had time to process his loss. Do you have Edwin Blair's address?'

He took a piece of paper from his pocket.

'I do, and the landlord's contact number. It's in an upmarket part of the city for a simple barman.'

I glanced behind me at the sound of plastic zipping around Blair.

'I'm guessing there'll be nothing simple about this whole thing.' I returned my attention to Jack. 'You speak to the landlord and tell him to meet us there. I'll get us some help.'

I left him on the phone and strode towards the two

policewomen keeping the public and the media from the scene. I wondered if the press and TV knew about our celebrity corpse.

'Move back now,' one uniform said to a tall bloke waving a camera in her face. He mouthed something about freedom of the press and how this infringed on his civil liberties.

I added another block of defence.

'You have my permission to arrest any troublemakers, Constable.'

The man scowled at me and stumbled away as a rack of expletives tumbled from his mouth.

'I don't think that'll be necessary, ma'am.'

She had stunning blue eyes. For one second, I nearly asked her if she had a brother who owned a comic book store. Steven Morris's name lingered in the back of my head, an image of his chiselled cheekbones living rent-free in my mind, as I turned to the other officer. She had pale brown eyes, not as distracting as her colleague. I wondered how much grief they took from the male officers. It was rare to see two policewomen together, but at least the numbers had increased since I'd joined. After more than a century since the first female police officers patrolled England's streets, now more than a third of the total force were women. Things had improved once traditional perceptions of male culture in policing had changed. Plus, many inflexible non-family-friendly working practices had been removed from the service. The Metropolitan Police led the way in equal opportunities for women, considering a quarter of the police forces in England and Wales had only one or no women in their top ranks. And yet my time in the Met continued to include snide remarks behind my back, but still loud enough for me to hear them, about the effectiveness of women police officers. It made me wonder how difficult it had been for Cane to get so far up the police ladder, and for a second, I felt some sympathy for her.

Job promotion was one of those things which fleetingly passed my mind dependent upon my current workload and how stable it was at home with my teenage daughter. Still, I always liked to give fellow officers a push in that direction if I could, and I felt like doing it right now.

'When did you join the force?'

'Two years ago,' blue eyes said. Her badge said Sutton on it.

'Eighteen months,' replied brown eyes. Her name was Grealish.

'Is this the most exciting thing you've done as a copper?'

They peered at each other, probably thinking it was another one of those regular wind-ups female police officers had to endure from their male colleagues. I had been fewer than three months into the job when a male copper placed a pizza box on the table in front of me in the police canteen one night. When I opened it, his erect penis winked at me. I told him chipolatas were no good and walked away as the rest of the shift burst into laughter. It was the first but not the last time one of my co-workers tried to harass me.

Blue eyes piped up.

'I've seen a dead body before, ma'am.'

'Staring at DI Monroe's palled complexion isn't the same as looking at a corpse,' I said as Jack returned.

He grinned. 'The landlord will meet us there with the keys.'

I pointed at the officers. 'Did one of you drive here?'

'I did,' said Grealish.

'That's great. You can shadow us and do some actual police work for once.'

Both of them tried not to smile as they followed us from the woods. Journalists and bystanders shouted questions in our direction. It was only when we reached the vehicles that someone recognised me.

She's the one who caught the Hashtag Killer.

4 INSIGHT

I switched on the radio to drown out the noise in my skull. Jack tapped his fingers on his leg.

'I love this song.'

It was *Don't Fear the Reaper* by Blue Oyster Cult.

'You dress like a dandy, but you're an old rocker at heart.'

I swerved around a sharp corner and he grimaced as his hips shifted. He held that pained look for longer than I expected.

'Are you all right, Jack?'

He'd suffered from stomach pains for a while, but was always reluctant to talk about them. What was it about blokes keeping their problems to themselves?

He gripped his side.

'I'm okay. We need a new bed at home. The old mattress is killing me.'

'I'll speak to your wife and tell her to spend more money on furniture and not your fancy suits.'

He forced a laugh, and I assumed it was because of the pain.

'I buy one set of clothes a year, Jen.'

'Yes, but a set for you is a dozen shirts plus shoes and suits to go with them.' I removed a hand from the wheel and pointed at his purple shirt. 'How much did that cost?'

'Would you rather I splashed it on booze and junk food?'

I didn't care what he spent his money on; I just enjoyed winding him up.

'Do you eat anything but burgers?' A healthy diet for Jack meant fries every other day. How he stayed so thin was one of life's eternal mysteries. He must have a speeded-up metabolism. But, as sunlight bounced into the car and warmed my cheeks, I noticed he'd put a little extra weight on his face. As he continued to hum along to the music, he pulled at his seatbelt, and I realised how much tighter his trousers were around the waist. Somehow I'd missed these changes in him; perhaps we'd both been stuck behind a desk for too long. And now we'd be at the beck and call of the Home Secretary, which was guaranteed to get Chief Super-intendent Cane breathing down our necks even more than usual.

The thought of The Prophet made my fingers tense, and I gripped onto the wheel so hard, I expected my bones to pop out of my flesh like that comic book character whose name I'd forgotten. That led me to picture where I'd sat not so long ago and the comic book man with the searing blue eyes. Was I contemplating throwing myself back into the dating scene with him? I'd only played along to pacify Abbey, but now, I had to admit, the thought of it excited me.

Jack's voice quickly shattered that excitement.

'I can feel The Prophet's beady eyes on us even from here.'

I knew what he meant. Chief Superintendent Cane is

the woman on *Come Dine With Me* who expects to win a grand by cooking chicken wrapped in parma ham. She's the NHS executive made to carry the can for an IT project that's gone massively over budget, the person ambivalent about Marmite. She's the one who informs the airline cabin crew she's listening intently to the safety demonstration, the woman who thinks she's become excellent friends with a maid on holiday. She's a vegetable curry in a world full of madras and vindaloo. I imagined her back in her office, working out all the ways she could absolve herself of blame if Jack and I messed up this investigation. She'd have a drawer full of excuses ready-made from the last high-profile case she handed to us.

I remembered what those people said about me as we left the Blair crime scene. The Hashtag Killer investigation was a year ago. I'd become something of a minor celebrity in its wake, but it soon wore off once the public and the media found someone else to obsesses over. But some of my colleagues, including Chief Superintendent Cane, believed I'd sought that fleeting fame to prove I was better than them. I'd also identified a serving police officer as a serial killer, which didn't go down too well with some in the force; especially when that serial killer was only targeting criminals. It meant I was never too far from barely hidden resentment from those supposed to have my back. Thankfully, none of that nonsense affected Jack.

'This is the place.' He pointed at the expensive-looking construction on our right. I pulled into a parking lot. A bloke with nervous eyes greeted us on the steps. He introduced himself as the landlord and let us into the building.

'How many flats are there, Mr Crilly?' Jack asked him.

'There are eight. Mr Blair's is the last one on this level.'

He jingled his keys and moved towards it. I faced my uniformed colleagues who'd followed us there.

'Speak with the neighbours about Blair.'

They nodded acceptance as Jack and I followed the landlord into the dead man's flat. We slipped on our plastic gloves in unison before putting latex covers over our shoes; this process always made me feel like getting ready for a spot on the space shuttle. I told Crilly to stay by the exit and touch nothing. A forensic team would be here soon enough to gather evidence, take photos and, hopefully, find something useful for the investigation. Jack switched on the light, and I closed the door.

It was sparsely furnished, with a large sofa in the middle of the room facing a sixty-inch flat-screen TV which had multiple gaming systems hooked up to it and a state-of-the-art sound system. I couldn't see a laptop or computer anywhere: Edwin Blair must have been one of those people who avoided connecting to the digital world. It seemed idyllic; on the rare occasions I saw my daughter, Abbey was so buried in social media apps, all she could do was grunt when she wanted something. I put it down to her going through that troublesome phase all teenagers did.

I scanned the room. The walls were bare and the carpet clean. It didn't appear as if much happened in Edwin Blair's flat. Jack checked out the kitchen and bathroom while I spoke to the landlord.

'How did a barman afford this place?'

He rolled his eyes.

'All I know is someone paid the rent by direct debit at the start of each month. That was better than the old system.'

'What do you mean?'

'Mr Blair always wanted to pay in cash, but that meant

me coming here when I didn't want to, plus more often than not, he wouldn't have the money. Six months ago, it all changed and he set up a direct debit. It's been much better since then.'

Jack joined us. 'What changed?'

Crilly shrugged. 'I don't know, and I didn't ask.'

'The kitchen looks unused, and the bathroom is spotless,' Jack said.

We strode into the bedroom together. There was a shelf stacked full of DVD horror movies in the corner, and obvious signs in the bed that more than one individual had occupied it recently. This room smelled lived in. Jack lifted the top sheet and peered under it.

'Do you reckon good-looking barmen have busy social lives?'

'You're asking the wrong person.' I opened the wardrobe. A few shirts and trousers hung there, nothing else. A bundle of socks and underwear sat at the bottom, and I was about to close it when I noticed the bit of cardboard peeking through the mess of clothes. I moved the outfits to the side to reveal a large box.

Jack let out a loud whistle. 'Maybe he dealt drugs, and his stash is in there.'

I helped him drag it out. 'You think his murder could be drug-related?'

'I'm not sure, you?'

'It appeared too clean and precise. Drug dealers are notoriously short-tempered, and they usually want their kills to be messages to others. No; this must be more personal.' Those penguin tattoo stamps were a message to someone.

We lifted the box onto the bed and opened it. It was full of papers; I grabbed some from the top and removed them.

As I did so, our forensic colleagues entered the flat; familiar dulcet tones greeted us.

'Well, well, if it isn't Flowers and Monroe, London's very own Batman and Robin. I thought you two were dealing with the river murders.'

'We follow Her Master's Voice, Athena.'

Athena Temple gave me that grin which said we should move aside and let her team do their job.

'What's that you've got hold off? Is it a suicide note? A confession? The winning lottery numbers?'

I read the words printed on the first page.

'*The Mage of Avalon. A Novel of High Fantasy* by EE Blair.'

Temple snatched the paper from my hands.

'He's the Home Secretary's son and an author. They'll rack up the security alert even further now.' I didn't correct Athena on the use of present and not past tense.

'What do you mean, security alert?'

'Cane has ordered extra police protection for the families of the cabinet.'

'She thinks this is terror-related?'

'Anything is possible in this corrupt world of ours, Jennifer. We can't take any risks with the lives of the higher orders.' She leant in close to me, both of us aware most of the people in the room were more than capable of telling tales when they shouldn't. 'I don't believe our superiors would do this for a homeless person, do you?' Athena kept her working-class background from most people, but she'd always seen me as a kindred spirit.

'Terrorists didn't kill Edwin Blair.'

I grabbed the pages from her and returned them to the box.

'And how do you know this, Jennifer?' Athena removed

her long plastic gloves as if she was auditioning for a seductress role in a film noir.

'Because we'd have heard from them by now; terrorist organisations aren't shy about broadcasting their actions.' I watched Athena's scrupulous gaze examine the room. 'Why are you here, Athena? There are no bodies to poke and prod.'

She glanced at Jack. 'Oh, I wouldn't say that.' Then she pushed her head close to mine. 'I'm assessing a new member of my team.' She touched her nose. 'But they don't know that.'

I shook my head, unwilling to get involved in any more departmental shenanigans. I strode past her and out of the bedroom. As Jack and I left, my uniformed assistants were waiting for us. Constable Sutton spoke first.

'Edwin Blair took a jog at seven o'clock every morning, Monday to Friday.'

'He must have been super fit.' Jack seemed suitably impressed. 'He never ran on the weekend?'

'No,' Constable Grealish replied. 'He kept to a strict routine during the week. It was different at the weekend.'

'How so?' I said.

'According to the neighbours, that's when he did all his partying. They say he had women over every Friday and Saturday night.'

Jack clutched at his hip. 'It's a hard life for some.'

'We should head over to that nightclub.' I was about to give the uniforms more instructions when my phone rang. I scowled when I saw the name on the screen. 'Are you after an update, Chief?'

'No. I need you to see the Home Secretary. He wants to speak to you immediately.'

'We're on the way to the nightclub where Edwin Blair worked, ma'am.'

'It's too early for that. Go there tonight and interview the staff and customers when it's open. Sir Oswald Blair is waiting for you at his club.'

'Club?'

'He's at the Mongoose Club in Westminster. Do you know where it is?'

'I'll find it.' I assumed The Prophet was more than familiar with the place herself unless it was one of those men-only joints which still operated under the radar.

'Don't let me down, Flowers.'

She ended the call.

Jack didn't look happy. 'It's going to be a long afternoon, partner.'

Didn't I know it? And it had started so well.

5   IN A LONELY PLACE

'This is my movie night with Abbey.'

'What was tonight's viewing supposed to be?'

I got my phone out.

'We've been alternating over the weeks. She shows me one of her modern films between me introducing her to the classics. Last week it was some terrible horror flick with aliens where everyone is deaf. Tonight it's *The Maltese Falcon*.'

'It's a classic. She can still watch it on her own.'

I clicked on Abbey's number.

'I can't do that. Part of the enjoyment is watching it together.' It rang for two seconds before she answered.

'How did it go, Mum?'

My daughter's voice lifted the gloom from my heart. I glanced over at Sutton and remembered my session with the comic book man.

'I'll tell you all about it later, but there's a change of plan tonight.'

'Oh.' Those two letters held so much disappointment.

'I've got to work. Let's save Sam Spade for another time,

and you can watch one of your shows instead. Order enough pizza and I'll have some when I get back.'

'That's if there's any left.'

'I love you.' I wasn't sure Abbey heard my words before hanging up.

Jack stared at the uniformed officers.

'Are we taking the rookies with us?'

'They're hardly that.'

Although Jack was a happily married man with two kids he loved dearly, he was not averse to flirting with pretty women, but he'd barely said a word to either of them since we'd arrived.

'They can type up the reports at the office.'

'Shouldn't you ring the wife and tell her you'll be late?'

He avoided my gaze and headed for the exit.

'She's used to it by now.'

I turned to the two policewomen.

'At the station, Chief Superintendent Cane will set up a Murder Investigation Team. Process your notes and email them to everyone on the team. And we'll see you tomorrow.'

They looked at me with equal surprise in their eyes.

'You want us to continue on this?' Sutton said.

I nodded as I left. 'And ditch the uniforms. Wear proper clothes from now.'

Jack didn't speak until I pulled the car from the kerb.

'Are you taking those two under your wing?'

'The sooner we have this sorted, the sooner we can get back to the river murders, so their help should speed this along.'

'You think this is political?'

'The murder or the reaction to it?'

'Both.'

'I don't know. Perhaps this conversation with Oswald Blair will answer that.'

Twenty-five minutes later, a morose man ushered us into a private room inside the Mongoose Club. As we entered, I wondered how many other women had walked through those same hallowed doors. It already felt like the kind of party you want to leave the moment you arrive. Blair stood in front of an unlit fireplace, his face passive and unresponsive.

'Was it a random attack?'

Jack glanced at his watch, a subtle message to the Home Secretary that we'd been on the case for fewer than two hours.

'I doubt it, Home Secretary.' I showed him my ID card.

'I know who you are, Detective Inspector. I asked for you.'

That was just great. Blair stared at me for so long, the heat burning from his eyes, I thought I'd dissolve into a puddle of water. Perhaps he wouldn't mind me asking him some problematic questions.

'Did your son have any enemies?'

He poured himself a drink and considered my question.

'My knowledge of Edwin's social interactions became limited once he left home and pursued a life I never approved of.'

There was no sympathy or sadness in his voice, but I couldn't judge him for that. Every person deals with grief in their own way. He could weep all he wanted once we left. Peering into those intense eyes, I assumed that wouldn't happen.

'You didn't like him working behind a bar?'

'Would you be happy with your child doing that, Inspector Flowers?' I didn't answer such a loaded question.

He finished the drink in one go before pouring another. 'But I suppose once Edwin left school with no qualifications, he would never do what I wanted.' I noticed the weight in his voice then, unsure if it was for his son's loss or because of his perceived failings in life. 'Do you have any leads? Is it connected to that club where he worked?'

'We're keeping an open mind at the moment, Home Secretary,' Jack said.

Blair looked at him as if he was invisible.

'You'll provide regular updates, Inspector Flowers.' It was a demand, not a request.

'Could this be connected to your work, Sir Oswald?'

His eyes narrowed as he pondered my question.

'Connected to the government?' He shook his head. 'The security services have overreacted. I wouldn't waste your time pursuing that line of investigation, Inspector.'

'I was thinking more about your previous employment.'

The glass was empty when he placed it on the table.

'My work as a lawyer?'

'You prosecuted people for twenty years; someone must hold a grudge.'

His shoulders slumped as he leant against the fireplace.

'You think one of them would hurt Edwin to get back at me?'

'I've known criminals do worse for a lot less.'

He stared beyond me at an empty spot on the wall.

'Yes, yes, you could be right.' The confidence that men of his upbringing and stature carried with them drained from him.

'I understand you're still a partner in your original firm?'

'Yes, a non-participating one. I intend to return to it once the politics is over.'

Jack stared at his phone. 'That would be Blair, Burnell and Cornwell?'

'That's correct, Inspector.'

'Has your firm kept all of your case files?'

'Lawyers throw nothing away, Inspector Flowers.'

'I don't suppose there are digital versions?' It was a long shot quickly shut down.

'I'm afraid not. The papers are all stored in the office's basement.'

'How many prosecutions did you handle in twenty years?' Jack said.

Blair shrugged. 'I didn't lead on all of them, but perhaps ten a year.'

'Christ!' Jack failed to contain his irritation. He stared at me and I felt his pain, thinking about two hundred files to read.

'Can we get access to those documents, Mr Blair?'

I was uncomfortable addressing him as Home Secretary, or calling him Sir. The thought of it transported me back to school days I hated.

'You can't remove them from the building, but I'll let the staff know you want to see them.' He turned from us and we took it as a dismissal. We glanced at each other and left him to his thoughts.

Jack checked the time as we got into the car.

'The Blitz nightclub won't open until later. Shall we head to the law firm?'

'No. Let's save that pleasure for tomorrow. I need something to eat. What about you?'

'Italian or Indian?'

HE WAS SIPPING his second glass of wine when I reminded him we were still working. He poured us both water, downing his in one go.

'Don't worry; I'll mix my drinks while we're here.'

I'd chosen the closest Italian restaurant to the nightclub. With Jack's delicate stomach, I didn't want to risk Indian food setting him off. I scanned the latest news on my phone while we waited for the food.

'There's no mention of Edwin Blair or a body in the woods.'

'And the terrorist threat to the government?'

'Nope, that's quiet.' I placed the mobile on the table. 'Perhaps they called it off once they realised how unlikely it is.'

'You think Blair's murder has anything to do with politics?'

'I'm not ruling it out, but it wouldn't surprise me if it's linked to his father.'

'How so?'

'Don't you think it's a coincidence the Home Secretary's son is murdered, by hanging, when Oswald Blair is a long-time advocate of the return of capital punishment to the British legal system?'

'Since you put it like that. Is it hanging he recommends?'

'It is.'

'In public?'

I grimaced as the waiter brought our cheese and tomato garlic bread to the table. If someone dropped two eggs in the middle of it, it would look like Edwin Blair's dead face. I suddenly lost my appetite and the wine appeared more of a temptation than it did sixty seconds ago.

'No, he hasn't mentioned that yet, though I bet when

he's in that little club of his, they all have a good laugh about it.'

The aroma of garlic was strong enough to fell a herd of vampires. I slipped back into the chair to avoid it. Jack took more of his wine, the deep red of it sparkling against his teeth, the words tinged with bitterness as they came.

'How come we're always working for those who had a better education?'

How much had he had to drink?

'You've answered your own question, partner.' Two gin and tonics arrived at the table next to ours, and I'd swear they called out to me. 'We'll find who killed Blair, and then move onto the next body.'

That's how it worked, one death followed by another and on into infinity. If you lined up all the violent crime victims since I'd joined the force, I wondered if they'd reach the moon and back. I considered all the coppers who came before me and the people they'd tried to help. It didn't matter how many killers I caught, how many criminals I put behind bars; there would always be others to replace them.

Jack burped, and then apologised. His alcohol consumption distracted me from my thoughts. I was happy to see him dropping ice into his wine, finding it easy to avoid falling into the bottle with him.

'You're discounting this as a terrorist attack?' He bit into an ice cube.

I nodded. 'Someone would have claimed credit for it by now. They'd be rubbing our noses in it, shouting out about how vulnerable we all are. This seems more personal to me.'

He finished a slice of bread and started on another, crumbs dripping from his teeth as he spoke.

'Let's hope we get something useful from the nightclub, then.'

'It could be a drug deal gone wrong, an irate customer, or a jealous boyfriend or girlfriend.'

That's what I wanted: for it to be simple. I kept that thought in my head during the meal, but by the time we left, I doubted it would be.

———

JACK BELCHED out pasta as we approached the queue outside the venue. His ID card was in his hand as I told him to put it away.

'We'll get better results going in undercover.'

He scrutinised me as if he realised what I was wearing for the first time today; black jacket, black top and black jeans.

'Are you wearing Abbey's clothes? You look like a middle-aged woman going through a Goth phase.'

'Middle-aged? I'm younger than you.'

'Only by a few months.' He grabbed at his lapels. 'And you know I wear it well.'

'Let's hope you can charm information from someone inside.'

We joined the end of the queue as it shuffled towards the entrance, a mixture of people who appeared to live on nothing but steroids and tanning machines.

Jack scowled at me. 'It's ten quid to get in.'

'That's half a sock to you.'

I held the money as security ushered us towards the counter. The biggest of them peered at me and I realised I'd put his brother away last year. I ducked past him, paid the cash, and trundled inside. Jack touched my arm.

'I'll go to the bar and ask the staff about Blair. Why don't you speak to some customers?'

'Okay. But soft drinks only for you.'

He gave me a mock salute and headed off.

I removed Blair's phone from my pocket and went through the photos he'd taken of women he knew. Were they conquests from here? They had a similar look about them, with long blonde hair and a shovelful of makeup. I'd been like that, trying to use cosmetics to turn me into someone else in my teenage years. My parents nagged me out of the face gloop before I left home to go to university, but it took me a lot longer to find comfort in my own skin. As I glanced into the large mirror at the back of the bar, I still wasn't sure how comfortable I was.

I scanned the corners of the room as my ears throbbed from the music. A few customers flexed their hips on the dance floor while everyone gazed through me. Jack was speaking to a barman, so I headed for the ladies toilets. It was empty when I walked in. There were fresh flowers at the sink and it smelt of violets. I turned the tap on and threw warm water over my face. As I used a paper towel to dry my cheeks, a gang of giggling women entered. They ignored me, delved into their handbags, and applied lip gloss and foundation to their faces as they spoke about the men outside. They didn't appear to be impressed by the slim pickings on offer; apart from one.

'Did you see the old guy with the purple shirt? He's dapper.'

'His shoes are lush.'

'You'd break him in two, Lacy.'

Then they all cackled like demented hyenas.

'Are any of you friends with Edwin Blair?' I said.

They continued to dabble at their faces, throwing me the occasional cursory glance through the mirror.

'Is Eddie working tonight? I didn't see him when I came in.'

'Lacy must have tired him out this morning.'

The room buzzed with amusement again. I assumed the redhead with the massive cleavage was Lacy. I stepped next to her.

'Were you with Blair last night?'

All four of them turned from their reflections and glared at me.

'Are you his wife?'

'Eddie's not married.'

'Maybe she's his mother.'

They blurted out laughter like asthmatic ducks.

'Someone murdered Edwin Blair today.' I stared at Lacy. 'You might be the last person to see him alive.' She dropped her lipstick into the sink. It rattled around in the bowl, leaving a red smear all over the porcelain.

'Eddie's dead?' Mascara melted across her face.

'The killer hung him from a tree this morning.' There was no point being sensitive. 'Do you ladies know why anyone would want to kill him?'

They stared at each other, then at me, then at each other again.

'Eddie wouldn't hurt a fly. Everybody loves him.'

'No jealous boyfriends or husbands creeping around?'

'Eddie isn't like that.'

I had to admire how they continued to talk about him in the present tense. I gave Lacy my card and told her to give a statement at the station in the morning. They huddled together and sobbed as a group as I left. Jack was waiting for me outside.

'No one has a bad word to say about him. Apart from

serving booze here, he had nothing to do with drink or drugs.'

'The women I spoke to were equally vociferous in their praise for him.'

I glanced across the nightclub as the music increased in volume.

'So, what now?'

'We go home and start again in the morning. Come on, and I'll drop you off.'

The queue had doubled in size when we left. Jack whistled as I headed for the car, the phone in his other hand.

'I'll see you in the office tomorrow, Jen. A mate lives around the corner, and he needs a favour.'

'Are you sure?'

He pulled from me.

'Absolutely. You need some rest. When we wake up, some terrorist group might have good news for us.'

I watched him walk off and doubted we'd be that lucky. I had a sneaking suspicion the mystery of Edwin Blair's murder would get murkier before it became clearer.

Something was sizzling in the kitchen when I entered, finding Abbey getting creative with a frying pan.

'Did I miss the earthquake?'

She shovelled food into a dish and placed it on the table.

'What did you do last night?'

Whatever she'd cooked, it looked as unpalatable as it smelt.

'I returned before midnight, early enough for my teenage daughter not to wait up worrying about me.' I used a fork to poke at the shrivelled husk on my plate. 'What is this pale excuse for nutrition?'

'It's vegan sausages and eggless eggs.'

I made the mistake of tasting the yellow muck, not embarrassed enough to spit it back into the grave I'd scooped it from. I stood and reached for the coffee, praying she hadn't substituted it for something fake. Sugar and caramel swam down my throat, brown tendrils tickling at my synapses and bringing my brain to life.

'Do you want a lift to school?'

She scowled at me, then at the plate, before peering into my eyes.

'What happened yesterday afternoon?'

I sipped before scratching my chin.

'Yesterday, yesterday, you know it feels so... so...'

'Stop messing around, Mum; did you meet anyone?'

'Ah, you mean at the speed dating session you forced me to go to.' I wiped imaginary stress from my forehead. 'Now, did I meet anyone yesterday?'

Abbey slammed the frying pan onto the cooker's top, sending warm fat flying into the air.

'I knew I should've followed you to that bar again.'

I scrutinised her face, wondering if she spoke the truth. In the last six months, she'd become so expert in deception, I'd started worrying about it.

'Well, I stayed for at least an hour, so I think...' I held my hand up and counted along my fingers. 'I met five people before I left.'

'How many of them were interesting? Did you get any phone numbers?'

I removed the business card from my pocket and handed it to her.

'I got this.'

Abbey narrowed her eyes. 'Soapbox Comics?'

'I met the guy who owns it.'

She stared at me open-mouthed, her blue lips quivering in astonishment, her eyes wide enough to crawl into and peer at her mind. I wondered what that would be like and if I really wanted to know what was in there.

'Get out of here.'

'Okay.' I picked up my bag and headed for the door. Abbey stood in front of me, blocking my way before I reached it.

'Mum, you can't leave before you tell me more about this bloke; at least say you'll see him again.'

I put my hand on her shoulder.

'We'll speak about it tonight, Abbey. I've got a new case to solve, and the top brass has given it the highest priority.'

She frowned. 'You've stopped investigating who killed those homeless people?'

The disappointment in her eyes mirrored mine.

'Hopefully, Jack and I will get back to it once we clear up this latest investigation.' Was I as confident as I sounded? 'Do you want a lift to school?'

She shuffled away from me.

'No, that's okay.'

Her shoulders slumped and I didn't consider why. A few times in the last month, I'd got back late from work, and she hadn't been home. When I'd questioned her about this, she'd explained it away as trips to the local all-night shops while I worked. She was always home before ten and kept in touch through text, yet it was difficult to pinpoint why, but I guessed she'd lied to me about these nights out. I kept promising myself I'd sit down with her and talk through it, but hadn't found the time.

'If I return early enough, I'll cook us a meal.'

She only grunted in response, now engrossed with her phone. I pushed Abbey and her world to the edge of my mind and went to the car.

THERE WAS NO MORE news about the murder on the radio or the websites I checked on my mobile; no updates from Jack or the station, so I assumed no progress as I headed into work and our depleted resources. More than half of London's police stations had closed since I'd joined the force, and staff numbers had reduced dramatically in the last ten years. But the government and this Home Secretary had promised a massive recruitment drive to improve policing across the UK; we just hadn't seen it yet.

I strode past reception and up one flight of stairs. I expected to see The Prophet waiting for me as I arrived, thankful she wasn't. The morning shift officers were attending their briefing session as I entered the building. These were the uniformed bods who the public got to observe in their local communities. They were the lowest rank on the police service's totem pole: the Police Constable; the foot soldier in the fight against crime. They had the most direct contact with the public, not just arresting criminals, but conducting community outreach, collecting information at the scene, submitting reports, and working crowd control. They were most often the officers who discovered the initial crime, keeping onlookers from interfering with the scene, doing office work, or running errands for the higher-ranking officers. This was where I'd started my career as a copper, and I was glad to be out of that daily grind.

Jack was sitting in the office as I headed for my desk, which still contained my files from the river murders. I picked them up and turned to my partner.

'Hasn't this been handed over to someone else?'

'I think they're waiting for you to confirm them as murder and not accidental deaths.'

'I don't have time for that now.'

Jack shrugged. Politics outvoted justice again. 'I was informed this is our priority.'

'Has the Major Investigation Team been set up at least?'

'Cane didn't waste any time. We're in the first suite.'

Scotland Yard's murder investigation unit had lost a quarter of its officers and staff in ten years, during which the number of major investigation teams (MITs) had decreased from twenty-six to eighteen. Each team comprised police and civilian personnel, usually totalling about thirty people.

I followed Jack from the office and down the corridor. The room was buzzing as we entered, with computers humming and evidence boards placed near the far wall. With no sign of the Senior Investigating Officer (SIO), I was told everything I needed to know regarding who should have been present.

'Is DCI Merson in charge?'

Jack rolled his eyes. 'Who else?'

Often, SIOs found they had several cases to investigate simultaneously and prioritised and delegated to others. Sometimes this caused confusion and demanded more of the staff in the incident room to ensure they allocated reports, statements and papers to the correct accounts the system used for homicide investigations. This was called the Home Office Large Major Enquiry System (Holmes), and we used the latest version.

'Have they assigned a category to Blair's murder?'

'Because of his father, it's been designated as a Category A investigation.'

That surprised me. Category A is a major investigation of grave public concern, such as a child victim, the murder of a police officer, multiple murder, or where vulnerable members of the public are at risk, where the identity of the offender(s) is not apparent, or the investigation and the securing of evidence require a significant allocation of resources. Eddie Blair's murder covered none of those conditions. At least the powers that be weren't taking it so seriously to call in the National Counter Terrorism Security Office.

This meant we took the lead, likely doing all the work and getting none of the credit. Jack and I would manage the core team under Merson's supervision. I walked over to the uniformed officers from yesterday, both of them now in their civilian clothes.

'Constables Sutton and Grealish, do you have any news for us?'

Sutton was the one with the sea-blue eyes.

'I've updated all the reports onto the system, ma'am, including the autopsy, forensics and what Cybercrime got from the victim's digital devices.'

'Do we have any leads?'

Grealish replied.

'Forensics discovered fibres on Blair's neck from a skipping rope usually found in sports clubs or schools.'

'That'll be easy to narrow down.' Jack never did well at hiding his sarcasm.

There was a large TV monitor on the far wall. As I spoke, I stared at the screen, watching the images from Parliament as the politicians debated the Bill to alter the sentencing laws for convicted criminals.

'Any updates on the terror alert they upgraded because of Edwin Blair's murder?'

Jack replied. 'Cane told me this morning it won't change until we come up with something which convinces them otherwise.'

I grabbed a seat next to Sutton and the spare computer.

'Then we'd better find it quick sharp.' I opened the file containing the list of people who worked with Blair at the Blitz. Someone had staked out his flat and knew his jogging routine, so they must have observed him going to and from work. 'Constable Sutton, can you get me the names of anyone who left their job at that nightclub in the last twelve months.'

She nodded and reached for the phone.

Jack sat opposite me. 'You think it could be someone he used to work with, possibly a disgruntled former employee?'

'It wasn't random, Jack, because it's personal, and our killer has a grudge.'

'That's if it isn't an indirect attack on Oswald Blair or the government.'

I sank into the chair. 'There is that.' I peered across the room at the pile of papers stacked on the far table before pointing at them. 'What are those, Constable Sutton?'

She removed the top two sheets.

'It's the manuscript you found in Edwin Blair's flat, ma'am.'

'Damn,' Jack said. 'I'd forgotten all about that. Has anyone read it?'

Sutton handed the paper to me: the title page of *The Mage of Avalon. A Novel of High Fantasy* by EE Blair, and the start of the story.

'I flicked through it yesterday.'

I glanced at the text and knew it wasn't to my tastes as it proclaimed the tale of a chosen man come to save the world from dragons and demons. I returned them to her.

'Is there anything helpful in it?'

Sutton shook her head. Then Constable Grealish placed an envelope in front of me.

'This arrived for you today.'

I stared at it, and then turned it over. It had no return address, only my name on the front. It was rare for officers to get personal mail at the station, but after the Hashtag Killer case, for a while, I'd received hate mail and hero letters in equal measure. They'd stopped arriving a few months ago. I tried to return it to Grealish.

'You can throw this away, Constable.'

'I think it might be important, ma'am.'

She pointed at the front, in the space between the typed letters DI and Flowers, at something small near my name, an image I'd missed.

Jack leant over my shoulder and peered at it.

'You need a magnifying glass to see it.'

'Perhaps we're just too old for this.' I pulled the envelope closer to my face, squeezing my eyes to improve my eyesight. The paper was so close, I smelt stale bits of smoked bacon and cheese clinging to it.

And then I saw what Grealish meant.

'Shit!'

'What is it, Jen?'

I looked again, staring hard enough to make my head vibrate.

'Put your glasses on, Jack.'

He was so vain, he hated wearing them when other people were around, especially young women, but he reached into his jacket, removed them and did what I said. Then he saw what we all did.

'No way.' He checked the rest of it, front and back. 'The postmark is impossible to read, with no sign when and where from.'

I took my phone, turned on the video, and handed it to Sutton.

'Record this when I open it.'

She nodded.

I stared at the tiny symbol one last time before opening the envelope, knowing the small stamp of a penguin near my name wasn't a coincidence.

7 TRANSMISSION

Dear Boss,
   Choke the man in the woods. Hung out to dry and die. And watch him struggle and squirm. Perhaps I'll let him live. To dream he could have a better life. Ever eternal with no more suffering. Ready player gone. Only to die every day. Now send this out to the media so they'll know my message. Exquisite corpse with no tongue for tales to tell.
   From your devoted follower, the real Serial Killer.

UNDERNEATH THE TEXT was a large stamp of the same penguin found on Blair's palms. I twisted the paper between the plastic covering my fingers. Jack placed his phone on the table.

'Forensics are coming for the letter and envelope.'

My neck hurt as I shook my head.

'I doubt they'll find anything, but I suppose we have to try.' I turned to Grealish. 'Copy the text to a document on the computer.'

I reread it, watching Jack mouth the words.

'*Dear Boss* must be a reference to the Jack the Ripper murders,' Sutton said.

I watched her type the letter onto the screen.

'It's a homage to the hoax letters sent to the police and the papers, but it doesn't mean it came from our perpetrator.'

'You don't think this is our killer?' Jack said.

I wasn't sure what to think.

'It's been made to look like it's from the murderer of Edwin Blair.' I pointed at the envelope and the bottom of the page. 'These stamped images of penguins match those on Blair's hands. So perhaps whoever posted this is the killer, or knows who they are.'

Sutton finished typing. 'Why use penguins?'

The ache at the back of my neck increased.

'They mean something to the murderer, but it's not obvious to me. Stamping the image onto the victim's flesh, then sending another one along with this letter, is them communicating a message we need to work out. Whatever they're for, it's made things harder and easier for us.'

Constable Grealish stared at me. 'How so, ma'am?'

'The master criminal who likes to taunt the police and play games is a rare beast, found only in fiction. This letter implies more to come, which means more murders. More victims should produce more evidence, which makes things easier for us; but it will also produce greater scrutiny from the media, the public and our superiors. And create misery for more people.'

I stared at the page, going through each word, sentence, and paragraph in my head, hoping the longer I scrutinised the text, the sooner a solution would magically appear inside my brain. As the rest of the team read through the letter, a forensics officer entered the room, wearing protective gloves and with a plastic bag in her hand. Constable Sutton explained the situation while Grealish handed each of us a printed copy of the letter. Jack put the text onto the big screen as the woman returned to the lab with the evidence. I stared at her forlornly, hoping for a miracle but not expecting one. Someone who'd gone into this much detail, both with the murder and the letter, was unlikely to be sloppy; not yet, at least.

Sutton picked up her copy. 'She said she'd send the results as soon as possible.'

'Don't get too excited we'll find anything useful from the page or the envelope. Someone as precise as this killer won't make stupid mistakes like leaving DNA or fingerprints behind.' I strode to the screen and pointed to the first line. 'Can we decipher useful information from this text?'

'I hope so,' Jack said.

'We'll assume the *Dear Boss* opening isn't because this is a hoax, but has some other meaning for our killer. Perhaps they admire the Ripper and want to emulate them.' Which was a worrying thought. 'The penguin on the envelope matches Edwin Blair's palms' stamps, implying a connection to the murder. This penguin design means something to them, but we're unlikely to understand what that is until we see more of them; which unfortunately means we're looking at more victims.' I stared at my colleagues. 'What are your thoughts on the text?'

'It's like you mentioned,' Jack said. 'They're taunting the police, provoking us, and this is the most famous case in history where that happened. I doubt there's any other link to Jack the Ripper.'

Sutton swung her computer around, so we all saw what she'd found.

'And Edwin Blair doesn't fit the profile of the Ripper's

victims. They were all women from different parts of society compared to Blair.'

I went to the next line.

'You can't get more specific than this for the death of Edwin Blair: *Choke the man in the woods. Hung out to dry and die.*'

'What do they mean by dry?' Jack said. We all considered it for a minute. Grealish gave it a go.

'Edwin Blair worked in a bar serving alcohol for a living. Using slang terms that would be the opposite of being dry.'

I nodded at her. 'Perhaps this is a crime of morality; a judgement of what Blair did, where he worked and those he associated with. If that's the case, then it would have a connection to the Ripper crimes as some thought they were attacks on the so-called loose morality of the women he killed.' Constable Grealish made notes on the computer as I spoke.

'What do the next three sentences mean?' Jack said before he read them out.

'*And watch him struggle and squirm. Perhaps I'll let him live. To dream he could have a better life.*'

'Did our killer have second thoughts, possibly wanting him to live?' I'd known plenty of murderers who suffered from remorse because of their crimes. Many were driven by vile urges, pursuing their terrible actions, but claiming once caught that everything was beyond their control. 'This dreaming of having a better life implies the killer knew Edwin Blair and was aware his father is the Home Secretary; this was no random attack.'

'Perhaps the better life comment is another connection to morality,' Sutton said. 'If it's a message about Blair working in a bar, our killer would think he'd have a better life employed somewhere else.'

I agreed. 'If their morality is that twisted, they might see death as better than a life they perceive as immoral.'

Sutton read the next pieces.

'Ever eternal with no more suffering. Ready player gone. Only to die every day.'

'The first sentence might be a reference to the afterlife and eternal peace.' Jack scratched at his chin. 'Maybe our killer is religious with a warped sense of morality as you say, but the ready player gone bit means nothing to me.'

Grealish spoke up. 'It might be a play on the book and movie called *Ready Player One.*'

'Never heard of it,' Jack said.

Grealish grinned. 'I think you're older than the target audience, sir. Both the book and the movie are about teenagers using virtual reality to escape the real world.'

Jack shrugged. 'How is that going to help us discover the killer?'

I considered the question. 'Some might argue alcohol is an escape from the real world. Getting a hangover is like dying every day. This might be our killer setting themselves up as judge, jury, and executioner for things they disapprove of.'

My fingers clutched at straws inside my skull. I wondered if this sounded as desperate to them as it did in my head. I read the last two sentences.

'Now send this out to the media so they'll know my message. Exquisite corpse with no tongue for tales to tell.'

'Do we inform the media?' Sutton said.

I left the text on the screen and returned to my seat.

'Not for now, Constable. Our letter writer craves attention so we won't give it to them just yet.' I peered at the words. 'Why is the corpse exquisite? The no tongue line could relate to how Blair died, choking and swallowing his tongue.'

Sutton answered. 'Blair might be exquisite because he was popular with women or of his privileged family. Our moral judge might consider him promiscuous.'

Jack pointed at the last line of text.

'*From your devoted follower, the real Serial Killer*. Is this all for you, Jen?'

God, I hoped not.

'What do they mean about a real serial killer?' Grealish said.

Jack answered her question.

'That might be a reference to the Hashtag Killer; the killer who wasn't a killer.'

Sutton stared at me. 'Because she got others to kill for them?'

I didn't reply; the last thing I wanted to do was talk about Alice Voss. But Jack could be right; Voss manipulated others to kill for her, hoping those actions would inspire vigilante copycats, and they did. This new killer might be another copycat; which was all I needed. The more I stared at the text, the more I read those words in my head, the less I liked it. I turned to Jack.

'This could be a terrorist threat, a fresh way to spread fear; and that's why they want this sent to the media.' How bad was it I wanted this to be about terrorism? How bad was I to think about it?

'They don't need us for that,' Jack said.

I pointed at the copy of the original text on my screen.

'They want to keep this between them and us: the penguins.'

He scratched at his face again. 'Why the penguins?'

I pondered that question as we all went to work looking

for meaning in that symbol. An internet search using the terms "penguins + murder" returned over two hundred results, the first of which was the South African penguin murder mystery. It sounded like cosy crime fiction until I clicked on the link and read the details about the events of 27 May 2001, when a group broke into an aquarium in South Africa and bludgeoned nine penguins to a pulp. I was into the second paragraph when I realised it was the synopsis for a short film.

The next search, "penguins + serial killer", gave up one hundred and forty-one results; it was two pages of complete nonsense. I closed the web browser and opened the folder containing the forensic files, reading through the details on the time of death and the rope. Apart from that, my colleagues had found nothing useful at the scene, with no fibres or DNA from the killer. Then I watched the CCTV footage of Edwin Blair's route from his house to the woods, frustrated at the few clips we had.

It was close to midday when Jack sidled up to me.

'I've gone through the statements from the neighbours and the staff at the nightclub; it sounds like Blair didn't have any enemies.'

'I wasn't sure before, especially with this so-called terrorist connection, but that *Dear Boss* letter makes me wonder if someone murdered Edwin Blair because of his father.'

This wasn't a chance attack; the penguin stamps and the letter proved the killer needed to communicate something to us, and perhaps someone else. All that meant to me was the murderer wanted to punish Sir Oswald Blair for some reason, and the easiest way for them to do it was through his son.

'It might make more sense than having a morality killer in our midst.'

I got out of the chair and stretched my legs, considering our next move as I received a message from Cane. I glanced at it and knew where we'd be heading this afternoon.

'You could be right, Jack. We've been summoned to a meeting with the Home Secretary.'

'Are we going back to his dodgy club?'

'No, but it's somewhere similar: he's waiting for us at Ten Downing Street.'

I was grabbing my jacket when Constable Sutton approached me with a look of complete shock on her face.

'I'm sorry, ma'am, but... but...'

'Spit it out, Constable.'

My mobile was in my hand when the new text popped onto the screen.

'It's about your daughter, ma'am. She's downstairs in custody.'

I didn't read the message from Abbey's school on my phone, pushing past Sutton and rushing towards the cells.

8 SOMETHING MUST BREAK

Two uniformed officers were watching over my daughter as I burst into the room. Abbey appeared bored as I stumbled toward her.

'What happened?'

She gazed at her fingers, avoiding the steam coming from my ears. A constable approached me.

'There was an incident at your daughter's school, ma'am. They called us and asked for her removal. We thought it best to bring her to see you.'

'What did you do?'

I stared at Abbey, but she peered at the floor. The officer handed me a phone.

'Everything is on video, ma'am.'

I took the device from her even though I was focusing on Abbey. She lifted from her seat, peered at her nails and ignored me. My head ached as the walls appeared to shrink around me, my fingers pushed into the mobile. I twisted my head from my daughter kicking her feet into the floor and played the video.

There was no sound, but the visuals spoke for themselves. I recognised the library from my visits to the school; it was empty apart from two girls sitting at a table and talking as books lay unopened in front of them. My eyes wavered for a second, returning to Abbey with her head away from me, her shoulders relaxed.

Then Abbey appeared on the screen, one from earlier in the day, striding towards the teenagers in the library. She seemed more focused than the one sitting near me, with a smile on her face so wide, I wondered why she was that happy. The on-screen Abbey carried an enormous book with her, something so substantial it took two hands to hold it. She grinned like I'd never seen before, a malicious smirk which made the phone shake in my fingers. Part of me was glad she was so happy, considering how difficult things had been for her in the past six months, but I was also aware nothing good was going to come from whatever this was.

Abbey was close to the girls when I realised what she was about to do; I saw it not only in her body's movements, but also in that malevolent smile. It was a smirk which never wavered as she swung the book hard into the head of the nearest girl. Even in the silence, I imagined the crack of bone as flesh met heavy paper, and the kid flopped to the side. Her friend threw up her arms and a soundless scream engulfed her horrified face. Abbey kept on walking, still holding the book, and disappeared from view. The screen froze on the image of the victim slumped on the table, her long hair strewn over the wood, as the other girl delivered a muted howl.

My fingers trembled as I returned the phone to the constable.

'Who filmed this?'

I had other questions to ask, desperate to turn to Abbey and scream: *Why did you do this? What's wrong with you?*

Instead, my mind told me to be a mother, but I fought to stay a copper and remain calm. To my shame, I hadn't thought about the girl Abbey attacked.

'The school has cameras everywhere.' She glanced at her colleague and then back to me. 'As you're a parent of a child there, I assumed they would have informed you of this, ma'am.'

I recognised the struggle in her eyes between addressing me as the guardian of this violent thug and a superior officer in this police station.

'They probably did.'

How many times had I ignored or pushed to one side letters sent to me from her teachers? There was a drawer full of them at home, left for when I had some spare time.

'We spoke to the principal. She mentioned the trouble Abigail had at school last year. She thinks it may be a mitigating factor in this incident.'

Abbey scrutinised the table. I wondered if she was embarrassed, or perhaps she didn't care. I left the room and indicated for the constable to follow me.

'Has my daughter spoken to you about what happened?' I was reluctant to say it out loud, but had no choice. 'Did she mention why she attacked this girl?' Was it connected to last year's problems, a reaction to the bullying and online grooming she'd suffered?

But Abbey didn't have a violent bone in her body, or so I thought.

'Abigail has given a statement about the incident, ma'am. She claims the other girl was harassing younger pupils at the school. I understand your daughter runs a counselling group for victims of bullying. We've asked her for the names of these girls, but she refused, saying it was confidential information.'

I leant against the wall, letting the concrete seep into my flesh. Halfway down the corridor, Jack stared at me; I didn't know he'd followed me. I returned my attention to the constable.

'Did you talk to the girl she hit?'

The violence of that video duplicated itself inside my heart, a whack which nearly knocked me over. I placed my hand on the wall to steady myself; it was cold and sent a shiver through every part of me. The corridor appeared to be constricting around me, suffocating my body as I struggled to breathe.

'Her jaw is cracked in three places; she's unable to speak right now and is in the hospital receiving treatment. We'll go there once we've handed Abigail over to you.'

'She hasn't been charged with anything?'

That was a relief and a surprise.

'The school principal said she wants to talk to you first, and the girl's parents are still in a state of shock.' The constable sighed. 'But, to be honest, with this clip, we have enough to send Abigail to a youth court.'

My shoulders slumped as I watched Jack approaching. Young people who committed minor offences were dealt with outside of the court system as much as possible, but for serious felonies, they visited a youth court; and this looked like a severe offence. Abbey might have killed that poor girl. I dug my nails into my leg as the video played in my head again.

Jack came closer as I considered what would happen to Abbey if she went to court: kids at a youth court can be bailed, or remanded into custody. I rested my free hand over my heart; they could lock Abbey up. It would depend on whichever of my colleagues was in charge and what they decided based on the evidence; and the girl and her parents' testimony. And the school; I assumed they'd expel her after this.

As for charges, the police would make a recommendation to the court about how to proceed. If the offender pleaded not guilty, they moved forward to a trial at the youth court later; if they pleaded guilty, sentencing followed. If their crime were severe, the case would go to the Crown Court for either sentencing or trial.

How serious was this? It looked terrible on the video. How much damage had Abbey done to the girl? She could be scarred for life; emotionally and physically. I had to find out why she'd hit her. Bullying other kids, younger kids, didn't sound like a justifiable reason to me.

'Is everything all right, Jen?' Ominous shadows consumed most of Jack's face.

'Abbey attacked a girl at her school.'

He ran one hand through his hair.

'Christ!'

'You can take her home, ma'am; we've finished with her for now,' the constable said.

I nodded and returned to the room. Abbey had lifted her head and stared at the door when I walked in. I kept all the emotion from my voice.

'We're leaving, Abigail.'

I left without another word. The recriminations would begin at home.

Jack waved his phone at me in the corridor.

'You need to check your messages, Jen; we've got to see the Home Secretary now.'

Abigail joined us, my focus switching between her and my partner. My daughter and I were overdue for a long talk, but maybe it would be better if I waited until the fire inside my head dissipated.

'That's okay; we'll take her with us.' I resisted the temptation to grab her by the arm. 'You're coming to the Prime Minister's house, Abigail; I wonder what he'll say about your actions today.'

I marched down the corridor, leaving Abbey to make small talk with Jack as we headed for the car. We took the stairs down and into the parking garage, finding my car near the exit. I let them decide who would get into the passenger seat, relieved when Abbey slipped into the back. After wanting to stare at her inside the station, now I had a hard time looking at her.

Jack strapped himself in.

'Did you check your messages? The Prophet seems irate.'

I pulled the car out and headed towards Downing Street.

'I've been too busy to look at my phone. Why are we seeing Sir Oswald Blair at the Prime Minister's residence?'

'There's a Cabinet meeting going on, and the Home Secretary wanted us there yesterday. I got the impression it's a command and not a request.'

'Great. It means we'll be treated like servants while informing the Home Secretary we're no further forward in finding his son's killer.'

'You can drop me off here and I'll get the Tube home.'

It was the first thing Abbey had said since I burst into the custody room. I didn't reply, letting the silence lie heavily on all three of us until it got too uncomfortable for Jack.

'Do we tell Blair about the letter?'

'I don't believe it's a good idea to keep secrets, do you?'

He shrugged as I drove through Westminster. There were twenty minutes of quiet apart from the occasional groan from the back and Jack tapping on his knee. I resisted the urge to turn the radio on, instead wanting Abbey to suffer in silence.

I couldn't think about the Blair investigation or the strange letter we'd received this morning; my only focus was on what I'd do about Abbey. She'd committed a violent assault, and I wasn't sure if she was aware of the seriousness of it or not; she didn't appear to be worried about it or my reaction. The ramifications of what she'd done stabbed at the insides of my skull until I thought it was about to explode. I kept seeing the clip of her attacking that girl, my imagination creating the sounds of the violence, the crack of bone and the screams of the others; and there was Abbey and that devious smile. I refused to stare at her in the mirror and pushed thoughts of the assault to one side. Now I needed to concentrate on this meeting with a murder victim's father.

I drove past the Cenotaph and took the left turn into Downing Street. There didn't appear to be an increase in security along the route; perhaps things had eased off since last night, and someone had realised Edwin Blair's death wasn't terror-related. However, I still couldn't dislodge the feeling of a connection to Oswald Blair.

Uniformed police officers waved me into a parking spot close to Number Ten. A black ironwork fence with spiked posts ran along the front and up the steps to the door. Outside of seeing it on the TV, I'd never got close to it.

I turned to Abbey.

'You stay here while Jack and I go inside; we shouldn't be too long.'

That's what I hoped, though I wasn't looking forward to having to deal with the teenager scowling at me.

'You can't leave me here on my own, Mum; what am I going to do?'

'Use your phone to find out the history of this building.' Her scowl transformed into a thunderous grimace of flesh. 'Or you could search online and discover how long you get in a juvenile detention centre for violent assault.'

I climbed out of the car and left her with those words. Jack looked worried.

'Is it that bad?'

'It could be.'

I had my ID badge in my hand, but I didn't need it. The door to Number Ten opened and I strode through the gap. As I marched to meet the British Home Secretary, all I saw was Abbey smashing that book into the girl's head again and again.

9 DAY OF THE LORDS

The blast-proof steel door of Number Ten closed behind us as I shut out the thoughts about Abbey's criminal behaviour. I surveyed our surroundings: black-and-white marble tiles covered the entrance hall floor, with a guard's chair in one corner. Once used when policemen sat on watch outside, it had an unusual "hood" created to protect them from the elements and a drawer underneath containing hot coals for warmth. Scratches on the right arm were from their pistols rubbing up against the leather; opposites brought together, but clashing as they did so.

Our guide spoke.

'The Home Secretary is waiting for you in the Cabinet Room.'

We followed him there, watching as ministers filtered out and barely acknowledged us.

The Chancellor of the Exchequer, his hands in his pockets, was laughing with the Secretary of State for Defence. Perhaps I should have brought Abbey inside to have a word with him. The Health Secretary wiped the sweat from his forehead as he glanced at me, while the

Minister for Transport showed someone photographs of an expensive-looking car. The Leader of the House of Commons sat slumped in a chair, while the Attorney General whispered to a woman I didn't recognise who was at least half his age and probably not his wife.

'Remember to doff your cap to your betters, Jack.'

It irked him, having to settle into his "proper" place in society. We were both raised on northern council estates, but his upbringing seemed to irritate him more when he stepped out of his comfort zone. I knew my place wasn't here, but I wouldn't let it faze me. The advantage of a privileged upbringing and going to better schools may have surrounded us, but it meant nothing in the grand scheme of things; that's what I told myself as I watched the members of the British Government pretend not to notice us in their midst.

'You can enter,' our guide said.

I followed Jack into the Cabinet Room, seeing the Home Secretary – official title the Secretary of State for the Home Department – talking to the Prime Minister and the Foreign Secretary. That's when I wondered if this was all for our benefit, to show us how important our victim's world was by association. Why bring us here if not to highlight who our lords and masters were? I shook my head, concerned that Jack's persecution complex was rubbing off on me.

The room focused my attention away from Jack. Painted off-white with huge windows along one of the long walls, it felt stuffy and warm. Three brass chandeliers hung from the high ceiling. The Cabinet table dominated the space; blotters inscribed with the ministers' titles marked their places around it.

The Prime Minister and Oswald Blair broke off their

conversation, and the leader of the country strode towards me with his hand outstretched. I stared at the glistening sweat in his palm as my eyes played tricks on me, seeing a stamped penguin winking at me before it vanished.

'Detective Inspector Flowers; it's a pleasure to meet you.'

His teeth sparkled as if covered in fresh paint, his vibrant hair perfectly styled. Before entering politics, he'd worked as a catalogue company model, and for one second I thought he might try and sell me a cardigan. There was a long-standing rumour our Prime Minister only needed to touch a woman to get her impregnated, which meant I peered at his outstretched fingers while terrible images ran through my mind.

I hesitated in taking his hand, before grasping his skin, which was warm, and allowing him to cling onto me for far longer than he should have. Up close in the flesh, he had a faint aroma of cheap aftershave wafting from him. Eventually, he let go, and I stepped back. His jacket and trousers were mismatched; his shirt may have glanced at an iron sometime in the past, but hadn't seen one today. Jack scratched at his neck, resplendent in his new shirt and Armani suit, providing a striking contrast to the country's leader. Seeing them together rekindled memories of my school days and the teachers badgering the kids about dressing smartly; uniforms were necessary, they said, because they represented you to the world. There were no mirrors in the room, so I couldn't check on what I was projecting to society's highest pillars.

'I'm surprised you know who I am, Prime Minister.'

His grin was reminiscent of one of those laughing policemen you used to find in seaside arcades.

'Poppycock, Inspector; the entire country is aware of the woman who caught the Hashtag Killer.'

His teeth shone like a shooting star, distracting me enough not to remind him I'd had help from Jack and dozens of others.

Oswald Blair stared right through me.

'Such a shame to discover the murderer was a police officer.' A block of ice covered his face. 'It hasn't left the service in a good light and has led to attacks on officers.'

He gazed at me, and I wondered if he held me to account for what he'd said.

The Prime Minister's smile disappeared.

'Best not to talk about that, Oswald; the public is easily upset.'

'Nobody likes to see privileged people get away with murder, Prime Minister.'

Jack's words surprised me; I was stunned to hear him openly mock our so-called superiors.

I addressed Blair. 'You wanted to speak to us, Home Secretary?'

The Prime Minister and the Foreign Secretary untangled themselves from us and left the room without another word. Blair led us from the table and towards a large painting on the other side. Jack peered at the portly figure in the frame.

'I was never good at history, but I assume he was important.'

Oswald Blair laughed, producing a noise I wouldn't have expected from a man with such a sizeable physique, a faint lilt like a nightingale singing. It was off-putting.

'You could say that, Inspector; this is Robert Walpole, 1st Earl of Orford, regarded as the de facto first Prime

Minister of Great Britain, and one of the greatest politicians in British history.'

How far we've fallen since then, I wanted to say but didn't.

The talk of history drew my mind back to Abbey in the car; I still didn't know what I'd do about her situation. Perhaps it was all beyond my control. I had a terrible vision of her in a prison uniform sitting behind bars, even though it wasn't like that in juvenile detention centres. It was my job to ensure it didn't come to that.

'I'm guessing we're not here for a history lesson, Home Secretary.'

'That's correct, DI Flowers. I have some information for you.'

'Since yesterday?'

He ran his fingers across the mantelpiece underneath the painting, tutting when he found dust there.

'No; I'm afraid I was reluctant to tell you this at our first meeting.' His eyes betrayed no emotion as he spoke. 'You can view it as the stupid worries of a man unsure of how to grieve the loss of his only child.'

He walked over to the table and took a seat; it amused me to see it labelled as the Prime Minister's chair. He motioned for Jack and me to join him. I got the Chancellor of the Exchequer's spot at the table, while Jack settled for the Foreign Secretary's chair.

'This is about your son?' I said.

Oswald Blair placed one hand on the table and pulled in his chest.

'I lost Edwin a long time ago, Inspector Flowers, even though I tried my best to stay in contact.'

'When did you last see him?'

'It was five or six weeks ago. I disliked going to his flat; it always smelt as if he'd hosted a drugs party or rave. It's also why I was reluctant to give him money because I guessed that's what he spent it on.'

I was unsure why, but I felt I should say something nice to him about his dead son.

'Our preliminary enquiries indicate Edwin never touched drink or drugs, Sir Oswald.'

He stared at me with eyes as big as saucers.

'That's good to hear, Inspector Flowers. Have you learnt anything else significant to the investigation?'

It hadn't taken him long to turn the questions on to us, but I wouldn't play his game.

'The landlord told us Edwin's rent was paid by direct debit every month; I assume by you?'

'That's correct, but I also transferred funds into his account when he begged me for it, which he frequently did.'

'Did you do that recently?' Jack said.

Blair removed a small notebook from his pocket and flicked through its pages. I got the impression he could pluck from memory all the times he had given his son cash.

'Yes, this is what I wanted to tell you face to face. I transferred a thousand pounds into Edwin's bank three days ago.'

I turned to Jack. 'Has the team gone through his financial details?'

Someone should have, though I had to admit it hadn't struck me as necessary when I checked his flat and employment history. Murder for money was one of the oldest crimes in the book, and I gave myself a mental slap for not considering it.

Jack stood and removed his phone.

'I'll ring the office and find out.'

He moved away as I faced Blair.

'The government don't think this is terror-related anymore?'

He shook his head.

'It seems unlikely, once you received the letter from the killer.'

Why wasn't I surprised he already knew about that?

'Were you informed of its contents?'

'I memorised each line of text by heart, Inspector.' He glanced around the room. 'I spent most of this meeting unaware of what anyone was saying since all I heard were those words.' He looked up to the chandelier. '*Exquisite corpse with no tongue for tales to tell.*' He returned to me. 'What does it all mean, Inspector Flowers; that and those stamps of penguins?'

What could I tell him that he didn't already know? Jack spoke before I thought of a satisfactory reply.

'Your son's bank account is empty, Home Secretary. He withdrew the money you sent him an hour after he received it.'

Oswald Blair gripped his hands together.

'Do you know what happened to it?'

Jack shook his head. 'No; not yet. It's one of our current lines of enquiry.'

'What are the others?'

It was a command, not a request. Jack looked at me to take the lead, and I obliged.

'The nature of the crime shows the killer, or killers, had observed your son for some time. This includes watching him at his place of work and recording when and where he went for his daily jog.'

'This was no random attack?'

'It seems unlikely.' I held his gaze, and he never blinked. 'We're considering if your son's death may have some connection to you, sir. Our officers will collect the information from your law firm, which we talked about yesterday, and then the team can go through what we have.'

Blair got out of his chair.

'You're wasting your time with that, Inspector Flowers, but I thank you for coming on such brief notice and keeping me updated.'

That sounded like a dismissal and, as if it had triggered a silent alarm, our earlier guide entered the room. The Home Secretary turned his back on us and moved to the window. We left the building without another word.

'We were summoned just so he could mention the money?' Jack didn't sound convinced, and I agreed with him.

'I think it was more of a reminder who we're working for.'

It didn't bother me too much. The bank account information and the missing cash might prove useful and mean it wasn't a complete waste of time. Would someone stalk and strangle Edwin Blair to send a message to others? I'd known drug dealers carry out more extreme acts of violence to make a point. In one case, when I first joined the force, a big-time dealer kept a swimming pool surrounded by mannequins looking as if they were having a party. Only when the police raided his mansion did they discover some of those dummies were dead bodies, with flesh preserved like animals from a taxidermist. It was a warning to any others who considered stealing from him. Blair's death could be such a warning as well, unless it was the work of a morality killer as that letter seemed to imply.

That thought slithered through my head when I got to the car and realised Abbey had gone.

10 SHE'S LOST CONTROL

I was on the phone and calling Abbey's number before I reached the car. She didn't pick up.

'Why don't you go home and see if she's there, Jen?'

I slammed my hand on the bonnet.

'We've just been told in no uncertain terms who we're reporting to on this case, Jack; I can't afford to get distracted.'

'You need to sort Abbey first.'

He was right, but I didn't want to admit it. And I didn't want to admit to myself I wanted to avoid a confrontation with Abbey for as long as possible. I was glad she wasn't in the car, turning my anger at myself for being so selfish.

I gripped the phone in my hand to regain a semblance of control; the longer I put off seeing her, the worse it would get. I peered at Jack.

'What will you do?'

'I'll go back to Edwin Blair's place, see if there was anything we missed regarding this money, possibly arrange for the sniffer dogs to pay a visit.'

'Okay. Will you ring the team and see where they're at with those files from Blair's law firm?'

'I will; you just make sure Abbey's okay.'

'Do you want a lift?'

He got his phone from his pocket.

'Nope; I'll call the office and get Sutton and Grealish to take me, and they can organise for a dog to be brought to the flat.'

I waved him goodbye and slipped into the car. I drove away, but didn't head home; I needed to do something before speaking to Abbey. This wasn't me still avoiding her, but needing to quell the guilt growing inside me. I reached the hospital twenty minutes later. Abbey hadn't replied to my texts, and I read the one from the school; they wanted a meeting with Abbey and me as soon as possible. I held back my reply until I'd done what I had to at the hospital.

The reception was busy when I showed a stressed member of staff my ID card. Her complexion was poor and her eyes bulged as she spoke to me.

'Can you sort out the idiots in Accident and Emergency, Inspector? I think there'll be a riot in there sooner rather than later.'

'Don't you have security?'

She shook her head. 'They're worse than useless.'

I searched through my head for the name of the girl Abbey attacked, the one the constable provided at the station. It popped into my brain at the same time as I saw the book smashing into her skull again. I winced as I shook the memory away.

'Can you tell me where Olivia Coates is?'

The receptionist checked her records on the computer.

'She's up on the second floor with an oral and maxillofacial surgeon.' She pulled the glasses from her nose. 'Some of your uniformed colleagues are already with her.'

I got directions and gave her my thanks. I took the stairs instead of the lift, using the time to consider what I'd say to this girl. I had nothing as I reached the corridor and saw the constable. I went up to him and showed my badge.

'How badly injured is she?'

A doctor stepped out and replied before the PC could.

'Ms Coates has fractures to the nose, cheekbones, the surrounds to her eyes, and the lower jaw. She'll be going for x-rays soon to check for other damage.'

Christ! Abbey did all that?

'Can those injuries be treated?'

'That depends on the type and extent of the fractures, which we won't know until after the x-rays. We'll likely need to bring the broken bones back into normal alignment and keep them in place, preventing further injury. We might need to operate to do this, possibly use plates, screws or wires inside or outside the bones to hold the fractures in position.'

My stomach lurched from side to side, imagining Olivia Coates leaving the hospital looking like the Bride of Frankenstein.

'How long before she heals, Doctor?'

His cheeks were hollow and gaunt, his eyes indicating someone who hadn't had a lot of recent sleep. I knew how he felt.

'There's no guarantee she'll recover from these injuries, and it'll be an arduous process, but I'd say two to three weeks minimum.'

Then he left. It sounded like a horror story; my brain was awash with images of those appalling injuries created by my daughter. Didn't she deserve juvenile court because of what she'd done to this girl disfigured for the rest of her life? If it had been anyone else other than Abbey who'd attacked her, then I'd expect the full force of the law to come down on them. If it had been in reverse, if Abbey had been on the receiving end of the attack and had all those injuries, wouldn't I have screamed blue murder?

As a thousand and one terrible things raced through my mind, two nurses wheeled Olivia Coates from the room. Bandages covered Olivia's head; her body was slumped in the wheelchair. What little food I'd eaten seemed desperate to get out of me. The constable looked at me for guidance. I forced the bile back into my gut.

'You need to stay with her. When the doctors give the okay, you can take her statement.'

'Yes, ma'am.'

He followed the injured girl down the corridor. As he left, two people I assumed to be Olivia's parents stepped out of the room; I guessed they realised who I was from the looks on their faces. I'd have put money on it being the father who'd erupt in a volcano of anger, but he was emotionless. Instead, it was the mother who turned into a human Krakatoa an inch from my head.

'This is your fault, Flowers.' She wagged her finger so close to my eyes, I worried one misstep would blind me. 'She's your kid, and you didn't bring her up properly; I bet you left her alone all the time and didn't teach her what's right from wrong, did you?'

The sweetness of her perfume couldn't hide the aroma of her rage. Was this my fault? Abbey hadn't had the upbringing I'd wanted her to have, but she understood the difference between right and wrong; she'd have to take responsibility for this and accept the consequences.

'I'm sorry, Mr and Mrs Coates.'

I didn't know what else to say, but from the mother's puffed out ruby cheeks and swollen eyes, it didn't appear to have a calming effect.

'We know who you are, Flowers, that you're a copper, but don't think that will let her get away with this.' Her hand rose and fell like a drunken lift. 'We'll take you to court and sue you for all you've got.'

The husband had his hand on her arm and pulled his wife away before I could muster a reply. I watched them shuffle down the corridor, heading for wherever their daughter was getting those x-rays. A nurse approached me as I imagined Abbey behind bars and our house and savings disappearing down that violent hole she'd created. Two teenage girls whose lives would never be the same again, and parents who'd wonder where it all went wrong.

As my mind ran through every possible terrible scenario, a woman's voice brought me back to reality. I turned to gaze into a glittering, infectious smile.

'The parents are likely suffering from post-traumatic stress caused by the realisation of their daughter's injuries.' She held out her hand to me, and I discovered she wasn't a nurse. 'I'm Dr Felicia Nelson, a clinical psychologist.' I shook her hand, unable to think of a reply. 'And you're Mrs Flowers, the mother of the girl who allegedly caused the injuries to Olivia Coates?'

She framed it as a question, but it was a statement of fact.

'There's no allegedly about it, Dr Nelson; it's all on video, and it's Ms Flowers.'

Dr Nelson clutched a clipboard to her chest.

'Ah well, I guess it simplifies the legal matters surrounding these injuries; but you'd already know that, being a Detective Inspector in the police force.'

'Have we met, Doctor Nelson?'

She shook her head and continued to smile at me.

'No, no, of course not, Ms Flowers.' She placed one hand over her mouth, and then removed it to reveal an even wider grin than before. 'Don't worry, I'm not stalking you; it's just, well, you were all over the news a few months ago and I heard your colleague talking about you and your daughter when Ms Coates arrived at the hospital, and... well, now I'm rambling, aren't I?'

I looked at her properly for the first time, her long chestnut hair tied back against her head and dark skin contrasting with the bland whiteness everywhere in the hospital. I would have guessed she was younger than me, but there was weariness in the lines on her face, which showed she'd had little sleep recently. It was a feeling I recognised only too well.

'Fame is doing its best to cling to me no matter how hard I try to shake it off, Dr Nelson.'

And everyone from doctors to serial killers knew as much about me as I did.

She placed her fingers on my arm and nudged me away from the corridor and the people bustling past us. Before I realised what was happening, we were inside the same room Olivia Coates had vacated. It smelt of blood and antiseptic, and when I glanced around, I imagined the poor girl screaming as the medical staff tried to help her. A scene from one of Abbey's favourite horror films popped into my head and I had a sudden shock, thinking that all the movies I'd watched with her recently, the psychological thrillers and film noir and horror movies, may have affected her behaviour. It took me two seconds to dismiss the idea as ridiculous.

'I don't want to pry into your personal life, Inspector

Flowers, but I understand your daughter had some issues about the same time you dealt with the Hashtag Killer.'

I peered at Nelson's name badge and her overall, wondering if she really was a doctor. It wouldn't be the first time someone had slipped on a white jacket and pretended to be medical staff in a hospital.

'Do you have some identification, Dr Nelson?'

She threw up her hands in horror, her eyes widening as if ashamed of something.

'Of course, Inspector Flowers; please accept my apologies.' She reached inside her coat, her fingers fumbling as she retrieved her photo ID. 'It's a terrible image, much worse than my passport, but I think you'll see I'm who I say I am.'

There was nervousness in her voice which hadn't been there before. I scrutinised the card before returning it.

'What's the difference between a psychologist and a clinical psychologist, Doctor Nelson?'

Her eyes sparkled as she replied.

'General psychology is the study of cognitive behaviours and psychological functions. Whereas clinical psychology is not merely a scientific study, but a step further and deals with the assessment and then treatment of mental illnesses.'

I returned her smile with my own.

'That's fascinating, but why are you talking to me about my daughter?'

She handed me a card and edged towards the door.

'I'm not trying to pressurise you, Inspector, but if you feel you and Abigail need someone to speak to regarding what happened today or last year, then please contact me. Mental health is the thing most of us push into the shadows when we should shine a light on it. If certain issues are left untreated for too long, it's no good for anybody.'

Her smile disappeared as she did, leaving me alone. I peered at her card and wondered if this was fate conspiring to force me to do something about Abbey's behaviour. As I considered that, a message beeped into my phone; it was from Abbey. Maybe it was fate. I stared at the image she'd sent, a mixture of relief and confusion concocting a heady cocktail inside my brain.

This is where I am.

I left the hospital and tried not to rush my way out. I was in the car and pulling it towards the main road in less than a minute, heading for Soapbox Comics.

11 NOVELTY

I strode into the shop. I'd expected it to be full of kids and comics, but there were groups of all ages and very few comics, with toys, games, statues and even some superhero-related clothes on racks. Two teenage girls laughed as they flicked through a book; a woman about my age held onto a *Game of Thrones* DVD box set, staring at the photo of Jon Snow on the back. The older bloke with her gazed at a poster of some scantily clad female aiming a futuristic pistol at a bug-eyed monster.

There was no sign of Abbey. My apparent confusion must have triggered sympathy in the teenage boy near me as he pointed to the stairs in the corner.

'They keep all the comics and the graphic novels on the next level up.' He scratched at his acne and smelt of bubble gum. 'It's annoying having this tourist stuff down here, and I have to go upstairs to get my pull-list.'

I didn't ask him what that was, imaging many salacious things blokes did with their pull-lists when they got home; instead, I marched towards the counter where two staff members were speaking to a customer. All three of them were unshaven, and it looked like hairbrushes or combs didn't exist in their shared universe. They were arguing about which fictional character was the stronger, Thor or the Hulk, as I approached them.

'Excuse me; is the owner here?'

They stared at me as if I was a shark in a goldfish bowl. The taller guy behind the counter, with shaved eyebrows and nails hanging from his ears, answered me. Construction nails, not human ones.

'Is it a complaint, love? We can deal with that.'

The three stooges smirked at me. The customer had a comic in his hand featuring an extravagantly dressed man wearing what looked like blue pyjamas and a billowing red cloak over his shoulders. The name on the cover said *Doctor Strange*, who appeared to be *The Master of the Mystic Arts*. The title reminded me, as if I needed anything to jog my memory, of the hospital I'd visited, and the teenage girl Abbey had injured. I reached into my pocket and touched the business card Dr Nelson had given me; if I convinced Abbey to speak to Nelson, it might be a mitigating factor if, when, she faced a juvenile court. And perhaps she might uncover why my daughter did what she did.

I peered at the three blokes, guessing they were five years older or five years younger than me; they were smirking so much it was difficult to tell. Then I showed them my police ID and watched the humour drip from their faces.

'The customer is always right.'

I turned to face that familiar voice. Steven Morris wasn't wearing his smart suit and tie, but was dressed in jeans and a t-shirt adorned with a bunch of comics bursting from a box. The top was tight-fitting and highlighted his impressive muscular torso; had he been this attractive the first time I met him? I disregarded any formalities and shook an unusual and inappropriate image from my head.

'I'm looking for my daughter, Abigail. I think she's here somewhere.'

His lips curled upwards to reveal the warmest of smiles. He placed two fingers on my elbow, his touch sending a shiver through my skin. I'd generally flinch from unwanted physical contact or give the person a quick slap, but I let him lead me from the startled blokes at the counter.

'Follow me, Jen. I'll show you where she is.'

He let go of my arm, and we strode past displays from films I didn't recognise. These included giant posters of costumed violence and a life-size cut-out of a woman with unreasonably large breasts and a minimum of clothing. Her face growled like a wolf, with one arm outstretched and a fist ready to punch an invisible assailant.

'She's here, then?' That was a relief.

'Abbey told me her name and who she is when she arrived.' We headed towards the back. Glass covered the top half of a door while shadows moved on the other side. Morris stopped a foot from it, his expression changing from joy to concern in an instant. 'And she mentioned the trouble she's in. I wanted to get her involved in an activity to occupy her mind.'

I didn't like the sound of her confiding in him. He moved to the side and I approached the door, leaning forward to peer through the glass. At one point, it might have been a storeroom; now the room housed a table and chairs where a bunch of teenage girls chatted while throwing dice, turning over cards and moving figures over a board game. Vague memories of playing Cluedo with my mother skipped around in the shadows of my skull; then I remembered it wasn't like that. She'd never play games with me because I'd be sent early to bed while she entertained her friends named Walker and Daniels.

Abbey sat at the far end, a massive grin on her face. I couldn't remember the last time I'd seen her so happy. I turned to him.

'What is this?'

'You need a ticket, and I'm the inspector.'

My mouth dropped open and something resembling a word stumbled out.

'Huh?'

'I introduced Abbey to this female-only TRPG. It allows them to focus on tactics and characters without being distracted by the ego-driven guys who come here.'

'Pretend I'm an idiot and explain what a TRPG is.'

'It's a tabletop role-playing game. To be honest, the games' playing isn't that important as the kids, and the adults, use the sessions as small social gatherings. It's a brilliant way to meet new people.'

I peered through the glass again, watching Abbey smile and laugh with a crowd of people I assumed she'd never met before today. I searched my brain, trying to recollect the last time she'd had any friends over to the house. I had no memory of her mentioning anyone she was friendly with. Even with the anti-bullying group she'd started at school, I'd always seen that as a support network and not a bunch of mates getting together. She acted like an adult with them and not another teenager. It must have been stressful for her, dealing with other people's problems. And she was only thirteen. Perhaps that was what tipped her over the edge to attack Olivia Coates.

'So I need to be invited in?'

He laughed at me.

'They're gamers, not vampires, Jen. You can go in.'

My fingers were on the handle, the tremble in my arms transmitting to the wood so it rattled. Abbey's joy beamed from that room. If I entered, would my presence wipe that away? Of course it would.

'No, let's leave her to finish the game. I'll speak to her later.'

I turned to leave. Morris strode with me; his walk was light, soundless like a ninja.

'I've put aside some graphic novels for her to read at home. She should enjoy them, and they might help her.'

We were close to the exit and the staff were nowhere in sight. His eyes sparkled blue and put me at ease. The tension of not knowing what had happened to Abbey after she left the car, and the memory of her violence, seeped out of me; I was more relaxed now than when I'd entered the shop.

'Okay, thanks for that and letting Abbey join the group.' I dug into my pocket and pulled out a twenty-pound note. 'Can you give this to Abbey and tell her I'll see her at home?'

He nodded and took the money. 'It's my pleasure, Jen.'

I remembered her laughter and felt good.

'I'll be in touch.'

I was only delaying dealing with Abbey's troubles, but better then than now. I left the comic shop, glancing at Morris as I went with a sweet smile drifting across my face.

I GRABBED something to eat on my way to work, visiting a drive-through for fast-food which was neither quick nor particularly edible. I couldn't get the bad taste from my mouth as I entered the station and headed to the team.

The investigation had acquired several people since the morning. Sutton and Grealish had distributed the files from Oswald Blair's old law firm over four tables, and there were boxes of them stacked against the wall. Other officers looked through the paperwork and transferred information onto computers. This should give us a searchable database to find links between Blair's cases, and possibly something to tie into his son's death.

A map of the crime scene adorned one wall, and someone had connected coloured tape to it to show where Edwin Blair had jogged before his unfortunate demise. Telephones rang, notes were taken, and each face looked focused. There was a duty roster pinned to a wall. It was a waste of time putting Jack and my names on there as we'd be working every hour possible until we caught the killer, but it was essential the others got time off, or mistakes would happen. And I knew from bitter experience even the smallest mistake could lead to more deaths.

I walked to my desk and checked for messages, finding nothing from Oswald Blair but a reminder to see Merson in her office. I removed my jacket and went to the coffee machine; that meeting with the SIO could wait, or she'd come to me.

Jack strode over and handed me a sandwich.

'How's Abbey?'

I told him about the comic shop and the possibility of arranging a session for Abbey with the clinical psychologist.

'I need to be careful about how I approach her with it.'

Jack sipped at his coffee.

'Perhaps you should tell her it's part of a programme she has to take to avoid juvenile court.'

'I'll see what happens first. I haven't heard from the officers who brought her in since I spoke to them earlier.'

I was reluctant to approach them; hoping ignorance would make the incident disappear.

'But she doesn't know that.'

'You think I should lie to my daughter?'

'You would, wouldn't you; if you thought it would help her?'

He wasn't wrong, but I didn't want to talk about it.

'Has there been any more mail?'

'No. Are you're expecting another letter?'

I was, but unsure if I wanted another one.

'I'd be surprised if there isn't one. These killers don't appear out of nowhere; they're created over time, taking years to formulate their plans and grandiose schemes. Someone knows them, works with them or lives with them; and maybe helps them.'

'What's our next move?'

'We might have to go public on this sooner rather than later.'

'Go public with Blair's name? I'm not sure how the Home Secretary would take that, or Chief Superintendent Cane.'

'We'll keep the penguin stamps and the letter out of it, but the rest should go to the media; you can wear your best jacket when you appear on TV.'

He spat bits of coffee onto the floor.

'Oh no, Inspector Jennifer Flowers, famed catcher of the Hashtag Killer; you'll be the poster girl our superiors will want for that.'

'I'm fairly sure you and about two dozen others played important parts in that investigation.'

Jack grinned. 'Perhaps so, but you know going to the media is risky.'

I sat in front of my computer and switched it on.

'There'll be anonymous tips by the lorry load, none of which will be useful. Added to that will be the false confessions, the nervous next-door neighbours twitching behind their curtains, and the people with grudges who want us harassing any number of innocent citizens of this city.'

He shook his head. 'Once the circus starts, it won't be long before all the clowns come falling out of the woodwork.'

I scanned the file Sutton or Grealish had created for the letter. I spent the rest of the day reading and rereading it until I got word blindness. The more I stared at the text on the screen, the more I thought of that big book smashing into Olivia Coates's head.

12 DISORDER

I didn't go straight home, my mind a box of confused emotions, unsure of what I'd say to Abbey which wouldn't make the situation worse. I left the station and entered the hub of tourism around the area.

Shops lined the streets: antique and art stalls, jewellery and junk stores, boutiques, souvenir kiosks selling London tat, and mobile phone retailers. All fought for space with the big names in food and drink and a bunch of vegan and vegetarian places. I crossed the road and marched into the nearest place which would sell me a cup of strong, sugary caffeine.

The air was thick with coffee as I strode to the counter. A cocktail of teenagers and pensioners stood in the queue before me. Legend had it that 9th-century goat herders noticed the effect caffeine had on their goats, which appeared to dance after eating the plant's fruit. A local monk then made a drink with it and found it kept him awake at night, thus the original cup of coffee was born. I pictured myself as a criminal herder failing badly.

I picked up a newspaper from the counter as I waited,

flicking through it to see if there was news about Edwin Blair. There was plenty of death inside: stories of mothers murdering their babies, husbands slaying their wives, multiple incidents of fatal stabbings, but there was no mention about the son of the Home Secretary. I guessed someone was working overtime to keep the story from the media.

But it couldn't last long. The adherents of the internet and social media would discover it soon enough, and then it would be in every newsfeed and notification. Once we released the letter's details to the press, which we would eventually, then it would be Christmas come early for crackpots and conspiracy theorists everywhere. Perhaps Jack was right and we should get ahead of this, to control the narrative before having it snatched from us. I wondered how to do that as I considered if I had the ingredients at home for an Espresso Martini.

The queue strolled forward and I ordered a black coffee; it was tall, thick and hot, and I hung on to it like sunken treasure as I found somewhere to sit. I wrapped my fingers around the mug, enjoying the heat spreading through my hands. I took a sip, the fire biting at my lips. It wasn't sugary enough, so I dumped more sweetness into it.

I hoped the mixture of caffeine and sugar rush would inspire me in what to say to Abbey when I got home. Playing the board game at the comic shop and meeting new people could be useful for her; it might be the perfect environment to show her what she did was wrong. Or maybe it would only fuel the violence which had been inside her all along. As the drink warmed my throat, I dredged my memories for what I was like as a teenager, searching for examples of me misbehaving when I was Abbey's age. There were a few, even some as violent as what she'd done to Olivia

Coates, but I'd always told myself I had a good reason for my actions then.

Most kids can be troublesome, but they grow out of it, especially with the right guidance. My parents were useless at that, but at least their behaviour taught me what not to do: I just had to put those life lessons into practice with my daughter.

I clenched my fist as the caffeine kick-started my brain, remembering days long past and the fights I'd got into at school. Those kids had assumed a preacher's daughter would be all sweetness and light, most of them shocked to hear the language shooting from my mouth. My knuckles cracked and I smiled at the memory of it, recalling how joyous it felt to exercise power over those trying to harass me.

The noise in the café increased as a group of kids barged through the door, their enthusiasm for life annoying some customers. Theirs was the future Abbey could have, as long as I sorted her present problems.

More people came and went, bringing the smell of the street with them, a bouquet of car fumes, old clothes, and fresh sweat; thankfully none of it was strong enough to over-power the coffee aroma. I was savouring my drink when someone slipped into the chair opposite. The woman held out one hand, her mocha steaming in the other. She had hair so black against skin so white, it was as if she'd fallen out of the frame from a Victorian Gothic picture.

'My name is...'

'I recognise who you are, Ms Nightingale. Every police officer in London is aware of the criminal's favourite defence lawyer.'

She pushed her cup to the side.

'Did you know some 16th-century Italian clergymen

tried to ban coffee because they thought it satanic?' I wasn't a connoisseur of the drink, but that seemed rather excessive. She withdrew her hand and smiled at me. 'My friends call me Charlie, but Charlotte will do for this conversation, Detective Inspector Flowers.'

'To what do I owe this unwanted intrusion into my privacy, Nightingale?'

Her smile grew large enough to consume the room as her pale-eyed, haunting face gave me the shivers.

'I was about to visit you at the police station when I saw you come here.'

'Visit me about what?'

'I need to speak to you about Alice Voss.'

And then the shivers increased, and cold swept through my body. I grabbed hold of the drink and willed the heat into my head.

'Are you her latest lawyer? Is she finally going to confess?' If so, it would be the first good news I'd received today.

'I thought I should warn you, Inspector, that Ms Voss will tell her life story in a series of podcasts starting tomorrow.'

I nearly spat caffeine all over her, instantly regretting not doing so and gulping down the warm liquid.

'And why should I care about that?'

Nightingale stood, leaving her drink untouched.

'Because you'll feature heavily in it and my client wanted me to make sure you're aware of this.'

It took ten seconds for my blood to stop boiling.

'How much is she getting paid?'

'There is no profit in this for Ms Voss, Inspector. I'm sure you know that, under the Coroners and Justice Act 2009, convicted criminals can't profit from publishing their autobiographies.' Her lips trembled slightly as she spoke. 'But she can tell her side of the story.'

'Voss had her day in court, Nightingale. She had plenty of time then to tell the entire world how she manipulated vulnerable people into committing her crimes.'

I resisted the overwhelming temptation to crush the bowl of sugar cubes next to me.

The lawyer smiled and left without another word. The steam drifted from her mocha and wafted over my face as an image of me sitting on a satanic goat as I'm led through the city gates obscured my vision. I made a mental note to check on her as I watched Charlotte Nightingale disappear into the crowd of tourists outside.

I PICKED up pizzas on the way home, the heat of the boxes warming my arms as I entered the house. I headed to the kitchen, noticing the colourful books spread across the table; they must have been the graphic novels Steven Morris promised for Abbey. I placed the food on top of the oven and slipped off my jacket. How long should I wait before calling upstairs for her? Abbey strode in as I was thinking about it.

'I didn't know you liked comics.'

I couldn't hide the surprise in my voice.

She reached over and plucked a book from the table. It had a colourful cover, and she handed it to me.

'This is Ms Marvel, a teenage female Muslim mutant.'

I didn't know what a mutant was, but I guessed a female Muslim would be unusual in the world of superheroes. I flicked through the pages, intrigued by the artwork and the dialogue. How come I'd missed my daughter's interest in this? I handed it back to her.

'Did you have a wonderful time in the comic shop?'

It was anything to avoid asking her the most important questions.

Abbey clutched the book to her chest as the cat wandered into the kitchen.

'It was great, Mum; all the girls are friendly. It makes a change from school.'

'How are things at school?'

It was a roundabout way of asking why she'd broken that girl's face. Abbey returned the book to the table.

'The support group is going well. We've had a few fresh recruits in the last month. I think everyone is enjoying it.'

But was she? I glanced at the clock on the wall.

'Is Olivia Coates in your group?'

Abbey's shoulders slumped, her hand shaking as she placed it on the table. Her eyes avoided mine as she spoke.

'Initially, but then I asked her to leave.'

'Why did you do that?'

She let out a loud sigh, the fingers of both hands digging into her palms.

'She bullied some younger girls.' A fire burned in her face, simmering anger I'd never seen before. 'I guess she thought it was funny, being in an anti-bullying group and then harassing others.'

'You did the right thing asking her to leave, Abbey. Did Olivia leave the group?'

'Eventually, but she continued to pick on those smaller than her. It started with words, ripping into the others with disgusting insults, but she couldn't stop at that; then she beat up a few of the kids, leaving bruises where you wouldn't see them under their clothes. It got worse every day; she got worse every day. The kids wouldn't tell their parents or any adults, so I couldn't let it go on.'

'Did you tell a teacher?'

Abbey laughed, her eyes dismissing my words as much as the tone of her voice.

'As a group, we're supposed to deal with things ourselves and not rely on adults to stand up for us; but yes, I spoke to teachers in school, but none of them believed me. Olivia is pretty and charming. She's one of the top students, and all the teachers love her.'

'Why was she in the group?'

Her laugh didn't wipe the disdain from her face.

'She's a chameleon who can adapt to any situation. Olivia was the most popular kid at school until what happened to me and I started the group; she hated that. All she wants is attention.'

'And now she has it.'

Was that it; was it that easy to understand why Abbey had committed such a violent act, why she'd done something inconceivable? Did the other girl use violence for attention, and then Abbey reacted with the only course of action she thought possible to protect others?

Fear crept over her face.

'What will happen with the police, Mum? Will I have to go to court?'

I remembered my conversation with Felicia Nelson.

'Perhaps not if you agree to visit a clinical psychologist.'

How easily the lie dripped from my lips.

She pulled a chair to one side and slumped into it, her hands grabbing at her hair and the sparkle vanishing from her eyes.

'A clinical psychologist? Would I have to tell them about my innermost secrets?'

Secrets? What secrets did my daughter have from me? She'd be fourteen this year, and I considered what I was like at the same age; recalled the secrets I'd kept from my parents. A sudden memory surfaced from the dark waters where I'd hidden it, a flash of pain which made me recoil from the table. I fumbled into a chair to steady my legs and heart; the voices in my head told me how terrible I was.

You're not our daughter.

I tried to focus on Abbey.

'You won't have to tell her anything, but it'll show willing on your part in understanding why you did what you did.'

I couldn't say the words: *we need to understand why you attacked that girl.*

'I told you why I did it: she bullied the other girls.'

I placed my hands on the table and gave her a smile which I hoped would comfort her.

'Of course, Abbey; but the authorities, the school and social services, will have to see something on your part which shows you want to deal with your actions.'

And prevent it from happening again. And what if it doesn't stop you from going to juvenile court, anyway?

I left my hands there, waiting for her to take them. Instead, Abbey hauled the chair across the floor as she got up, the wood scratching against the kitchen surface and making the cat jump. She stormed off and left me with a head full of confusion.

I waited downstairs for half an hour before going to bed, my heart heavy with a thousand tortures and my mind consumed with thoughts of comic books and killer penguins.

Charlotte Nightingale was twelve when she made two decisions which shaped the rest of her life. The first was proclaiming she would be called Charlie, not Charlotte. The father who'd abandoned her years before had given her only one decent thing, which was her surname. Charlotte was her mother's choice, and though she didn't mind it, she much preferred to be Charlie. Her second came after she fell in love with the novel *To Kill A Mockingbird* and decided she'd be a lawyer when she grew up, defending those who couldn't protect themselves. It had been a long and challenging process to get to where she was in her professional life, made even harder by coming from a working-class background, but she only reverted to Charlotte when working.

As a teenager, she was the odd one out at school; not because she dressed like a Goth and listened to 80s music, but the fact she was the only girl her age who didn't want to be a YouTube star or win a reality TV competition. Charlie couldn't see the point of spending all her spare time in front of the TV or on the internet; not when she could read and listen to music. Most of the kids she hung around with, including her many friends, spent their lives glued to mobile phones and playing games, which Charlie knew were empty calories for the brain. Her father had wasted his life on meaningless pursuits, and she was determined not to follow him down that path. Even at an early age, she was driven to succeed in life while her friends fell away into pointless marriages or dead-end jobs.

Her dedication to studying and love of education earned her the nickname of The Professor. She'd acquired several worse *noms de plumes* since she began pitting her wits against the police and the legal system, none of which were very flattering, but she'd enjoyed every minute of it. But she'd never seen a case as fascinating as this: Alice Voss, the so-called Hashtag Killer, even though there was no proof she'd ever killed anyone. The police and prosecution described her as a mastermind, an expert manipulator. They'd found plenty of evidence she'd had conversations with those who'd committed the crimes attributed to the Hashtag Killer; that she'd encouraged and helped them to kill. But she'd never laid a finger herself on any of the victims.

The case fascinated Charlie at the time, but she soon focused on her clients once Voss was convicted; so why was Voss asking for her now?

And why should Charlie be bothered?

She didn't know, but if the biggest case to hit the media in years didn't grab her attention, then maybe it was time to be searching for a new career.

Charlie read through Voss's file, ignoring the details about her crimes and focusing on the woman's life before joining the Metropolitan Police Force's Cybercrime Unit. Like Charlie, Alice was born in Yorkshire; Sheffield for the incarcerated ex-copper, Barnsley for the lawyer.' Her parents took the family to Australia, but Alice returned to England as a teenager. At twenty-eight, Voss was twelve years younger than the woman now scrutinising her life. One of the best in her school, she excelled in her exams, and did even better at university, gaining a First Class degree in computing from Oxford. No wonder the police snapped her up.

As impressive as this was, none of it was what interested Charlie. It was Alice's identical twin Beth she wanted to learn more about. The girl had disappeared when she was seven, an assumed abduction. According to the prosecution at Alice's trial, this had triggered her plans of revenge years later. Revenge not against the unknown person who took her sister, but anybody else suspected of getting away with a violent crime.

Charlie read through everything twice and found nothing she could use to get the conviction overruled. Yet Voss wanted to see her. Why?

Two hours later and Charlie Nightingale sat opposite Alice Voss inside a cold prison room. That's when she got the answer to her question.

'I need someone to be my voice,' Alice Voss said. 'I'm not allowed access to the internet or any social media or even the telephone. And all my letters are vetted before leaving here. I need someone to tell my story to the world.'

Charlie placed her phone on the table.

'I'll use this to record our conversation.'

She didn't ask for permission. Alice pointed at it and grinned.

'Mobile phones are cigarettes for the eyes and ears.'

'Some would say you couldn't have committed your crimes without it.'

'The prosecution did.'

'And they won their case.'

Alice shrugged. 'And I'm refused access to things most other prisoners take for granted.' Her fingers moved towards the phone before pulling away. 'While in the real world, there are kids reared by smartphone-addicted parents, the children competing with the screen's chemical glow for attention. Every sphere of contemporary civilised life will highlight a swarm of the population in complete thrall to devices they're unable to withdraw from, with neon displays attached to their eyes and ears like tubes pumping drugs into hospitalised cancer patients.' She paused for a second. 'I can only hope in the future in places like this the authorities dole out smartphones to pacify the prisoners, with any threat of rebellion from the incarcerated snuffed out with the promise of zero access to what's trending on Twitter or Instagram, or the opportunity to wallow in the latest and hippest games. Remove the chance for selfies, and people will crumble.' She pointed at the phone. 'Instant photos are the new chains around our necks.'

Empty calories for the brain.

'The significance of photographs has changed during our lives.'

'How so, Ms Nightingale?'

'One aspect of modern life differing from previous generations is the context of time through photos. In the 19th century, they captured the moment, but without the commonality and regularity they did in the 20th and do today. In the past century, people more vividly witnessed the passage of time and measured those comparisons more startlingly. It brings home the variance of an individual's existence.'

Voss leant forward, excitement dripping from her.

'Absolutely, yes; but photos have now morphed into video clips and internet postings: it's a collection of our lives which would seem like magic to our great grandparents.'

'How can I help you, Ms Voss?'

Her eyes were bright enough to lighten a darkened room.

'You'll be the guardian of my legacy, Ms Nightingale; the person to direct it down the ages.'

'And how can I do that?'

'You and I must grab onto the coattails of the popularity of True Crime stories, Ms Nightingale; it will make you famous and reveal the truth about the Hashtag Killer and me.'

Charlie Nightingale peered across the table and wondered how famous she wanted to be.

14 ATROCITY EXHIBITION

Tiny nails clawed at the insides of Clive's chest. He couldn't remember the last time he'd brought anyone to his studio, let alone allowed them to watch his latest work before completion. There was no sound for thirty seconds, the drama unfolding along the old woman's black and white face: the lines were deep and many, stretching across her head. Her wide eyes moved randomly, their whiteness obscured by cataracts. Her hair was wispy over her scalp, and she placed trembling fingers over stray strands. There was frustration in those weary eyes. Her lips shivered as the words struggled from her mouth.

'How do these people fit inside the box?'

She held her hand to the camera, struggling to count her fingers. Her eyes turned from the lens, her ears listening to someone unseen. A single tear slipped from her eye as the scene changed to a man of a similar age. He leant towards the lens, the light illuminating a lifetime of experience in every nook and cranny of his flesh. His yellow teeth glistened as he spoke.

'What's this for?'

Clive's voice sprang from the video screen.

'It's a collection of memories, Richard. Look at me and say whatever you want.'

Aged eyes sparkled inside the digital world. Clive understood what came next, his heart thumping at how his guest would react to this.

'Whatever I want?'

'Take your time, Richard.'

Richard's wrinkled face crumpled as he rubbed at it with his spotted fingers.

'I've killed people.'

'I know; you were in the army.'

'No, after that. Innocent people; I murdered them. I enjoyed it.'

His eyes were midnight black, shimmering with raven wings. They held the type of darkness that sucks you in like a magnet and refuses to let go of your soul. The video froze on the image of Richard's eyes pouring through the screen. Clive leant over and turned it off. His guest gripped the glass of wine in his hand.

'What's this project?'

He'd told Clive his name was Frank, but Clive didn't believe him. He knew most people on the dating app never gave out their real names, and this bloke was no different. Clive always used his real name, and he didn't care, just like he didn't care it was a sex app.

'They're interviews with dementia patients, maybe the last ones they'll ever give. I'll enter it into an art funded competition, but my agent says I should direct music videos.'

Frank pointed at the screen.

'Do you believe this guy is telling the truth about being a murderer?'

Clive drank half of his wine.

'I'm unsure; I only got this one interview with him. I need to go back to the care home where he lives.'

'If it's true, and he tells you more, think of what this project could morph into.'

Clive hadn't stopped thinking about it since taking the film two days ago. He finished the drink as Frank wandered around the studio, examining everything he saw.

'What's with all these tools?' Frank stood next to a bench full of knives, axes, saws and hammers. 'You can't make many videos with these, can you?'

'They're for a future project, mixing traditional working tools with those of the new century; computers, the internet and social media. I want to draw a historical line between the first industrial revolution and today's technological one.' He scratched at his chin. 'But I don't have a theme for it yet.'

Frank picked up the biggest of the hammers.

'I have one for you: instruments of torture.'

'What?'

'From the hammer to the mobile phone, and everything in between, these were created to make life easier, but more often than not, are used to inflict pain and suffering; that's the theme you should use.'

Clive strode towards him.

'That's a great idea, Frank.' He shook his head and laughed. 'I must add your name to the list of acknowledgements; that's if you tell me your real name.'

Frank grinned at him. Then he swung the hammer into the other man. Clive's skull cracked like a sonic boom. Strength vanished from his legs in an instant, his flesh and bones giving way as he crumpled to the ground. Frank checked his clothes, making sure there was no blood on him.

He returned the hammer to where he'd got it and used his sleeve to remove any fingerprints.

'Do you have any towels or plastic sheeting in here, Clive?'

He left his victim quivering on the floor. Frank didn't know much about video artists, but he hoped they were like other visually creative people and kept plenty of material in the workshop. He checked the cupboards and shelves in the far corner, finding what he wanted on the last one. He pulled out the large sheet of clear plastic and dragged it towards Clive, who was trying to crawl away.

Frank knelt next to the broken man and took Clive's mobile from his pocket. He removed everything from the video artist's phone. Then he added it to what he was about to create. He draped the plastic sheet over Clive's body and turned to the bench full of tools. Frank had planned to strangle Clive, but this was easier; messier, but easier. He dug into his trousers and removed the penguin stamp. He lifted it and used the symbol on the struggling man's palms; then he replaced the sheet and the penguin.

Frank put on his gloves and peered at the instruments in front of him. He started with one of the smaller hammers; it wouldn't do as much damage as the other one, but it was lighter to swing. The bones in Clive's legs took longer to break, but it didn't matter; he had plenty of time. And how useful was it to have a soundproofed workshop?

He hoped his future victims would be this thoughtful.

15 DEAD SOULS

We drove to the scene of the crime, an artistic workshop and place of residence. I followed the blue lights into the backstreet and parked alongside the rest of the police vehicles; we left the car and headed for the building. It was one of four that made up the cobblestoned alley, three storeys high with most of the windows broken or boarded up. If challenging environments created the best artists, I assumed many Picassos and Jim Morrisons lived around here. Rats and feral cats ran between the bags of rubbish piled on either side of the alley. It stank of piss, shit and discarded food even the starving wouldn't eat. Empty cans of super-strength lager littered our route into the house.

Scene of Crime Officers were taking photos and bagging bits and pieces as we approached. I spoke to the uniformed officer at the entrance.

'Who called this in?'

'A neighbour got upset when she found groups of rats outside her flat. She rang us when she saw what they were chewing on.'

'And what was that?'

'The victim's flesh.'

Jack gulped and grabbed at his guts as we strode through the door and followed the noise and flashing lights. We stepped inside and observed the carnage across the ample space; blood lay everywhere, and it smelt like an abattoir. But that wasn't the worst of it: the body was in pieces, chopped up like a leg of lamb at a butcher's. The torso sat in the middle of a coffee table; the hands and feet were on opposite shelves acting as bookends. The legs were stacked with pots and pans in the sink, the arms hanging from the main ceiling light, while the head peered from the top of the TV; a face with wide eyes and a gaunt, expressionless stare.

Technicians from pathology took photos and videos while forensic officers continued their work. Constable Sutton stood nearby and headed towards me when I waved her over.

'This is a different MO from Edwin Blair's murder, so what's the connection and what do we know about the victim?'

I glanced away from the decapitated head staring at me, those haunted eyes lingering in my vision.

'We're waiting on a formal identification, which is difficult considering the state of the body.' I followed her gaze around the room, noting the array of limbs; was the placement random? 'But this is the combined workshop and residence of Clive Hamilton, a twenty-five-year-old video artist. The connection is the penguin stamp on the palms.'

'I used to own a dog that ate its own shit; that's what it smells like here.'

I recognised the voice.

'It's only the best for you, Sam.'

The attending pathologist, Dr Samantha Cooper, squeezed my hand. I'd met Cooper before, a tall, thin woman with cheekbones not too dissimilar to the bodies she dealt with, cold and angular looking. When you added that to her brown eyes, which might freeze you with a stare, it appeared as if she was as unapproachable as a hornets' nest. Still, she had a sense of humour which could fell a herd of elephants at ten paces. And the one thing you needed to survive in our jobs was the ability to laugh at death in all its guises.

'At least I don't have to clean up.'

She was right. Once Forensics had collected the evidence, it would be a civilian firm that would deal with the chaos. I knew someone who set up her own company once she saw how the crime rate was rising in the capital. She went from cleaning ovens to wiping up blood and guts and making a lot of money.

'Have you worked out how the victim died, Sam?'

Cooper lifted her fingers to her lips and pulled on an imaginary cigarette. It was three years since she'd quit, but I understood why she found it impossible to lose that motion; we used to spend time after her autopsies sharing packets of cigarettes and moaning about our terrible romantic lives. I think we both gave up nicotine and sex at the same point. She pointed at the pile of tools: hammers, knives, and two electric saws, while I imagined Steven Morris removing his comic book shirt. It was an unwanted and inappropriate image, and I shook it from my head.

'I think they probably had something to do with it, Jen.' Officers were bagging the equipment as Cooper spoke. 'But I'll have a definitive answer once we move everything back to the mortuary. Would you like to come and watch?'

'Why not?' Jack said.

Cooper peered at him.

'Did you get a haircut or have your ears moved down, Inspector?'

He ignored her as she left. We tried to dodge our colleagues as they did their work, but Constable Sutton approached me with a bagged mobile phone.

'Would you like this, ma'am, or shall I take it straight to Cybercrime?'

'I'll have a quick look.'

She unbagged it as I put plastic gloves on. If it needed a code to unlock it, I wouldn't have it long, but the screen lit up as I touched it. I checked his text messages, going through the recent ones first, finding nothing suspicious. His last few calls only contained numbers from his mother and sister. I was about to hand it back to Sutton when something made me check the apps on the phone; one jumped out at me: Grindr.

Jack stood next to me.

'This wouldn't be the first time we've seen a link between a Grindr murderer and a serial killer.'

He was right. There had been several murders where killers had trawled gay dating apps such as Grindr, arranging sex, and then rendering their targets unconscious with surreptitious GHB doses. Social media and internet applications had become such breeding grounds for violence, manipulation, and perversion, they needed to come with warning signs like cigarettes and alcohol did.

I opened the app and checked Hamilton's contacts and messages; both were empty. His profile contained photos of him happy and smiling, his appearance far different from what I'd seen in this room. I showed the phone to Jack.

'Do you think we can get the company that owns the software to give us their records for this account?'

He shook his head. 'I doubt it; they'll just quote privacy laws at us. Perhaps Cybercrime will discover something.'

It was a longshot, but the only one we had. I dropped the phone into the bag and handed it to Sutton. Then Jack and I completed a fruitless search of the workshop. We went through everything there, from the pornographic magazines we found in one cupboard to checking the clothes hanging in his wardrobe. There was nothing which pointed to penguins or strange letters about serial killers.

'There's nothing useful here, Jack; let's hope we learn something with the body.'

We left our colleagues to deal with the scene and stepped into the alley; the rats had vanished, but it still smelt of the sewer.

THE JOURNEY TOOK HALF AN HOUR. We were greeted by a mortuary technician the spit of Ian Brady, a sight which made me more nauseous than the smell of death and embalming fluids hanging over the place. He led us into the post-mortem room. Thankfully, the days when the Victorians dressed up the dead and photographed them with the living as mementoes given to the loved ones were long gone, but Cooper had once smoked cigarettes with me while browsing through a book of such photos and I always pictured those images when entering a mortuary. I shook an image of a dead girl standing next to her sister from my mind as we stepped into the room. Even though I had no intention of getting too close to the examination, the technician handed us disposable long-sleeved cuffed gowns and nonsterile, single-layered gloves to wear.

About a dozen plastic bags were brought in and

emptied of their contents: Clive Hamilton's remains. I didn't envy whoever would get to complete the formal identification of Hamilton's head. The walls were pristine white and smelt of chemicals, reminding me of every mortuary I'd ever been in: cold enough to make me wish I'd worn a scarf and gloves over the protective gear. Dr Cooper cleared her throat.

'Let's get started.'

She turned to her technician to ensure the video recorder worked. I peered at the instruments on offer to Cooper, wondering how many were like the saws and drills the killer must have used to separate Hamilton into so many parts. The technicians took photographs of each limb before Cooper examined them and presented her analysis of Hamilton's remains.

'Your murderer is nasty and methodical, but I don't think the dismemberment of the body was for forensic countermeasures.'

'It's sending a message.'

'Yes, Inspector Flowers; just like these.' Cooper held up Hamilton's hands, so everyone in the room saw the penguins stamped on them. 'Do you understand the significance of these birds?'

'No; I hoped you might help us with that.'

Cooper laughed loudly enough to rattle the lights above our heads.

'Well, I'm sorry to disappoint you, Inspector, but the method of murder on display here, with broken body parts and severed limbs, has no connection, as far as I can see, to penguins.'

I examined Hamilton's hands inside their plastic containers.

'How long did it take to dismember the body?'

The pathologist answered.

'There's no distinctive medical knowledge or expertise evident here; it's a hack and slash job: arms, legs, feet, hands, torso, and the head; probably all done and dusted within twenty minutes.'

It was an impressively quick slaughter.

'Did the victim die before the mutilations started?' Jack said.

'From the condition of the arms and legs, it seems unlikely, though I assume the pain would have rendered him unconscious.'

Jack wiped at his face. 'Let's hope so.'

'There are no defence wounds to the hands and the arms, implying an attack from behind for the initial blow.' She moved across the table and retrieved the head. 'I found a small hole in the neck here, can you see?' Cooper held it to my face, my eyes peering into Hamilton's dead sockets.

'Yes; what is that?'

'I won't know until the results of the bloodwork come back. I suppose it could have been there before the murder, but it's a recent incision, and it wouldn't surprise me if the killer injected something into the man to render him more pliable before they chopped him into pieces.' She looked at me. 'I didn't do the autopsy on the first victim; did they have any drugs in their system?'

Jack answered. 'The report said no.'

Cooper flicked a stray hair from her eye.

'If it's the same killer, and the penguins would indicate it is, then even though they've changed their method of murder, I'd still guess they'd have used the same thing to pacify their victims. How else would your first victim, Blair, not be able to fight back while strung up with a rope?'

Dr Cooper had always struck me as a frustrated detective, which was why she appeared keen to offer theories along with the medical science.

I stared across the different body parts in their bags, contemplating how a human being could end up resembling a jigsaw in a place like this. I'd hoped this method of murder, with so many potential pieces of evidence, would help identify a suspect. But now, watching Cooper and her technicians file Hamilton away into separate drawers with the head disappearing into the biggest of them, I contemplated how hard it would be to find a killer ready and willing to change their modus operandi on a whim.

No, not on a whim; method directed the madness, and it was my job to figure it out before more people died.

Jack rubbed his hands as he stood next to me.

'Do you think we'll get a letter tomorrow?'

One part of me wanted to, while another desired the opposite.

'We could check all the post-boxes near Hamilton's house.'

Jack shook his head. 'We don't have the personnel for that, Jen.'

'What time does the first class mail normally arrive?'

'Around nine o'clock.'

I nodded and headed for the exit. Dr Cooper shouted to us as we left.

'I'll send over the internal reports when they're finished.' She winked at me. 'Don't have nightmares.'

As Jack and I exited the building, I wondered how many people would watch over my remains like an audience in a cinema when I eventually moved off this mortal coil.

Abbey was excited when I arrived home.

'You've got a date tonight.'

I dropped my jacket onto the back of a chair and opened the fridge, needing a drink more than anything else; something to wipe away those images of Hamilton's dismembered body. The metal was frosty against my skin as I grabbed a can of fruit cider, the sweetness of it chilling my throat.

'What are you talking about, Abbey?'

She grabbed hold of my free hand and dragged me into the living room; she pointed at the phone, and the answering machine connected to it.

'Comic book guy rang you earlier.' Excitement rippled out of her. 'Listen to it, Mum.'

So I did.

'*Hi, Jen, I hope this isn't too short notice, but I was wondering if you wanted to meet for a meal tonight. It's not a date, just food and drinks between new friends. Give me a ring if you fancy it.*'

'Call him back now, Mum, go on.'

I took two large gulps, the cider thrusting a spark into my weary bones. Perhaps a night out would do me good. At least it would be a release from today's events. I knew I'd do it as soon as she mentioned it, but I wanted to mess with Abbey.

'I'm too tired, love. Plus, he said it wasn't a date.'

I slumped into the sofa and glanced at the clock; it had just gone six, but it felt nearer to midnight. Abbey put her hands on her hips, her cheeks flushing so she resembled an agitated teapot.

Why wasn't I speaking to her about what she'd done? Because it was easier that way.

'You better do this, Mum; otherwise, I'll get angry.'

And we couldn't have that. 'Anything for you, love.' I sipped at the can. 'Did you give him the home phone number?'

I still had the business card he'd handed me, but I didn't remember giving him my number.

Abbey scowled at me. 'I did, so you'd better call him now.'

How could I argue with that? I rang him back and got the details, warning him it might be a long and drunken night. He didn't complain.

I TOOK the Tube to the restaurant, getting on at Dagenham to go to Barking. Abbey had told me to wear a dress and makeup and have my hair done because that's what all the boys liked nowadays. I reminded her I wasn't going out with a fourteen-year-old and that my date liked nothing better than wearing jeans and shirts adorned with costumed superheroes. Plus, I couldn't remember the last time I'd owned a dress, let alone worn one.

It was seven-thirty, so I'd missed the end of the rush hour and the herd of humanity scampering to get some-where, anywhere. It was quiet when I got onto the platform and waited for the next carriage, listening to a playlist Abbey had created for me with music she'd downloaded onto my phone. I'd wondered if it would be raucous and give me some insight into her current frame of mind, perhaps a load of shouty punk nonsense from the late 70s, but was pleasantly surprised to be serenaded on the brief journey with a mellow collection. However, the only song I recognised was by Fleet Foxes.

Twenty minutes later, I walked into a Chinese restau-rant to meet Steven Morris. He waved at me from a corner table, and I dodged a waiter and joined the comic book man. A waitress smiled with the whole of her face as I sat down and she handed us menus. Before she left, I asked my date if he wanted to share a bottle of wine.

'I don't drink,' he said. I gave him a curious look. 'Wine.'

'You're quoting Bram Stoker to me.'

He laughed and I ordered a glass of White Zinfandel. He asked for fizzy water.

'It's to cover my nerves,' he said, even though he didn't appear nervous.

'That's what the alcohol is for.'

He laughed again.

'I bet you deserve it. I read on the internet about the murders; they're saying there's another serial killer on the loose in London.'

'What?'

He showed his phone to me.

'It's all over the web; the media are calling him The Penguin.'

I grabbed it from his hands, scanning through the stories on two sites, my guts churning and not from hunger.

'Shit!' Someone had leaked details from the murders, including quotes from within the investigation. Cane, Merson and the Home Secretary wouldn't be overjoyed at this. 'They've even got photos from the crimes.'

The waitress brought the drinks over in super quick time, and I drank half of my glass before Morris had unscrewed the top from his bottle of fizzy water. He looked at me.

'Is that a bad thing?'

'My superiors won't be happy about this. And I expect when I get to work in the morning, we'll have received hundreds of useless bits of information.'

'You could receive good tips.'

The water bubbled into his glass.

'A body strung up in the woods and another chopped into pieces; I'm hoping someone knows something.'

I didn't tell him anything which wasn't already in those internet reports. At least they hadn't leaked the details of the letter or printed images of the penguins.

I shut up when the waitress returned, and we ordered our food. I asked for another glass of wine, regretting not getting the bottle as soon as I'd sat down. I grabbed my phone and made an excuse to visit the toilets. It was empty inside as I threw water over my face and scrubbed at the haze eating at my eyes and infecting my brain.

Who leaked these details to the media? It could only be someone from our team. I peered at my reflection in the window and considered all the options before giving up;

then I called Jack. He didn't answer after three minutes; perhaps he hadn't seen the news.

I returned to the table as the food and my next drink arrived. Steve didn't wait on ceremony to eat, talking as he chewed.

'It's weird about those penguin stamps left on the victims; it's the behaviour of a super-villain.'

The wine flowed and my mind turned to mush.

'What do you mean?'

Bits of sweet and sour chicken dribbled over his lips.

'There's a Batman villain called The Penguin.'

I searched my brains to see what I remembered about Batman and his villains. My focus was distracted by wondering who the leak was, so I shovelled noodles down my throat for a bit of inspiration.

'Isn't Penguin a little bloke who walks funny with a long cigarette and an umbrella?'

There were vague images from late-night movie watching when Abbey was in primary school.

'That's how he started in the comics and was portrayed in the 1960s TV show and the movies, but the characterisation has become more sophisticated over the years.'

'When we first met, you said comics weren't for kids anymore; is this what you meant?'

He wiped sauce from his face.

'I won't bore you with a lengthy history, but something created for youngsters has developed and changed over the last seventy years. You get comics for all ages now; and those characters perceived as children's entertainment, such as Batman, Superman, Wonder Woman, Captain America, Thor and others, are written with more adult readers in mind.'

I finished my drink and searched for the waitress to

order another one, happy to have something to talk about other than the investigation.

'When did these changes happen? All I remember from my youth is kids reading grubby copies of *The Dandy* and *Beano*. My mother told me she used to have comics just for girls when she was growing up, but I didn't see those.'

She allowed no entertainment in the house, and the only reading material I ever saw her with was a wine list.

His eyes sparkled as he spoke and I assumed he enjoyed talking about his favourite subject.

'To be honest, those are British comics, whereas the characters I mentioned are American. And in America, the publishers have always aimed their product at as many consumers as possible. In the 1950s, when the States was at the height of its communist and UFO paranoia, certain publishers put out graphic crime and horror comics which caused a moral panic across the country.'

The waitress finally brought me another drink.

'I heard about that. Didn't it have a name?'

His cheeks were full of colour, and I thought he might explode. I had a similar sensation running through me, but for an entirely different reason.

'Historians call it the Ten-Cent Plague. Moral guardians such as the police, teachers, politicians, and the church believed comics corrupted America's youth. Influential people talked about banning all comics, and not just the horror and crime ones. The two biggest publishers, what we now know as Marvel and DC, decided they had to do something before the government intervened. So they introduced a voluntary Comics Code, which meant everything would be wholesome and good from then on. Crime definitely wouldn't pay.'

'I guess this didn't last?'

'It lasted long enough for companies to go out of business and ruin careers. It was only in the late 60s, early 70s when publishers abandoned the Code and started printing things a little more grown-up.'

I sipped at the wine, an idea forming in my brain.

'Do you get many serial killers in comic books?'

He grinned and finished his water. The alcohol made me light-headed.

'In the 90s, a publisher put out a series of comics featuring notorious real-life serial killers. People like Ted Bundy, Jeffrey Dahmer, and John Wayne Gacy. I think they were popular.'

'That doesn't surprise me. The public has always been fascinated with murder and repeat murderers have held a particular interest for the British ever since Jack the Ripper. Was it regular comic buyers who bought those serial killer issues?'

He screwed up his eyes as he pondered the question.

'Probably. Villains are as big a part of comics as the heroes. It's the same for most fiction. Where's the tension unless there's an antagonist to the protagonist?'

'Are serial killers popular characters in today's comics?'

'I think they always have been, but they weren't known by that term in the early days.'

'What do you mean?'

'The same villainous archetypes have run through the entire history of comics, from the 1930s to now.' He'd settled into teaching mode, but I didn't mind. 'We'll ignore the supernatural and extra-terrestrial ones and the groups and focus on the individuals.'

The next glass of wine sank like the *Titanic*. A few prawn crackers soaked up some of the alcohol.

'I'm all ears, Professor.'

'First, you have the gangster types, what we'd call the career criminals. In the earliest issues with Superman, that's who he's always fighting.'

'That's not much competition for someone with superpowers.'

'This is true, and that's why they created super-powered villains. But Superman's greatest enemy is the prime example of the next archetype: a famous name even non-comic readers should know.'

I racked my wine-addled detective's brain until I found an image of a chubby bald man.

'Lex Luthor.'

'Correct, Inspector Flowers. Luthor is what we call the megalomaniac controller of the world type. You can find them everywhere in fiction, from fantasy to spy novels. But these have limited interest to some people, especially non-comic readers. That's why we have the next category, the crazed costumed characters whose villainy is typified by grandiose criminal plans. The comic book Penguin is one of these, but it's another of Batman's villains, probably the most famous villain in comic book history, who I'd argue was the first serial killer in the comics. You'll know his name from the movies.'

The alcohol sloshed through my skull, and I wanted more, but the restaurant staff were giving us a wide berth.

'The Joker.'

He clapped his hands together so loud it hurt my ears.

'That's two for two, Jen. Characters like the Joker are sociopaths who disguise their crimes behind extravagant plots against their nemeses, but they're just your common or garden serial killers like Bundy or Gacy.'

'Every protagonist needs an antagonist.'

'That's what they say.'

'Does that mean I'm our killer's antagonist or protagonist?'

'If the media are keen for this serial killer to be known as The Penguin, it surely won't be long before they name you as Batman.'

The thought made me queasy.

'Don't you mean Batwoman?'

Morris giggled like a teenager.

'Of course.'

I got up from the chair, my legs wobbling as I did. I removed money from my pocket and placed it on the table.

'This meal's on me.'

'You're leaving?'

Disappointment filled his eyes.

'Don't worry, Steve, I'll see you again.' I checked the unanswered messages on my phone. Jack wouldn't get away that easily. 'I need to speak to my partner about the leak to the media. One of us will give a press conference in the morning, and if you're right, it's probably best he does it.'

'If I'm right about what? All I did was talk about comic books.'

'You gave me an insight I didn't have before. Now I have to wait and see if it's true.'

I turned and left the restaurant. A chill wind swept across my face as I called for a taxi. As I waited, my addled mind was full of images of costumed superheroes and villains.

Maybe the only connection between the murders was me.

But was I the protagonist or the antagonist?

17   NO LOVE LOST

Jack didn't answer the phone, so I took the taxi to his house. It was ten o'clock when I arrived. Jean wouldn't be happy to get a visitor so late, but I hadn't seen her for so long, and she might have a bottle of wine chilling in the fridge.

It took two raps on the door before she answered. The bags under her eyes were heavy and thick, and it looked as if someone had scraped white paint over her cheeks. The conversation in the restaurant with Steve made me think of the Joker as I spoke to her.

'I'm sorry for turning up so late, Jean, but Jack's not answering his mobile, and I need to talk to him. It's important.'

Her eyes widened and she let out a shrill laugh.

'Why am I not surprised he didn't tell you?'

'Tell me what?'

'I've kicked him out.'

I'd have been less shocked if she'd told me she was the serial killer.

'Kicked him out?'

'Yes, kicked him out for his cheating. I'm not one of those dutiful women who stand by her man, no matter how much of a bastard he's been.'

Perhaps it was the wine or the chill of the night, but I was light-headed and was struggling to understand what she said.

'Jack cheated on you?'

She narrowed her eyes and scrutinised me.

'I was convinced you were in on his little secret, all things considering.'

'Considering what?'

'Considering who he's been having an affair with.'

'And who is that?'

'Your mate, Alice Voss.'

The world spun around as the food and booze returned to attack me. There was a rat in my chest, and it was on fire. I stumbled backwards and threw up in Jack's garden, all over the rose bushes and the Christmas gnome left there all year round. Bits of Chinese food and the smell of Zinfandel stuck to the gnome like glue as I stared at Jack's estranged wife. Jean didn't say goodbye when she slammed the door. I stumbled forward and sat on the wall, the cold of the bricks clinging to my hands. My fingers shook when I removed the phone from my pocket. I couldn't face going home, so texted Abbey.

I need to go to work. Don't wait up for me. I'll see you in the morning.

Her reply was instant.

Did you have a good time on your date?

Before I replied, a cocktail of wine and noodles erupted from my guts again and flew all over the pavement. A dog eyed me from the other side of the road before its owner shooed it away and glared at me. I staggered to my feet and phoned for a taxi. Then I texted Abbey while I waited.

It was great. We spent all the time talking about comics. I'll tell you about it tomorrow.

A tumble dryer was inside my stomach, churning away at my sides and punching up into my ribs. At least Abbey wouldn't see me like this.

It's all over the news about the serial killer.

Great. That's all I needed.

That's why I need to work.

Is he really called The Penguin?

That's nothing to do with me. And we don't know if it's a he or a she.

Okay, Mum. Speak in the morning. Goodnight.

Goodnight, love.

The taxi pulled up as I put the phone away. I wiped vomit from my chin and gave the driver directions to the station. Thirty minutes later, I lay on an uncomfortable bed in a custody cell. The sergeant placed a bucket next to me.

'You make any mess, and you clean it up.'

Then he closed the door. He didn't lock it.

The night was as bumpy as the bed, my sleep as restless as a choppy sea. I had a serial killer to catch, one who wanted to play games with me; and my daughter had turned violent. She was hiding something, plus there was the possibility she might end up inside a juvenile prison; and it appeared as if my partner was involved with the previous serial killer I'd put away. And that very serial killer was about to tell her story in a series of internet podcasts.

Yes, I wonder what kept me awake all night.

At seven in the morning, I crawled from the bed and stumbled to the bathroom, throwing hot water over my face and avoiding my gaze in the mirror. Station staff came and left as the shifts changed, both officers and civilians. Nobody spoke to me, and I returned the compliment.

I lurched outside into the light and crossed the road to the coffee shop. It contained fewer people than on my previous visit, but I got a similar drink and took a seat. As I let the caffeine kick-start my synapses, I trawled through the internet, searching for the latest on our so-called Penguin killer, finding nothing illuminating or satisfying. There were no newspapers in the place, sparing me the sight of glaring tabloid headlines.

Early morning workers filtered in as I closed all the webpages and checked my emails just as a new message pinged into my Inbox. It was from the lawyer, Charlotte Nightingale. I scanned the subject line, all in capitals so it had to be important.

YOU NEED TO SEE THIS

Inside was a link to a webpage and nothing else. I wouldn't usually click on a random collection of words and numbers, but I did this time. It opened onto a brief video clip, thirty seconds long, a promotion for a new podcast. I watched it a dozen times.

Available for download tonight, episode 1 of VOSS-CAST. Learn the truth about Alice Voss, the so-called Hashtag Killer.

Voss's photo collage played randomly, images of her as a baby through to one taken before her imprisonment. In it, she's leaving court after her sentence, her blue eyes wide, lips deep red, with long dark hair blowing in the wind. If it hadn't been for the officers escorting Voss to the vehicle, it might have been a photoshoot for a glamour magazine. And just over her shoulder was a shot of me smiling.

I closed the video and put my phone away. What was Voss playing at with this lawyer and the podcasts? I stared out the window and waited for my partner's car to enter the station. Perhaps one question I'd ask Jack was about the podcasts.

I'd finished two cups of coffee and a blueberry muffin before he arrived. I scrambled out of the cafe and followed him, dodging the barrier and nodding to the guard on duty. Bits of muffin clung to my fingers as I crept towards the car. Jack stepped out of it and headed to the lift as I came up behind him and placed my hand on his shoulders. He turned, and I pushed him against the wall.

'You bastard!'

I hurled the words at him. He never moved.

'What's wrong, Jen?'

'Why didn't you answer your phone last night, Jack?'

Two uniformed officers strode past us fifty feet away. They didn't look in our direction. It was a good thing considering the amount of steam blowing from my face.

'It wasn't me, Jen; I didn't leak the case to the press.'

My hands had turned into fists as I held onto his jacket. Blood pumped through my veins like a runaway train.

'Why didn't you answer your phone?'

The breath came out of him in short bursts.

'I was asleep.'

I let go as more vehicles entered the parking garage.

'I visited your house, partner. I spoke to your wife. Jean told me she kicked you out.'

The colour drained from his face.

'Did she tell you why?'

'Why don't you tell me yourself?'

Jack ran his fingers over his jacket, doing his best to straighten out the creases I'd created.

'It's just a misunderstanding, Jen. I'm sure it'll be sorted soon.'

'What type of misunderstanding?'

He steadied himself. I observed the movement behind his eyes, wondering if he'd lie or not.

'She thinks, Jean believes, I've met another woman. So she threw me out.'

'Have you met another woman?'

He pulled at his fancy tie, dragging it away from his throat so he could breathe.

'No, it's not like that.'

He wouldn't tell me the truth. We'd stand there all day, and he'd wriggle out of everything I asked him.

'Jean told me you're having an affair with Alice Voss.'

Jack's eyes bulged and his voice shook.

'It's not like that. She's in prison.'

'Tell me the truth, Jack.'

He thrust his hands into his pockets and his shoulders slumped against the wall.

'It started last year when she joined us on the Hashtag case.' His gaze was furtive, shifting from mine and glancing at the floor before staring at the walls. 'Jean and I were having problems, I was restless; I mean, I'm not trying to make excuses, but my mind wandered, and the stress at home and work go to me. And then I saw her.'

'Alice Voss.'

'Yes. I tried to ignore it at first, but then we talked as part of the investigation, and she complimented me, and then I couldn't stop thinking about her. I knew it was infatuation, but I couldn't do anything about it. Being around her made me feel wonderful and terrible. And then I told myself I was in love because every glance she gave me, I turned into something else. Each word became a secret message I translated into her telling me she felt the same.'

'And did she?'

God, I hoped not.

'I never got the chance to ask her. You arrested her and then she was in court.'

Thank goodness for minor mercies. They hadn't had sex, the thought of which churned my stomach. I rubbed at it as the remnants of the Chinese; and the wine continued to play havoc with my insides.

'So why does your wife say you're having an affair with Voss? Did you tell Jean about it?'

'No. She found the letters.'

'What letters?'

He ran his fingers across his cheek.

'Even when she was in custody, I never stopped thinking about her.'

'After what she'd done, and you discovered she'd recruited others to kill people, you still had feelings for her?'

'Have you never been in love, Jen? There's no controlling your emotions. If you don't act on your desires, a black pit of depression swallows you up.'

I thought I'd been in love once, a long time ago; but it was just an older man manipulating me for his own ends. The memory of him added to the volcanic lava swimming through my veins, and I had to resist the urge to smash Jack in the face.

'So you wrote to her?'

Jack stepped forward, his voice trembling as he leant against his car.

'I couldn't help myself. I poured all my thoughts into those pages and it made me better for a while. But I didn't think she'd write back.'

'How long has this been going on?'

'Five months.'

'Christ!' How did I not spot any of this, not recognise his emotional state?

'And then Jean found the letters?'

'She wasn't happy about them.'

'I bet she wasn't.' I glared at him. 'Stop writing to her, Jack.'

He hung his head. 'I will.'

'I mean it, partner. You can't keep doing this job if you're obsessed with her.'

I put my hand on his arm and he lifted his face.

'Will you tell Cane or Merson?'

'Not if you promise to stop writing to Voss.'

His eyes were glassy, his fingers quivering.

'I promise, Jen.'

'Okay, let's get back to work. We've got the fallout from this leak to deal with.' We stepped into the lift together. 'Did Voss tell you about these podcasts she's doing?'

He shook his head. 'I saw the advert for that online, but she never mentioned it to me.'

'Okay.'

Did I want to ask him what they'd talked about? I'd rather have all my teeth pulled out with no anaesthetic.

Both of our phones pinged with text messages as we stepped into the corridor. We checked them together; it was a summons to see the SIO.

This wouldn't be pleasant news for either of us.

We took the short walk past the Murder Room, which had flowed over into a second area, to Chief Superintendent Cane's office. She was sitting behind the desk, finishing a phone call as we walked in. She didn't ask us to sit down.

'You've got a leak in your team.'

Well, thanks for telling us the bleeding obvious, I wanted to say.

'It was bound to happen, ma'am,' I said.

Her scowl told me she wasn't happy with my reply.

'I've arranged a media conference for here in an hour.' She glanced at me, and then at Jack. 'I wanted you to take it, Inspector Flowers, but looking at you now doing your best Worzel Gummidge impersonation, I have my doubts. Have you not seen a mirror this morning?'

That's when I realised I smelt of yesterday and my breath was one long wine and Chinese burst.

'I've been rather busy with personal stuff lately, ma'am.'

'Yes, I'm aware of the trouble with your daughter.' She picked up her phone, and I waited for her to mention something about the apple not falling far from the tree. 'I hope everything gets sorted satisfactorily there. I'll rearrange the media conference for midday. I want you to go home and get fresh clothes, perhaps have a few hours' sleep, and then return to deal with the shit show one of your team has caused.'

She dismissed us with a wave of the hand. Jack seemed disappointed.

'I thought she might ask me to lead the conference.'

I shrugged. 'Feel free to take over.'

'No, Jen. You're the one they'll want to see.' He grinned at me. 'But not looking like that. Did you sleep here last night?'

I ignored his question and checked on the rest of the team. Both rooms were a hive of activity. I stepped into the first one and got Constable Sutton to drive me home. I left Jack to his own devices.

The cat was sitting on the doorstep when I arrived. I stumbled into the house, ready for a shower, as Abbey shouted to me from the living room. I presented her with my best weary smile.

'Mum, you look like someone dragged you through a hedge.'

I dropped onto the sofa opposite her.

'Thanks, Abbey.'

'Is this because of your date?'

She sounded concerned.

'No, love. This is all work-related.' I didn't mention the wine I'd had. 'The meal was great. I'll see him again.'

I noticed the books on the table between us. I picked up the biggest and heaviest of them.

'One kid from the gaming group gave that to me.'

'*From Hell.* Is it a horror story?'

'It's about Jack the Ripper, but not about Jack the Ripper.'

'You'll need to explain that to me.'

I flicked through the pages as she did.

'Did you know there's new evidence about the Ripper?'

'I do. DNA from one murder connects to the descendants of a suspect, Aaron Kosminski. Some critics still say it isn't strong enough to declare this case closed.'

'It doesn't matter. This book was written years before that and in the introduction, the author, Alan Moore, says it isn't about identifying the Ripper, but it's shining a light on British society through the ages. It's an exploration of how our perceptions, how societal expectations, shape all of our lives even when we don't realise it, how our connections as groups and individuals reach down through time; a story isn't what's on the surface, but what's underneath.'

It shocked me to hear her speak like this; as if she wasn't a child anymore, but an adult. I flicked through the book; the pages were stark black and white and beautiful.

'And you've read all this?'

'Yesterday; when I was on my own.'

'Well, I'm glad you didn't waste your time.' I placed the book onto the table. 'Now I need a shower and a change of clothes.'

'Do you want me to make you something to eat?'

'That would be fantastic, love.'

I trudged up the stairs, tired but happy because of the conversation with Abbey. I still didn't know what was happening with her and this Olivia Coates incident, but at least she was using her brain to think about things other teenagers wouldn't. I hoped that was a good thing. Or perhaps it wasn't, and she should behave like a typical teenager and not an adult. My childhood was cut short and look at how that worked out for me.

I threw my clothes onto the floor and stepped into the shower. I caught a glimpse of my reflection in the mirror before turning the water on, finding the bags under my eyes large enough for tourists to pack for two weeks on holiday. I experimented with the temperature, switching between too hot and too cold, letting the liquid sink into my bones. I pressed my face against the tiles, my mind a fog of a thousand different things.

When I finished, an aroma of fried bacon was sweeping upstairs. I wrapped the cloth around my head and slipped into a dressing gown. I couldn't find my slippers, so marched downstairs in bare feet, the damp seeping from my skin into the carpet. The floor was cold as I stepped into the kitchen. I sat at the table.

'I think I can get used to this, with you making me food instead of the other way round.'

Abbey grinned at me. 'You owe me big time for this.'

'I'll buy you more graphic novels, how does that sound?'

'That sounds great. Are you going on another date soon?'

Burnt toast crunched between my teeth.

'Hold your horses there, Speedy Gonzales. I've got a killer to catch first.'

'I've been reading about it online. Are you really calling him The Penguin?'

'That's not in my control, plus there's no guarantee it's a man.'

She narrowed her eyes. 'It could be a woman, like Alice Voss?'

'Well, let's hope it's not like her. If it's someone that clever, we'll need as much luck as detection to find them.'

'Do you know she has her own podcasts, starting tonight?'

'I'm aware of that.'

'Will you listen to them?'

'No.' I finished the food and stood. It was time to return to work.

'Why not, Mum?'

'There's nothing she has to say I want to hear.'

I went to my bedroom and got dressed. Abbey was reading *From Hell* when I returned downstairs. She placed it on her lap, the pages open.

'Are you coming home tonight?'

'I am, love. I promise we'll have some time together.' I pointed at the book. 'I guess that won't have a happy ending.'

She shook her head. 'Does anything?'

As I left, I wondered if Abbey reading comics was a good thing.

WHEN I RETURNED to the station, I gathered all the team into one room, half an hour before I was to deliver the media conference.

'Okay, people, it's time for an update.' I turned to Constable Sutton. 'Where are we with the files from Oswald Blair's former law firm?'

She walked to the front.

'We've checked over two hundred, finding thirty criminals prosecuted by Oswald Blair released in the last three years.' She let out a long sigh. 'I've narrowed that down to five, based upon people still living in London, the nature of the original crimes, and whether they have alibis for the first murder.'

'Well done, Constable Sutton. I need you and a colleague to visit those five and ask some pertinent questions.' I stared straight into her eyes. 'Don't take any risks.'

'Yes, ma'am.'

'Where are we on Edwin Blair's missing finances?'

Jack cleared his throat and stood.

'I nipped into the club last night and spoke to some informants of mine. They were all adamant Edwin Blair was neither a buyer nor a seller of drugs.'

'So what happened to the money he received from his father? It can't have just vanished.'

'I got the names of his most frequent girlfriends, half a dozen of them. I'll get their details today and contact them. One of them might know how his cash disappeared.'

'Okay, let's move onto the second victim. Do we have the blood analysis report from Cooper?'

Constable Grealish stood.

'According to the doctor, there was nothing unusual in the victim's blood. But she thinks the small incision found at the back of the neck could have been to inject a drug which inhibited Hamilton so he couldn't move. She's requested access to Edwin Blair's body to see if he has a similar cut.'

'Tell her to go ahead,' I said. 'Have we learnt anything about the dating app Hamilton used?'

A tall man with an impressive Afro haircut got up.

'I'm Officer Rey from Cybercrime.' He paused and glanced around the room. After the revelation of Alice Voss as the Hashtag Killer, Cybercrime's reputation had hovered somewhere just above the gutter. He coughed to clear his throat. 'Clive Hamilton owned four digital devices: two laptops, a tablet, and his smartphone. It was the phone he used for the dating app, Grindr. We assume the killer deleted all messages, images, and any information relating to them on the mobile. So we contacted the dating app, and they voluntarily provided us with the username, phone number, and email address.'

A sharp intake of breath ran through the room.

'We can trace the killer?' I said.

Rey shook his head. 'I'm afraid not, Inspector Flowers. The user name is Palpatine, the phone number attached to a disposable device, and the email address is from a North Korean server.'

He was about to sit down when I stopped him.

'Where do I know the name Palpatine?'

'It's a character from *Star Wars*, ma'am.'

I pushed out my cheeks and hid my frustration. The clock on the wall said I had five minutes before meeting the media.

'Do we have any other leads?'

Jack pointed to the row of phones in the room next door.

'Since the leak last night, we've had over a hundred tips. The team will sift through them this afternoon.'

My partner had mentioned the leak, and I should have addressed it then. But I didn't and headed off to the media conference. I spent thirty minutes answering questions and trying to set the record straight without giving anything important away. Merson stood at the rear while I spoke, her gaze never leaving me.

As I got up to leave, one of the tabloid journalists asked me a final question.

'Will you request a profiler to help you with the investigation?'

The lead in my shoulders nearly sent me back into the chair. Profilers were all the rage in a media obsessed with everything American, especially violent crimes and their mythological solvers. TV shows focusing on the FBI's behavioural unit and their unbelievable powers of deduction were no help.

'We have enough expertise at the moment. I don't see any need to add anyone else.'

I left as the cameras flashed across my face.

I was out the door and heading back to the team when Merson grabbed my arm.

'Maybe the profiler isn't a bad idea.'

'Is that what you want, ma'am?'

She let go of me.

'It's just a suggestion, Jennifer. You're in charge.'

Merson left me with a smile and an uncontrollable itch on the back of my neck. I took a sharp turn from my colleagues and headed towards the lift. I drove from the building as the groan in my stomach grew louder. I was unsure where to go until I removed the card from my pocket as I sat at a red light. The phone was on speaker and connected to the car as the lights changed. I dialled the number as I picked up speed.

'Hello, this is Dr Nelson.'

'It's Jennifer Flowers, Doctor. Are you at the hospital?'

'No, Inspector, I'm at home.'

'Can you give me the address and I'll come straight over?'

She was quiet for a second, before whispering to someone in the background. Then she gave me the details. I thanked her and said I'd be there as soon as possible. I entered the coordinates into the GPS and headed towards some psychoanalysis.

Nelson lived in a village an hour outside London. Her home was an idyllic setting down by the water, so I parked the car near the canal. As I knocked on the door, a strange sound came from inside the house, like a child crying. Nelson opened it before I banged again.

'Hello, Jennifer; how nice to see you.' It was two o'clock in the afternoon, and she was wearing long cycling trousers which appeared painted onto her legs and a sports top. There was a small towel in her hands, and she used it to wipe sweat from her forehead. 'Excuse my appearance; I've just finished a session on the spinning bike. Please come in.'

She stepped backwards, and I followed her in and through another door. It led straight into a long, narrow kitchen: dirty plates and cutlery littered the sides near the sink, with opened cereal boxes stacked against the window, and there was a group of empty cartons of fruit juice on top of the oven. I glanced over the mess.

'I'm sorry to disturb you, Dr Nelson.'

She went to the fridge.

'It's no problem, Jennifer; can I call you Jennifer? You

should call me Felicia. Would you like a drink?' She removed a large glass of something thick and green and held it towards me. 'This is healthy juice made from lots of different natural things.'

My guts rumbled as I got a whiff of cabbage and broccoli from the concoction.

'No thanks, Felicia, but you can call me Jen.'

I wanted a cup of coffee, but wasn't sure if my bloodstream could take any more caffeine.

'No problem, Jen.' She closed the fridge. 'Let's go into the living room.' Then she gave me a curious smile. 'Just watch out for my housemates.'

The living room contained a three-seater sofa and a TV screen. Further down at the back was an extension containing her exercise bike and a set of weights scattered on the carpet.

'You share this place with people?'

Felicia drank half of her green concoction, and I wondered if she'd turn into Ms Hyde. Some of it was stuck to her lips as she spoke.

'No, not people.'

She laughed and placed the glass on a coffee table as the cats crept from the woodwork. They emerged from behind the sofas, down the stairs, and jumping from the window ledge. It was a feline invasion, and cat hair suddenly worked its way into my nose and lungs. The place was so full of hair it was like staring up someone's nose.

'How many are there?'

I tolerated the cat we had at home because I knew Abbey loved the damn thing, but watching these gather around my feet unnerved me.

She scrunched up her lips as if I'd asked her about the secrets of the universe.

'I think I'm at ten now.' She scratched at the sweat slipping down her cheek. 'I lose count sometimes.'

'I bet you do.'

'Are you allergic to cats, Jennifer?'

'No. I'm not sure they like me, but my daughter has a pet cat.'

Felicia scooped up a massive ginger moggy as it sniffed at her drink.

'They're not pets, Jen.' She appeared hurt by the suggestion. 'I was a bit of a loner as a kid, so gravitated towards animals.' Her face took on a wistful expression. 'My mother said the only friends I'd ever have would be animals, and she wasn't far wrong.' She dropped the cat onto the floor and looked at the others. 'She'd probably view this as my collection.'

I scrutinised the rest of the room, expecting to see qualifications on the walls or some sign of her academic and professional achievements, but there was nothing to show she was a Doctor of Clinical Psychology. Most of the cats continued to purr around my legs; it would be murder trying to remove the cat hairs from my clothes later on.

'Do you want to get changed before we talk?'

She shook her head. 'There's no need for that. I'll be back on the bike later, so there's no point in me using a set of clean clothes in between.' She picked up her drink. 'Let's go into the backroom; most of the cats avoid going there when I'm exercising.'

I did as she said, wondering where we'd sit when I noticed the two chairs up against the glass doors separating the house from the garden. There was also a large computer screen facing the exercise bike. As I took a seat, the image of Alice Voss's podcast stared at me, frozen in time. I pointed at it.

'Will you be listening to that tonight?'

She sat opposite.

'I'll wait until all four are available and listen to them together. Once I've started something, I have no patience to find out what will happen next.' She picked up a remote and turned off the screen. Then she peered at me. 'I saw your news conference earlier; is that why you're here?'

One of the more curious cats, not much larger than a kitten, approached my feet. It was a ball of solid white fur with sparkling gold eyes. It sat and stared at me as I replied to Dr Nelson.

'No, Felicia; I'm here about my daughter, Abigail.'

'Did you speak to her about seeing me?'

'I did.'

I lied and maybe blackmailed her; some mother I am.

She reached over to the table and grabbed her phone.

'Shall we arrange dates and times for the sessions?'

'That would be great. Would they be at the hospital where I met you?'

The doctor picked up a pair of glasses and pushed them up her nose.

'It might be more beneficial if she had them here. What do you think?'

I glanced over at the sea of felines next door.

'She'd love being around the cats, at least.'

'Excellent. When do you want to start?'

I didn't know. This wasn't the real reason I was there.

'As soon as possible? It will show good intentions if she has to go to juvenile court.'

That's what I hoped.

Felicia scrolled through her screen before coming up with a solution.

'I could fit her in tomorrow morning, say nine o'clock.'

I got out my phone and made a note of it.

'That's great, Felicia. I'll confirm it with Abbey later today and text you.'

I gripped the device between my fingers and didn't move.

'No problem, Jen.' Felicia finished her drink. 'I get the sense there's something else on your mind. Do you want to talk about it?'

Of course I didn't, but I knew I had to.

'Could Abbey's actions, her recent violent behaviour, be hereditary?'

She slipped her phone into her lap and one of the smaller cats joined it, nudging at the screen and purring loudly.

'Well, decades of research have shown both genetic and environmental factors play a role in a variety of behaviours in humans and animals. The genetic basis of violence, however, remains poorly understood. Heritability models of violence are based on animals because of the ethical concern in using humans for genetic study.' She seemed disappointed by that. 'So, there isn't much evidence I can give you in answering your question.' She crossed her legs and folded her arms, her body language now of a professional at work. 'Why do you ask?'

The white cat gazed at me through watery eyes.

'I'm concerned her behaviour might be my fault.'

'I assume all parents, at some point, blame themselves for their children's deeds, no matter what they are. But even if it had something to do with your genetics, Jen, it still wouldn't be your fault; none of us can control our biological ancestry.' She gave me her widest smile. 'Is there something about your behaviour which might have influenced Abbey's actions?'

Was I there to unburden myself to a stranger? I suppose I must have been since the words flowed from me like rain in a downpour.

'When I was Abbey's age, I took part in several violent transgressions for around four years, which were the same or worse than what she did to that girl in the library. I'd forgotten most of it, or at least pushed the memories into the darkest corners of my head until they emerged recently.'

She didn't ask for specifics, instead doing her best to reassure me.

'Early childhood aggression may be mostly a result of genetics, but new research suggests that whether the tendency toward violence increases or decreases as kids grow up depends on environmental factors. Whatever you did as a teenager has no bearing on Abbey's behaviour.'

I guess her words were supposed to make me feel better, but they didn't.

'When you say environmental factors, you mean her upbringing?'

She must have recognised the apprehension in my voice.

'The family environment is significant, yes, but it's also imperative to understand the significance of outside factors, such as school, friendships, location, cultural influences, and so on.'

'Will you discover how important these things have been in moulding her behaviour during your sessions with her?'

'I hope so, Jen.' She unfolded her arms and uncrossed her legs. 'As long as you realise what she tells me is private.'

'I do, Felicia.'

The phone vibrated in my hands and I checked the screen.

'Is it anything important?'

'I set up notifications for responses from the media conference I gave, that's all.'

'It was an interesting question asked at the end, about the profiler.'

The phone buzzed again as I put it away.

'I don't know how much of that I believe. Most of what the public sees comes from TV shows and movies, such as exaggerated versions of the FBI's Behavioural Science Unit.'

She scratched at the cat's chin.

'Does the UK have a similar unit?'

'We have the National Crime Agency; it's the UK's national law enforcement organisation. A department within the NCA called the Serious Crime Analysis Section works to identify the potential emergence of serial killers and serial rapists at the earliest stage of their offending. They have a database of serious sexual offences committed in the UK. SCAS receives case files for offences meeting specific criteria from a network of contact officers in every police force in the UK. This information is coded onto the Violent Crime Linkage Analysis System, the in-house SCAS database, which allows specific details of both the offence and known suspects or offender to be captured.

'Cases are then subject to Comparative Case Analysis to identify any similar offences held on ViCLAS. Bespoke reports are sent out to forces including details of similar offences or potential suspects identified.'

Felicia's eyes lit up like fireworks, mirroring the gaze of the cat in her lap.

'So, you'll be using their facilities for this Penguin case?'

It was my turn to scratch at my head. Perhaps if I did it

hard enough, I'd unearth some brain cells capable of solving all my problems.

'The two murders we're investigating are in the SCAS database, but there's a problem with that.'

'I guess that's because the MO was different in both crimes.'

'And the fact we've found no sexual element to them.'

Felicia leant forward, pushing the cat closer to her knees.

'I thought the news reports said the second victim was out on a date organised through one of those smartphone apps?'

'He was, but I believe it was a ruse to get him alone. We discovered no evidence of sexual activity at the scene.'

The cat tumbled to the floor as the doctor was half out of her seat. The moggy landed safely and scowled as it scampered from the room.

'But I'm sure you realise, Jen, the physical act of the murders themselves could be the function of sexual release for the killer.'

'Considering the differences in the *modus operandi* and the locations, I think there must be something in the murders for the killer beyond the actual act of killing.'

'Can you tell me anything else about the crimes?'

I shouldn't, but I needed all the help I could get.

'Somebody strangled our first victim in a public place; the second was dismembered in their home. This killer is methodical in their planning and a risk-taker; they must have planned the murder in the woods weeks in advance, but still, they knew there was a high risk of someone catching them in the act.

'The murderer enticed the second victim through a dating app to meet a stranger in their home. This means our killer planned this, created a fake account and communicated through messages before they met, though they were all deleted from the victim's phone. Then they were confident they'd be able to overpower the victim before killing them.'

'Did they take the tools for dismemberment with them?'

'No. The victim was a video artist and he had all kinds of equipment where he lived, including a stack of hammers and saws.'

'So the method of murder was spontaneous?'

'That seems to be the case; which is another sign of their risk-taking.'

'How many body parts were there?'

'Ten.'

'And how were they placed around the crime scene?'

'You think it's a pattern?'

'Haven't other killers done that, especially ones who feel they're communicating a message to the authorities?'

'I suppose it's possible. I must check the videos and photographs when I return to the station.'

'Do you suspect your killer is male?'

'Statistics would say so, but I won't fall into the same trap again.'

'The images of the penguins stamped onto the palms; do you have any theories on that?'

'Not yet.' If I did, would I tell her?

If I was waiting for Nelson to provide some insight from what I'd told her, I didn't get it. My phone vibrated again. I got up from the chair.

'Well, I best get back to it.' She stood, and I held out my hand to shake hers. Her fingers gripped mine; her strength surprised me. 'Thank you for what you're doing with Abbey, Doctor.'

She smiled and let go. 'It's Felicia, Jen; remember.'

I headed out, past the curious cats, and into the idyllic surroundings outside. I checked the messages on the phone; Jack had sent me the team's updates: there was still nothing useful. Someone to profile our killer could be beneficial, but I knew it would only be worthwhile if one thing happened: there had to be another murder.

I returned to Felicia Nelson's house the next day, arriving five minutes before the appointment. Abbey had taken the news well; she hadn't bombarded me with questions as I'd expected, too busy reading *From Hell* to give it much concern. Now, in the car, her interest was piqued.

'How long will it last?'

'I'm not sure, love.' My fingers clenched as I spoke. 'See how this goes; if you're not happy, you don't have to do it anymore.'

'Will it help if I have to go to court?'

I didn't lie to her.

'It would impress the authorities.'

She reached over from the passenger seat and hugged me.

'Then I'll try. Will you pick me up when it's finished?'

'Do you want me to?'

She smiled and shook her head.

'No. I'll pop into the village and have lunch, then get the train to London.'

I wasn't happy with her wandering around on her own,

but I had to show her some trust.

'Okay, love; but stay in touch.'

'I'll need some money, though, for the journey and lunch and stuff.'

I dipped into my purse and gave her twenty quid.

'This should be enough.'

She grinned at me. 'And I can keep the change?'

I laughed as she got out of the car. I watched as she knocked on the door, waiting for Nelson to take her in. I hadn't told her about the cats. When she was inside, I left.

———

I ARRIVED at the station at ten thirty-five. Both rooms were busy as I entered the main one. I recognised what the fuss was as soon as I saw the big screen: we'd received another letter.

'You've missed all the excitement, Jen.'

Jack handed me a copy of the original.

'Any forensic results?'

He shook his head. 'No fingerprints, no fibres, and no DNA. There is a return address, though.'

I nearly fell to the floor.

'What?'

His grin annoyed me.

'Sorry, partner; I'm messing with you.'

The weariness had left his face, unless the growing stubble was hiding it.

I resisted the urge to slap him around the head.

'Do we know where it's from?'

'It was posted from outside London early yesterday morning: Watford High Street. And before you ask, I've sent uniforms to see if there's any CCTV footage.'

'Let's hope there is.' I walked towards the display and read the words.

CATCH *the blood from his neck. Harvest the organs into a fine pie. A tasty morsel for the masses to feast upon. Purse your lips before licking them. To eat is to live. Eager to dine on the divine. Resurrection of the soul. Two for the price of one. When day changes into night. Only the brave come out to play.*

CHRIST! Even more randomness. I read it in my head again, but it still made no sense.

'Very poetic, don't you think?'

For some reason, Jack appeared pleased with himself. Perhaps getting the truth about Voss and him out in the open had released some of the pressure he must have felt. But that's if he'd told me the whole truth about the two of them. Would Jean have kicked him out if their so-called relationship was only based on a few letters?

'I've always hated poetry; my school made us read Ted Hughes and Kipling endlessly.'

Jack laughed. 'I prefer his cakes.'

'Have any of the team tried to analyse the text?'

'Well, like the other one, it's in a fourteen-point Times New Roman font, probably created on a Windows computer.'

The lines on my face grew tighter, the shadows under my eyes dark enough to obscure my view.

'You know what I mean, Jack.'

'I waited for you; you're much smarter than me for this.'

I took a copy of the text and sat at the computer. I found

the file and opened it; I had three versions in front of me: big screen, small screen, and the one in my hand. I hoped the repetition would help the cogs spin inside my head.

'This sounds cannibalistic: using the organs for a pie, a tasty morsel, licking lips, eating to live and dining.' I stared at Jack. 'Do we know if we recovered all of Clive Hamilton at the crime scene?'

'You think our killer might have eaten some of the victim? Surely Dr Cooper would have mentioned if body parts were missing.'

'Someone contact her and ask.'

My voice was brittle, ready to break. Jack called Sutton over and repeated what I'd said to her. Then he turned back to me.

'*Two for the price of one* and *When day changes into night* sound familiar.'

'You're right; it's as if they're from a gothic text.'

I grabbed the mouse and opened the web browser on the computer. I typed in "two for the price of one" as a search. There were nearly two and a half million results, the first ten being an Abba song.

Jack leant over my shoulder.

'Perhaps our killer is obsessed with Abba, or Scandinavian murders.' He hummed the chorus from *Dancing Queen*. '*The Girl with the Dragon Tattoo* turns into the bodies with penguin stamps.'

The lyrics were beneath a link for a video of the tune. I didn't play it, but read through the text; the words made little sense. I moved onto another part of the letter.

'Perhaps this is religious: *Eager to dine on the divine* and *Resurrection of the soul*. This might be the morality theme we talked about.'

My partner scratched his head.

'This will take some unravelling; we haven't even figured out the first text yet.'

I threw the paper onto the table.

'That's what our killer wants, for us to spend our time going through this nonsense.'

'You think these messages are distractions?'

'That or to send us chasing down dark alleys or rabbit holes.' My mind slipped back to the conversation I'd had with Felicia Nelson yesterday. 'We could ask the Chief Super to call in a forensic linguist to analyse the letters.'

Jack scowled at the mention of bringing in outside help.

'There aren't many of those, are there? And from what little I've seen of their work, it's more about proving authorship of texts, like when killers send messages or postcards pretending to be their victims.'

'That's true, but they might be able to tell the gender of the writer based on the use of language, grammar, spelling, and syntax in the writing. I know there's a Department of Forensic Linguistics at Aston University in Birmingham, so it could be worthwhile getting in touch with them if we don't get any traction elsewhere. For now, we need to focus on the victims and the crime scenes.'

I returned to the computer for the photos of Hamilton's dismembered body.

'We've gone over these dozens of times, Jen; what do you think you'll find?'

I opened six of them onto the screen, each one showing a different angle of the limbs.

'Perhaps this is another message?'

It had to be; there couldn't be any other reason to place the body parts like the killer did if it wasn't to send a message.

The torso sat in the middle of a coffee table. The hands

and feet were on opposite shelves, acting as bookends. The legs were stacked with pots in the sink, the arms hanging from the ceiling's main light. Charles Hamilton's head peered from the top of the TV, a morbid achievement considering how narrow the television was. There was also a video of the scene. Jack and I watched it twice and were none the wiser. My partner chewed on the end of a pencil.

'If there's a message there, I can't work it out.'

'Me neither.' I closed all those files before they made my head ache more than it already did. 'Do you think we should bring a profiler into the investigation?'

He rolled the pencil around between his teeth.

'I suppose. Perhaps they can tell us all about our killer's childhood and how they used to dress up in the wrong clothes.' I snatched the pencil from his mouth. He grimaced and rubbed at his face. 'You could break a tooth like that.'

'You'll end up with lead poisoning.'

I checked my phone for messages from Abbey, finding nothing. I wondered about her time with Felicia Nelson. Jack must have read my mind.

'How's Abbey doing?'

I told him about the session with the clinical psychologist.

'I hope it does her some good, regardless if it's beneficial with the juvenile court.'

'Have you had any news on that?'

'Not yet, and I'm afraid to ask. Ignorance is bliss, as they say.'

But they, whoever "they" are, were wrong about that.

'Do you want me to?'

I shook my head. 'Thanks, Jack, but I don't want them thinking I might be interfering.'

'So, what's next for our investigation?'

'Where are you at?'

'I've spoken to three of Edwin Blair's lady friends. None of them saw him with drugs or heard anything about him involved with them. They said he was generous with money, though I guess it was the old man's cash, but not to the degree where he'd go through thousands of pounds quickly. I'll interview the others this afternoon. Do you want to come?'

'No. Take a uniform with you. I need to catch up with the case reports.'

That's what I did while Jack was out. Abbey texted me to say she was on the train into London, heading for a gaming session at the comic shop. I didn't ask how it went with Nelson.

I read through Sutton and Grealish's reports about Oswald Blair's former law firm's case files. The list they'd made from over two hundred prosecutions had been narrowed down to two, the rest of them eliminated by watertight alibis. I brought them up onto the screen. The names were from the opposite end of the social spectrum.

Devon Grace, thirty-five years old, prosecuted for the manslaughter of his girlfriend fifteen years ago; served thirteen in prison. He'd lived in a hostel in Croydon since his release. The file contained the reports from his probation officer. Grace worked in the kitchen of an Indian restaurant for six months. He'd always denied the killing, claiming an accident during their consensual rough sex. He'd strangled Debbie Morse, and Oswald Blair prosecuted him. Sutton had tried to contact him by phone and in person, had even visited his workplace, but with no luck. Grace had violated the conditions of his parole.

I stared at his photograph on the screen, a thin bloke with haunted eyes. Did he look like he could plan two murders, or throw a rope around Edwin Blair's neck, a much bigger, younger, and stronger man, and haul him up a tree to strangle him?

The second name was a different story. Carrie Spector, fifty-five years old, and financially independent even though Oswald Blair had prosecuted her for embezzlement from the family firm she worked at twelve years ago. Her sentence was eight years in prison, but she only did half of that. I wondered why Sutton had her on the list until I read the transcripts of the trial. When they removed Spector from the court, she served a volley of threats at Blair, promising to kill him and his family by stringing them up before chopping them to bits. Was that coincidence regarding how the victims had died?

She had two degrees, one of which she got while in prison. Again, Sutton couldn't contact her. She wasn't at her address, a million-pound apartment in Knightsbridge, and no relatives were willing to help. Since her conviction was for a non-violent crime, a probation officer had been deemed unnecessary.

I settled into the chair and stared at the two of them on the screen. I got up after five minutes of contemplation.

'You're coming with me, Constable Sutton.'

'Yes, ma'am.' She grabbed her phone from the table. 'Where are we going?'

'We're off to follow up on the excellent work you and Grealish did with the Blair's files.'

Absorbed in the scent and murmur of searching for a serial killer, we set off to explore the contradictions of the capital.

21 CANDIDATE

I informed Jack where we were going and headed to the car. He stared at me through curious eyes as I led Sutton from the Murder Room and down into the parking garage. A soundless breeze little more than a whisper rifled through space as I remembered my recent confrontation with my partner in this spot. I filed the concerns I had regarding Jack's separation from his wife next to the ones about Abbey and her state of mind. I glanced at Sutton as we strapped ourselves into the car.

'How well do you know London, Constable?'

I drove out of the building and into the heart of the city.

'I'm from Barking, ma'am, lived there all my life.'

'What's it like in Barking?'

She settled into her seat and considered it, glancing at me for a second. Perhaps she thought it a trick question.

'There's not much going for it, shop wise, and there isn't a lot to do for kids, so they end up messing around and getting into trouble.' There was sadness in her eyes until she must have remembered something nice to say, and her smile returned. 'The market is great, and the library hosts excellent events. There's a new independent coffee shop over-looking the water opened by the residents, and that's popular at the moment.' She placed one hand on her leg as I drove. 'It's like any working-class area in London, with good transport links and affordable housing. Like many places, it gets a poor reputation because of certain media outlets or ridiculous unfounded rumours.'

I nodded. 'What do you mean by unfounded rumours?'

I must have hit a raw nerve. She relaxed and didn't reply as if speaking with a superior officer.

'Many areas of London look rough, but are fine and not as crime-ridden as the media makes out. Most incidents affect those in the same circle. If there's a stabbing, it's not a random thing, but gang-related, or an argument between friends. Some people get scared if they don't see white faces at night or they hear others talking in a foreign language; ignorance and hatred fuel their fear, but what they believe isn't based on reality.' Her voice rose a notch as she spoke, her face like a flushed orange. I stared at her in the mirror. 'The point is, everywhere is fine, and yes, there are some undesirable places for certain people, but they're okay for others. Little Lucy born and raised in Hertfordshire coming to the city for the first time would freak out at those places, but they're nowhere near as bad as some say.'

She finished and let out a deep breath. I guessed she'd been holding all of that in for a long time.

'I agree, Constable. We should avoid little Lucy from Hertfordshire at all costs.' We laughed together, the sound of my enjoyment surprising me. A fist gripped at my heart as if I knew this couldn't last. 'Have you ever visited Knightsbridge?'

'No, ma'am. It's a bit out of my price range.'

She continued to laugh, the movement making the blue of her eyes shimmer like a warm Caribbean sea.

'Now you'll see how the other half live.'

The traffic slowed around St James's Palace and Buckingham Palace's tourist spots, and I parked on the double-yellow lines opposite the luxury flats, leaving a police badge on the windscreen. Police work was relentless, time-consuming and, more often than not, deeply frustrating, but at least we were out in the sun in one of the capital's most prestigious settings. A blazing blue sky poured down torrents of light as we strode to the steps of Carrie Spector's residence. Sutton's eyes were wide in awe as we approached.

'When you said the other half, ma'am, you meant the one per cent, didn't you?'

'It is impressive.'

'Not bad for an ex-convict to end up here.'

I paused before ringing the bell.

'Spector comes from a lengthy line of wealth and privilege. Don't let her stint in prison fool you.'

Sutton looked confused.

'So why would she steal money from her employer? Wasn't it half a million pounds?'

'That was her defence at the trial. Her family is worth millions, and she wouldn't need the cash.'

'So, what happened?'

'The evidence convicted her, Oswald Blair and his team proved that. It was quite a coup for them, prosecuting someone of Spector's status when most people expected her privilege to protect her. Spector claimed a setup, though there was never any proof, and she wouldn't name who framed her.'

'And that's when she freaked out at the trial and let loose a tirade of threats?'

'Spector had a troubled childhood. She has an IQ of 160 and a history of emotional problems going back to her primary school days. Perhaps she expected to get off and snapped at Blair when she didn't.'

I rang the bell, and we waited. A shiver of apprehension crisped my skin, and I scratched at it as the door opened; a woman with a lifetime of experiences etched across her face glared at us. She'd dressed in jeans, a hipster jacket and a neck scarf. Her face was made up, but not overdone, and her long black hair was pulled back into a ponytail. Her eyes moved quickly over both of us.

'I left the charity bags in the alley.'

I showed her my ID card.

'I'm Detective Inspector Jennifer Flowers, and this is Constable Sutton. Can we have a word, Ms Spector?'

'Of course, Inspector. Which one would you like? Vamoose or scat? Or possibly it's more than one word, like police corruption, planted evidence, or bent coppers?'

I let her have the little rant; we all deserved one now and then.

'I can return with a warrant, Ms Spector, if that's what you prefer. Turn up with flashing blue lights, so all your neighbours will know we're here. Maybe even inform the media.'

She studied me like a bug under a microscope.

'Well, since you put it like that.' She stood to one side and invited us in. 'Close the door behind you, Constable.'

Sutton did as instructed, and we followed Spector inside. The entrance hall was all sash windows, high ceilings and bespoke solid oak floors. Our host glided silently across the wood like a ghost, leading us through a decorative door on the left. Inside, a dozen large canvases covered the walls, most of which appeared to be artistic interpretations of London landmarks, but others were of locations I didn't recognise. I scrutinised the one closest to me, a watercolour of two dogs ripping at each other's throats with a canal in the background.

'Are you an art collector, Ms Spector?'

I thought it best to make at least an attempt at being cordial before questioning her about a murder. She ignored my question.

'I suppose you're here about Clive?'

I glanced at Sutton as something got caught in her throat. I admired the way she controlled herself.

'Clive?'

Her eyes narrowed as she scrutinised me.

'Hamilton. I hear he came to a sticky end.'

Sutton and I glanced at each other.

'What was your relationship to him, Ms Spector?'

She stepped next to me and pointed to one canvas. I moved closer to it, a disturbing image of a baby ripped from a man's stomach through ruptured ribs. Art was not my speciality, but this made my stomach churn.

'Clive painted this for me.'

I stared at the name on the painting.

'This is signed by Haz.'

'Clive wanted to be the Dickens of the modern art world, with a unique *nom de plume*, highlighting the inequities of contemporary society.'

Sutton took notes as I spoke to Spector.

'I thought he was a video artist?'

Carrie Spector sighed loudly.

'He struggled with his original artistic vision and switched to the medium of video out of desperation. My purchase was one of the last things he painted.' She gazed at the art on the wall. 'I wanted to gather a collection of unique images of my city while supporting as many unknown and struggling artists as I could.' She moved forward and touched the frame of Hamilton's painting. 'It was a terrible shock to learn what happened to Clive.'

'How did you meet him?'

She turned from the canvas and stared at me.

'I have several connections in the art world, Inspector. It's one of the few agreeable things my family name has given me.'

'Did you go to his studio?'

'I only visited him once to buy the painting. He was a nervous creature, always looking over his shoulder and jumping at shadows. It looked like he hadn't eaten for weeks.'

'Do you remember the date?'

She checked through her phone.

'It was last month, on the thirteenth. He said it was the best time for him to complete his artistic vision.' Spector peered at the painting. 'He was superstitious, but in a different way than normal. He believed in the opposite of anything else, so black cats were good, the number thirteen was lucky, the Devil a benevolent creature, that sort of mumbo jumbo.'

'So you weren't there two nights ago?'

Spector grinned at me. 'Am I a suspect, Inspector? I was here all day.'

'Where were you on Monday the 11th, between six and nine o'clock in the morning?'

She laughed. 'I was in bed.' She stepped towards me and put her hand on my arm. 'Did something terrible happen then?'

'Edwin Blair was murdered.'

She gazed at me.

'Am I supposed to know him?'

'He's the son of Sir Oswald Blair. Do you remember him?'

There was a glint in her eye as she spoke.

'How could I forget?' She let go of me and removed her phone to glance at the screen before slipping it back into her pocket. 'I didn't know he had a son.' She didn't hesitate in using the past tense and I knew she was lying. 'You believe I had something to do with his death?'

Sutton continued making notes as I replied.

'It appears you have a connection to two recent murders.'

The laughter roared from her.

'This seems very spurious, Inspector. Was Blair chopped up as well?'

'He was strangled while out on a morning run.' I waited for her to process that information. 'And you say you have no one to vouch for your whereabouts for both crimes?'

Spector shook her head and pointed at something behind me. I turned to see a stack of papers piled up on a table near the far wall. For a second, I tried to recall what it reminded me of until the memory of Blair's novel returned, that manuscript of dragons, demons, and chosen ones. I wondered which one I'd be when someone got around to telling my story to the world.

'I was working on my memoirs.'

'You're writing an autobiography? Does it cover your trial and time in jail? Is there any mention of the threats you made against Oswald Blair?'

She glanced at her art collection, and then back to me.

'I wasn't myself then, Inspector. I'm sure you could

forgive anyone a moment of madness given the circumstances. My writing is a thesis on what makes a criminal, based on my experiences of the justice system.'

'Are you still claiming someone framed you?'

'You must read my book for the answer to that, Inspector.'

A breeze drifted in from somewhere and rattled the pages on the table. Spector was connected to both victims and had no alibi for either murder, and she liked to write. Perhaps she also enjoyed sending letters to the police. I went to the papers and picked the first one from the top, reading the title aloud.

'*The Effects of Family Structure on Crime.*'

I scanned the introduction on the page, not taking in the content but checking the fonts and printing, and doing a spot analysis of the sentence and paragraph structure. It was a desperate hope I'd see something in the text reminiscent of the letters we'd received, but there was nothing. I returned the page to the pile.

'Would you like me to send you a signed copy when it's finished, Inspector Flowers?'

I didn't let her little jab get to me.

'Hasn't this subject been written about a thousand times before?'

'Are you suggesting there's nothing new under the sun, Inspector?' She didn't wait for a reply. 'Empirical evidence shows that many young men and women from broken families tend to have a much weaker sense of connection with their neighbourhood and are prone to exploit its members to satisfy their unmet needs or desires. This contributes to a loss of a sense of community and to the disintegration of neighbourhoods into social chaos and violent crime.' Her gaze lingered on me. 'I would have thought this would be particularly interesting to you, Inspector, considering your situation.'

I dug my nails into my palm.

'What do you mean by my situation?'

'With your line of work as a police officer, of course.'

She'd turned things around to put me on the spot with ease. I'd underestimated her and knew it was time to go.

'We'll be in touch, Ms Spector.'

I nodded to tell Sutton we were leaving. Spector showed us out, stopping me before we left.

'Tell me, Inspector, how does it feel?'

'What?'

'What's it like to be famous?'

She closed the door before I replied.

I spoke to Sutton as we headed to the car.

'When we get back, I'll sign off on the paperwork, and I want you to organise twenty-four-hour surveillance on Spector.'

'Yes, ma'am.'

'Now we're going somewhere a lot less salubrious than this place.'

It was time to visit Devon Grace.

The drive from Knightsbridge to Croydon took fewer than thirty minutes. I parked five hundred yards from where we needed to be. If I'd driven straight into the estate, the car might not be there when we returned.

Sutton checked the location on her phone. 'The address is in that block of flats across the road, ma'am.'

I peered through the window. Outside was a combination of mangled terrace houses and monstrous tower blocks, one of those schemes designed by people who didn't understand what it was like to exist in squalid depravation. With no prospect of progression, crime was inevitable for many. Perhaps Carrie Spector had visited places like this for her research into what makes a criminal. After twenty weeks of training at police college, my first night on the job had been on an estate like this. I ended up in hospital after being bitten by a Rottweiler, an event which gained me an impolite nickname from my colleagues for the next five years.

Sutton stepped out of the car before I could reply; perhaps her mind was still full of the wealth and splendour we'd encountered at Spector's luxurious apartment. Whatever it was, she was moving towards the building when I pulled her back. It was the whoosh through the air I heard first, and then the clatter of metal on concrete as the bombardment landed at our feet. Sutton flinched and bumped into me.

'What?'

About half a dozen tins of beans were rolling around in the road, the noise of them followed by laughter and shrieks from the direction they'd come.

'We're a huge target here, Constable. We have to ensure we're not in the centre.'

I strode further down the street, Sutton scampering to keep up as more objects dropped behind us. The estate smelt of dirt and desperation, frustration and anger mixed in with the aroma of fried chicken from somewhere. Dogs barked in the dark while small creatures scurried through the tall grass at our side. A large woman dressed in a Paddington Bear onesie tramped by, pushing a shopping trolley containing two mewling kids. She handed one of them the fag from her mouth to shut it up. I stopped Sutton from running to her.

'How do we get inside safely, ma'am?'

'We do it with great caution, Constable, with great caution.'

I led us from the front of the tower block and, hopefully, to a safe distance. I'd known some places which had used medium-sized catapults to bombard the police when they entered somewhere which didn't want them. We crossed the road and into the shadows next to the building. A chill wind cut across my face as the howling dogs got closer. The street stank of feral animals and open toilets; we dodged the broken bottles and crushed pizza boxes and reached the entrance to the high-rise flats with no other missiles aimed at us.

The contrast between this and where Carrie Spector lived was staggering; the highs of wealth and privilege compared to lack of opportunities and chronic depravation. I stepped into the building first, scrutinising the reception for a welcoming committee, relieved to find it empty. We needed to be on the eighth floor and moved to the lift.

There was an eerie silence in the lobby as we waited for the creaking metallic coffin to arrive, the vacuum only shattered by the screech and clang as the lift descended. A nervous twitch affected Sutton's eyes as our chariot arrived and the doors opened. The stink of piss and vomit assaulted my senses; we moved inside, and I pressed the button as the box swallowed us. The constable kept her hands glued to her sides, but she couldn't hide the trembling in her fingers. Butterflies fluttered in my stomach as we went up and the building whispered around us.

The aroma was worse when we stepped out, the corridor smelling like a human sewer. Thankfully, it was empty and the flat we wanted was close. Even before we'd moved two feet towards it, I saw the open door. I leant close to Sutton.

'Be extra vigilant when we get in.'

The door screeched as I pushed it aside; something sticky attached itself to my fingers, and I winced. The smell was even worse inside: a mixture of unflushed toilet fermenting with discarded chemical waste. I grabbed at my nose as we stepped over a school of used needles, dirty adult nappies and mouldy food. The room was devoid of furniture, apart from a stained sofa and a broken chair. My shoes stuck to the carpet as I called out for the tenant.

'Devon Grace, are you here?'

Silence surrounded us, only to be cracked by the rumbling of Sutton's guts. All the colour drained from her face. We had three rooms to check, but I didn't have much hope of finding him. I pointed Sutton towards the bedroom while I took the others.

The bathroom looked like it hadn't been used in weeks, clean compared to the rest of the flat. The kitchen was in a terrible state, dirty plates and cutlery everywhere, and rotten food clogging up the sink. I wasn't brave enough to check the fridge.

Broken beer bottles littered most of the floor. Breaking glass was the anthem of my childhood. A day never went by without the sound of a wine glass being smashed into a thousand glittering fragments somewhere in the house. My father tolerated my mother's excessive drinking only because he knew it made her easier to control.

I knelt to pick up a piece of shattered glass in Grace's kitchen, telling myself I was checking it for blood or a sign of foul play, but knowing deep down I was still trying to break away from those memories. It fell from my fingers onto the floor as I returned to the living room and found Constable Sutton waiting for me.

'The bedroom is empty, ma'am, but I discovered this under the bed.' She handed me a flyer for the club where Blair worked. 'I guess Grace could have met the first victim there.'

I was considering the possibility when a noise attracted my attention. A group of women – girls, really, since most of them appeared to be teenagers - stood in the doorway and blocked our exit. Their expressions were as harsh as the environment: screwed-up eyes and screwed-down hairdos. As the tallest one stepped forward, I noticed they all had the same tattoo on the back of their hands. Thankfully, it wasn't a penguin. I was trying to work out what it was when she spoke.

'You shouldn't ave done what you did, Flowers.'

It seemed my reputation preceded me everywhere in the city. She clenched her hand into a fist; I recognised her tattoo, and I knew what she meant. It was the symbol of a hashtag, and they all had it.

'You're talking about Voss?'

They stepped closer, weapons in their hands and hate in the air.

'She was protecting all of us, and you ruined it.' The group glared at us. 'You and all the other pigs.'

It seemed I'd never get away from what happened with Alice Voss, but to see these kids admiring her as a hero sickened me.

'She used people, kid, to do the dirty work for her.' Using the word kid might have been a mistake. The tension rose in the room, their faces a cocktail of smouldering resentment and anger. 'Voss is in prison because she deserves it; she killed people.'

The tallest one stepped forward.

'She didn't kill anyone.' The rest of the gang murmured behind her. 'Only scumbags died, and they deserved it. And you stopped all that.'

Quick as a flash, they all had blades in their hands. The glint of light from the silver helped me to count them: six blocked our escape, the smallest appearing younger than Abbey. Here were the continuing consequences of Alice Voss's actions, with violence begetting more violence.

I was struggling to think how we'd get out of this unscathed when Sutton moved between the group and me.

'I was like you at your age. I even had the gang stamp, but it differed from yours.'

She rolled up her sleeve and held out her arm so we all saw it: a mark six inches above her wrist, the scars of a former tattoo, but it was impossible to make out what it used to be.

The leader peered at it.

'What was it?'

Sutton pulled her sleeve down.

'You know the *Alien* movies? It was one of those creatures.'

The girls let out a singular gasp before the leader spoke.

'You were a Xeno?'

'For four years, starting on my twelfth birthday.'

'So why did you betray them and join the pigs?'

She flung the words at Sutton. The constable was unmoved by the venom facing her.

'Because I wised up and realised a group of older blokes were using me. I took control of my life, and you can too.'

The trembling and nervousness vanished from her. Determination filled Sutton's face, which must have impressed the gang as much as it did me. The leader spread her arms wide.

'It's women and girls only with us, copper.'

Sutton didn't back down.

'You say that, but I guess there're already guys creeping around you, if not as a group, then as individuals so they can break down your solidarity. It won't start as much, maybe the offer of free booze or drugs, then they'll worm their way in and convince you it would be better to join a larger gang. There might even be promises of shared power, but they'll prove false, and before you know it, you'll see splits in your friendships, and you'll end up as nothing more than accessories.'

She didn't hold back, and from the looks on some girls'

faces, she'd hit a raw nerve with more than one. There appeared to be a silent communication between them as they parted down the middle and offered us a way out. Sutton glanced at me, and I didn't hesitate, striding through them but never avoiding their gaze. They were young, a few of them younger than Abbey, but a lifetime of pain seeped from their eyes.

We got outside and Sutton headed for the exit. I pulled her back.

'We'll take the stairs. The residents might have sabotaged the lift.' Sutton looked horrified. 'I knew a colleague who got stuck in one for twelve hours before any of us realised it. Some thugs had disabled the alarm and intercom while jamming it between floors.'

I pushed the door open and we motored down eight flights, never looking back and ignoring the weird sounds coming from above and the stench of decay oozing through the concrete. We got downstairs and outside in record time. All the tins had vanished from the street as we hurried to the car. Luckily, it was where we'd left it and untouched.

I had been driving out of the estate for at least a minute before Sutton spoke.

'I hope I didn't overstep my position, ma'am?'

I stared at her in the mirror.

'Is it true what you told them?'

She grabbed hold of her wrist and pulled at her arm.

'It wasn't so long ago, but it seems like a different lifetime.'

I didn't ask her anymore, satisfied to leave her privacy alone for now. I concentrated on what we'd seen during our road trip.

'What did you make of our visit to the flat? Do you think Devon Grace could be our killer?'

'No, ma'am, I can't see it.'

'Why not?'

'The circumstances of the murders are clear indicators we're dealing with an intelligent, highly focused and organised individual. And Grace's flat was evidence of the opposite of that.'

'What about Spector?'

'I think she's the poster girl for the description I gave for the killer.'

I didn't disagree as we returned to the station.

And then I got the call.

There'd been another Penguin murder.

23   THE DRAWBACK

As I stepped from the car, a siege was waiting for me; two sides pushing and shoving while teetering on the edge of unnecessary and unwanted violence. A scrum of reporters and gawkers had gathered outside, crowding the space in the narrow street. Uniformed officers struggled to hold them back.

Constable Sutton and I approached the scene, watching the public spectacle while they watched us. Elvis Costello sang inside my head as the crowd pumped themselves up into a stage of near frenzy. The Penguin murders had got the city on edge, and that was without the majority of them knowing about the letters the killer had sent to the police.

In the excitement, someone had kicked over a large green bin, spilling its contents over the pavement between us and the house. An empty bottle of wine rolled next to me, and I remembered my time at the restaurant with the comic book man and what the booze did to my insides. It was a strange thing to think about at that moment, but I needed to get back in touch with him at some point.

I marched over a cluster of ready-meal boxes and side-stepped the fresh fruit and rotten vegetables attracting the neighbourhood dogs' attention. The street stank of things long dead, and I pushed through the bodies towards my stressed-out colleagues. Some hacks must have recognised me and lights flashed in my face as they called my name.

'Flowers, Inspector Flowers, has The Penguin struck again?'

'Flowers, why don't you protect us?'

'Why can't you catch the killer, Flowers? Is this because of police corruption?'

And then, for good measure,

'Will you listen to the Alice Voss podcast, Inspector Flowers? Is Voss innocent, and did you get it all wrong, Inspector?'

As I got through the crowd, Jack strode towards me; Sutton was at my side, looking as perplexed as I felt inside. My partner wore a new suit, or at least one I hadn't seen before, dark blue contrasting against the pure whiteness of his tie. I had a sudden urge to ask him about his love letters to Voss, but let the noise sweep such a stupid idea from my brain.

Jack nodded at me.

'It looks like there's another one.'

I followed him and Sutton inside. It was a narrow street house, probably built in the 19th century and likely costing an arm and a leg to buy now. Broken pottery littered the corridor as the three of us walked over it and entered the living room.

The smell hit me first, sweeping through my nose and into my lungs; intense and cloying, it pressed against my senses, wanting to trigger every button which said I should throw up. But I'd done enough of that in the last twenty-four hours. A woman lay on the floor, her face forced into the ground so I couldn't guess her age, her legs and arms twisted in unnatural directions. A lake of blood surrounded her head and had turned the carpet a thick shade of red. Scattered around her were broken ornaments, with bits of them sinking into the ruby liquid. Her hands lay at her side, pointing out like a crazed clock. On the back of them were crude carvings of penguins, probably created with the same blade which killed her.

I knelt to get a closer look, my initial thoughts confirmed. I moved to let my colleagues take charge. Forensics officers turned her over. Her throat had been cut so deeply it had nearly severed her head. This had been a frenzied attack; with no sign of control, no evidence of planning. Constable Sutton asked the question.

'Was this our Penguin?'

Jack shook his head and aired the concerns I'd kept to myself.

'It's a copycat and not a very good one. The murder is too messy, too undisciplined. And those penguin cuts are crude and in the wrong places.'

He let out a tremendous sigh, and I wondered if it was because this wasn't our killer or because of the troubles in his love life. At least his IBS hadn't flared up in a while. Perhaps arduous affairs of the heart outweighed medical problems where the human body was concerned. Given a choice between the two, I questioned which he'd pick.

I moved from the victim, staring at the photos on the bookcase.

'Whoever did this used the descriptions in the media, which have been exaggerated or inaccurate.' The noises from outside grew louder and swept through the open door. I walked across the room and picked up two framed photographs. The blonde in them was the body on the floor.

I handed them to Sutton. 'I'd suggest you look for the brunette in these photos.'

Jack stood at my side as Sutton gathered the other uniformed officers and they searched the house for the woman in the images.

'What shall we tell the reporters?'

I contemplated his question, my mind wandering back to my recent conversation with Dr Felicia Nelson and her army of felines.

'Leave it to me, Jack; I'll put the cat amongst the pigeons.'

My smile didn't mirror his confused face. He followed me outside as I stood before the mass and cleared my throat. The crowd had grown, rumours of another Penguin attack spreading far and wide into the next streets and neighbourhoods. Mixed among the professionals were the public with their cameras and smartphones, glittering screens reaching out for me, ready to drag my image into the digital world. I guessed some of them were streaming the whole thing live, and that my appearance and voice would soon be broadcast across the country and the world. I waited there and glanced at my fingers, imaging every inch of me converted into a million dots and dispersed through the universe.

Then the questions flew at me.

'Inspector Flowers, is this a Penguin murder?'

'Was the body chopped up, Inspector Flowers?'

'How many are dead?'

'Why have the police no leads?'

'Did another copper do this?'

'Have you caught The Penguin?'

Jack was standing at my side when I raised my arms, waiting for my audience to quieten. The hush settled as

Jack stared at me. Heavy oppression seemed to brood upon the air as I spoke.

'I can only give you a brief statement.' They groaned at me. 'I'm sure you'll appreciate this is an ongoing investigation, and we cannot reveal too many details of this murder at the moment.' There was intense murmuring in the crowd.

'Have you caught him?' someone shouted.

I waited for thirty seconds before the question came again.

'Have you caught him?'

'Have you caught The Penguin?'

Have you caught him? Have you caught him? Have you caught him?

The sounds spread through the throng like a mantra. I raised my hands again for the hush to descend.

'No, we haven't caught him.' An omen full of possible danger swept through me. 'We've caught her.'

Then I turned back and returned to the house as chaos erupted outside.

Jack ran after me.

'What have you done?'

I ignored him and searched for Sutton. There was a commotion in the kitchen, so I followed the noise. When I got there, Sutton and two other constables were dragging someone from a cupboard underneath the sink. Bottles of bleach fell to the floor as she kicked out and knocked over a cup of washing powder; puffs of it drifted up into the air, and it smelt of lavender. Her body was all bent from the time she'd been there, and you couldn't miss the blood on her clothes; it was the brunette from the photographs. Tears streamed down her face as a flame of scarlet crept in a diagonal across her cheeks. It seemed to be a crime of passion, hastily arranged to be something else.

'There's our murderer, Jack.'

He leant into my face.

'You know she's not our serial killer, Jen. What are you playing at?'

'I never told them she was; I only said we'd caught her for this particular crime. They can spin whatever they want from that.' What did I care if they looked foolish because of it?

Jack grabbed my arm.

'You know what I mean. The media will take your words and stitch them to this killing. When she's dragged from here, hundreds of photographs will be all over the media and the internet, and every one of them will name her as a serial killer. Is that what you wanted?'

I pulled from him as the suspect screamed behind us.

'Our murderer has been ahead of us from day one. Hell, they've been in front from before that. Now we've thrown a spanner in their works. Maybe they'll make a mistake and help us.'

'And what if they don't, Jen? What if they strike again because of your words?'

I stepped past the officers arresting the woman and headed out the back door. Hopefully, I'd get to my car with none of the press spotting me. I turned to Jack before I left.

'They were always going to kill again, Jack; we've just been waiting for it to happen. At least now we have a fraction of control.'

There was rubbish piled high in the yard. I avoided it and wrenched open the door which lead into the alley at the rear of the building. The cobbled path was empty. I made it to the car unseen and headed to the station.

QUIET GREETED me when I walked into the Murder Room. I'd expected SIO Merson or The Prophet to be there considering what I'd said to those reporters, but they were keeping their heads down. Jack and Sutton hadn't returned yet. Grealish approached me.

'Do we continue to go through the information we have, ma'am?'

'Nothing changes, Constable Grealish; we keep working, and DI Monroe will interview the suspect when she arrives.'

And once she gets a lawyer. I guessed there would be plenty of them lining up to represent her now I'd implied she was the notorious Penguin. Should I feel guilty for putting her in this spot? Perhaps I did for a second, before remembering what she'd done to the woman she'd lived with. Those photographs from the house were in my head as I considered what terrible things people do to the ones they claim to love.

Messages bombarded my phone, all about the news going viral: texts from Jack, Abbey, Felicia Nelson, and Oswald Blair. Blair's was simple.

Is it her?

My reply was just as simple.

I'll keep you informed.

I felt terrible misleading him, but my brief show at the copycat house was a sign of how desperate I'd become; a rash move which might backfire on many people, not least me. Perhaps this was where Abbey got her impulsivity from, and I couldn't blame her at all for attacking Olivia Coates. I put the phone on my desk and stared at the computer. I sat like that for an hour before Jack returned, unhappiness etched into the lines underneath his eyes; lines growing by the day.

'She's singing like a bird.'

'That would be the brunette?'

He nodded. 'Her name is Cathy Daniels; the dead woman was her girlfriend, Lucy Smith. Theirs was a heated relationship; the neighbours confirmed frequent fights between them, and sometimes they spilt over into the streets. This one went too far, and Daniels grabbed a knife and slit Lucy's throat.'

'Then she panicked and carved those penguin figures into the back of her girlfriend's hands?'

'That's what she said. A neighbour heard the screams and called the police. When the uniforms turned up, Daniels hid in the kitchen. Now she's panicking, thinking we'll pin the other two murders on her.'

He couldn't stop his teeth from grinding as he spoke.

'Are you mad at what I did?'

He grabbed the seat near me.

'Is this about my letters to Alice Voss, Jen?'

A sharp pain stabbed into my chest as I burst out laughing.

'Not everything is about you, partner. I told you why I did it.'

He crossed his arms and sighed.

'So what do we do next?'

'What we always do, Jack: we work, and we wait.'

And I wondered how much trouble I was in.

A sense of desolation and disillusionment overwhelmed Mags as she ignored Billie's scowl and dragged her friend through the pile of pizza boxes and disused needles scattered in front of them. Fat cats chased after scrappy rats, and the two young women paused outside the broken door of the entrance and held their breath. The river spat out effluence, which settled over the building and made Mags grab at her throat. Billie continued to glower at her mate.

'Are you sure this is the venue for the photoshoot?'

'Why do you never believe me, Wilhelmina?'

The pout transformed into a grimace, before settling on a frown. Billie hated anyone using her given name, but she knew Mags was the same.

'Because you're a practised witchery of fiction, Mary Evans, and you haven't told me the full story about this latest Instagram adventure of yours.'

The early evening rain drizzled over them as they pushed their way inside the abandoned warehouse.

'It's an adventure for both of us.' She smiled at her best friend. 'This is our big chance, Billie; you know that.'

Mags showed her the message on her phone again.

Photoshoot for new Instagram Influencers to promote the restoration and gentrification of the Amex building on the river. Thursday 14ᵗʰ @5pm. Be there or be square.

Billie shook the damp from her flowing red locks.

'How many of these fake events have you been to?' The water dripped from her head. 'You waste so much time standing around in dumps like this, and nothing comes from those texts and emails. You know it's scamsters after your money, Mags.'

Mags ignored her friend and strode down a corridor strewn with rubbish towards the main hall. Lights flickered at the end, blending in with the shine on her face. Billie scampered behind her as they pushed through the doors.

It was an impressive construction, three storeys high with one more underground, but it hadn't always been that way. The building was old; two centuries of stories witnessed by those rafters and support structures. At some point, it was used for manufacturing; perhaps during the war, armies of women slaved inside, creating armaments for the war or materials for the soldiers. After the conflict, they would have trooped back to their domestic duties, their husbands, brothers and sons returning to find jobs in what was by then a factory producing electrical goods. It would keep doing that for over three decades, the sons and grand-sons of the original workers putting their shifts in before heading for the pub and the football at the weekend.

And then the recession hit and the employees disap-peared to be replaced by cats and mice and feral dogs and birds discovering sanctuary amongst those towering rafters. Occasionally, children and teenagers would stumble their way inside and use the building for sex or drugs or drink; and sometimes all three together. But not all the intruders discovered their escape in that manner; others hid in the shadows, finding solace from the terror at home or in school.

A decade of such intrusions passed by before a larger invasion happened. Some local entrepreneurs saw a gap in a developing market and converted part of the building. Hence, it housed regular rave parties where euphoric participants danced on the ground where their ancestors once sweated blood.

Eventually, those gatherings were deemed illegal as the country prospered once more. The structure was cleaned and sold to a telemarketing business, the staff phoning people and selling them things they didn't want or need. After a decade, the work emigrated across the planet, and the building stood empty once again; the animals and the vagrants returned to that gloomy interior, desperate to find shelter from the harsh world outside.

Now Mags and Billie shivered inside its abandoned limbs and searched for those who would make them famous. They'd been friends since school, and now, on the cusp of their twenty-second birthdays, Mags was convinced her new life was about to begin. They'd soon leave the gloom of the city and head for the beaches at Bali or the glitter of Dubai. Then she'd laugh in the faces of her parents and all those teachers who'd said she'd never amount to anything.

'What's an Instagram Influencer?' Mags's father had asked her.

She'd snubbed the ignorance in his face.

'Well, they have the power to influence their audience to do something.'

That's all Mags desired, to have someone listen to her and respect her. She pulled at her skirt and hobbled in high heels across broken concrete and towards a sizeable area at the back of the hall. Lights flickered along the edge, but there was no one there.

Billie grabbed at her arm.

'Shouldn't there be more people here?'

Mags was glad there weren't.

'It means there's less competition.' She shook herself from her friend's grip and peered into her face. 'What makes us different from all the rest? That's what you need to concentrate on, and be willing to show everyone your uniqueness. This means we're special, sets us apart and makes an impact.' She lifted her arms in the air. 'In a sea of over four hundred million Instagram users, we must highlight our exceptionality. We find that distinctiveness and FOCUS on it! It may be uncomfortable at first, but it'll be worth it. Trust me, Billie.'

They held hands as they moved towards the lights up ahead. Mags was focusing on looking forward and didn't see the figure step from the shadows behind them. Billie's fingers slipped from hers. Mags's head twitched to the side as Billie slumped to the floor. A circle of red liquid seeped from her throat and congealed around her hair on the ground. The scream was nascent in Mags's mouth when the blade swept across her flesh. Her legs gave way as her fingers shook and reached for her face.

As her skull hit the concrete, she stared at her friend before slipping away, her last thought of an exotic beach she'd never get to see.

Jack arrived at the scene before me. He must have gone straight from his new residence. I'd barely got out of the station and was heading home when I received the call to divert to a disused industrial estate in West Hendon.

The flashing blue lights guided me into the front of the building. As I got out of the car, mountains of construction materials greeted me, many of them reaching into the dislodged metal fences supposed to be for security. Scenes of Crime Officers, Forensics, and uniformed constables gathered around the side and the warehouse entrance where I met my partner.

'It looks like our killer is accelerating, Jen.'

'Give me the terrible news.'

'You need to see this for yourself.'

Was it another hanging or more dismemberment? A bouquet of death lingered in the air as we pushed through a narrow door and entered the main hall, dodging years of detritus littered everywhere. Light filtered in through a gigantic hole in the roof and every broken window. As I glanced up, birds beat their wings between the rafters and clouds of dust floated down to the bodies: two of them, face down over tables, the blood dripping from their throats and onto the ground.

They were young women, dressed as if at a fashion show or a disco. One of them had long flame-red hair which made me recall a Pre-Raphaelite painting I'd seen in the Tate once. That hair was the colour of the blood seeping onto the floor. I held my fingers to my nose as I spoke to Jack.

'Who discovered them?'

He showed me his phone.

'We did. This photo and message were posted on Instagram forty minutes ago, and several users called the police, worried about what they'd seen online.'

I stared at two pictures of the outside of the building and a caption.

I died to be here.

'We're unsure if the posting came before or after the murders because we're waiting for the medical examiner to arrive,' Jack said.

'Who posted it?'

'It's on Wilhelmina Moore's Instagram account. She's the one with the red hair.'

I returned his phone and stared at the two women.

'Both with their throats cut?'

'That's what it seems like, sliced open from behind.'

I glanced around the building.

'Why were they here?'

'We don't know yet; Cybercrime needs to check the phones and social media accounts.'

I didn't like this additional aspect of social media introduced into the crimes.

'This is a step-up in confidence for our killer, slaying two people together. Why are we sure it's the same perpetrator?'

Jack moved to the victim closest to me and lifted her hand to show me the bird's unmistakable image from the other murders.

'The penguin is only on this victim.'

I took her hand from him, the chill of it seeping through the glove I wore.

'Perhaps the killer was interrupted. Do we have both their names?'

'The one with the penguin stamp is Mary Evans; her friend is Wilhelmina Moore, both twenty-two years old.'

I moved closer to the tables and bent my knees, twisting my head to have a good look at their faces; their eyes were wide, mouths red with fresh lipstick, cheeks hanging on to life now gone. Had they been placed like this, posed to leave a message? More murderous messages from a warped morality of someone passing judgement on those they deemed unworthy?

One of the forensic team was checking the victim's phones. I wondered where Athena was as I spoke to my colleague.

'Have you got anything from those?'

He acknowledged me with a nod; he appeared not much older than the victims.

'There are a lot of photos on both devices, hundreds of them. A glance through each shows no images taken today.'

'So someone else took the photo posted on Instagram. Can we trace that account?'

He shrugged. 'We'll try, but I'd expect it to be a dummy. Both women had their internet connections active and logged into their Instagram accounts. It looks as if they tried to make careers out of using that app.'

'How do you do that?'

I limited my familiarity of social media to what Abbey taught me.

My colleague with the phones grinned at me, an expression out of place for where we stood.

'These types of Instagram users want to get hundreds of thousands of followers to their account; it doesn't work otherwise. Then they can attract advertisers to their posts, and those advertisers use them to sell their products: the media call them Influencers.'

This was a whole new world for me.

'Is that why they were here?'

He nodded. 'It seems so. On Mary Evans's phone is a text asking her to come here today for a paid job as an Influencer.'

'Do you know who sent the message?'

'I'll do a full trace on it when we return to the station, but I'd expect it to originate somewhere in China or Russia so it'll be impossible to find the sender.'

I gave him a resigned nod and re-joined Jack with the bodies.

'It seems these women wanted to get famous using the internet.'

I explained about the Instagram app, assuming he was as clueless as me about these things. Maybe Sutton or Grealish could help us with a better understanding of the technology.

'That means the last two crime scenes for our Penguin have them meeting their victims through different mobile software: the dating app for Clive Hamilton, and now Instagram here.'

The connection troubled me; a murderer using the internet to choose victims made me uneasy. It meant our killer or killers were skilled enough in utilising the software, so it would be difficult to trace them. Things were getting harder with each crime and not easier.

I watched as my colleagues dealt with the bodies.

'Someone needs to tell their next of kin what's happened.'

'That will be us, partner.'

'Do you have the details?' Jack nodded.

The concrete was stained red as I prepared to deliver the worst kind of news and we left the scene. We drove to Mary Evans's parents first. She was an only child, and I expected a combination of tears and anger from her mother and father, but they were both as cold as ice.

'I told Mags she spent too much time on Instagram, but she wouldn't listen,' the father said as the mother stared into space behind me.

There was a row of figurine ducks of different sizes on the wall, laid out as if ready to fly from the house. Mary's mother fixated on them. Grief is a terrible thing, and she barely registered her daughter's death.

'Do you mind if we check her bedroom, Mr Evans?' Jack said.

The father nodded and led my partner upstairs. I stayed with the mother, waiting for her tears to come. I thought about how I'd react if I'd received this news about Abbey. The sound of Jack going through the young woman's room filtered through the ceiling.

'Do you know who your daughter met tonight, Mrs Evans?'

I hated intruding in people's lives like this, but I had no choice. Her face never moved as I got ready to ask again.

Then she reached across and put her hand on mine; it was as cold as her daughter's when I'd touched it not so long ago.

'She always went out with Wilhelmina.' A brief smile crossed her lips. 'Though Wilhelmina hated her proper name. It was Billie and Mags getting up to their adventures.'

'Do you know of anyone else Mags met on these adventures, Mrs Evans? Perhaps she spoke to you or her father about other people, perhaps a boyfriend.'

She shook her head. 'No, there was never anything like that. Mags said she didn't have time for boyfriends. She was always too busy trying to be famous on the internet, even though her father laughed at her.' She gripped onto my hand, her nails digging into my flesh. 'It's our fault, really.'

I eased away from her, ignoring where she'd broken the skin and the bruise forming on my palm.

'Why do you think that, Mrs Evans?'

She clasped her hands as ominous shadows consumed her face.

'We were never there for her as she grew up, you see. We both worked and wouldn't give up our jobs, so we had childminders when Mags was young. When she got to thirteen or fourteen, we decided she was old enough to look after herself.' She took a tissue from her pocket and dabbed at her eyes. I had a sudden vision of myself in ten years. 'That's when she turned to the internet for affection and attention.'

'None of this is your fault, Mrs Evans, or your husband's.'

She didn't appear to hear me.

'Mags's dream was to be famous.' She gazed at the wall as she spoke. 'We tried to talk her out of this Instagram nonsense, but she wouldn't have it. Her dad ridiculed her when she told us about all the exotic places she'd visit.'

'It's a different world for young people now, Mrs Evans, compared to the one we grew up in.'

I guessed her to be a similar age to me, regardless of the thick shadows spreading around her eyes. She lifted her fingers to her face.

'If she'd taken the nursing course we arranged for her, Mags would still be alive.'

I couldn't say much to that, reluctant to tell her violence against women and girls was increasing every year, irrespective of where they lived or worked.

'Did your daughter have many friends?'

Perhaps one of them could provide more details about this ambition to become famous using social media.

'Wilhelmina was her only friend; you should speak to her.'

I was about to give her more unwelcome news when Jack and Mr Evans returned from upstairs. I recognised from my partner's face he'd found nothing useful. The father folded his arms, his expression emotionless. We left them with their grief and headed to deliver to another set of parents the terrible news about their daughter.

WILHELMINA MOORE HAD two younger sisters, one of whom opened the door to us. Her father had died five years ago, killed by a hit-and-run driver who escaped. I think her mother realised why we were standing there before we spoke. I hoped she'd take the girls into another room. They looked about seven or eight years old, but she kept them there as Jack delivered the grim news. The girls broke down in tears as the mother sat stony-faced. I sat the kids down while Jack delivered the same awkward questions we'd asked at the Evans house; I listened to the answers while trying to console the sisters, unsurprised to get the same unhelpful results.

It wasn't the parents' fault we left with no greater knowledge of who'd committed the crimes. Young people, especially daughters, were usually unforthcoming when informing adults about their lives.

An hour later, we were at the station with nothing useful to show from visits to two sets of grieving families. The investigation now included evidence, photographs, and notes from four murders.

And we were no further forward.

A jigsaw surrounded me, and I couldn't see how to put the pieces together. A barman hanged and strangled while out jogging; a video artist hacked to bits in his studio; and now two young women with their throats slit after being lured to a fake social media event. Jack handed me a cup of warm coffee.

'Do you think there's more than one killer?'

'I suppose it's possible with all the different methods of murder. The only things linking them together are the penguins and the letters.'

Yes, the letters; would another arrive in the morning? And would it be helpful? As I was considering this, I got a text from Abbey. Was it wrong that, because of this afternoon's events, I'd forgotten about her making her way into London by train?

Something dark and terrible nibbled at my brain as I checked her message.

Can you pick me up from the comic shop?

She didn't state which shop, but I guessed she meant Steve's. My frazzled head hurt, and I was getting nowhere with the investigation. I made my excuses to Jack, who appeared glad to see me leave early. Since I'd discovered why Jean had kicked him out, it hadn't returned to normal between us. I wondered if it ever would as I set off to get Abbey.

The comic book store was busier than on the previous occasion, with a greater smattering of women and young girls than I'd have expected. A faint smell of lemon air freshener drifted above my head as I strode towards the back. I stepped beyond the two blokes discussing how bad some *Star Trek* movie was and to the room where I'd seen Abbey with her new friends the last time.

'Over here, Mum.'

Abbey's voice came from my right. There was a large display of Superman with his arm around Batman in the way. I moved past it and found her sitting at a table with a spread of opened comics near her. I pulled aside a chair and sat down.

'I thought you would have gone straight home after the session.' I wanted to ask her about it. I glanced at the colourful pages in front of me instead. 'What are you reading?'

She stared at me, her nose curled up, her mouth pouting.

'These are graphic novels, Mum.'

I picked up the closest to me, the cover featuring a girl with purple hair, purple lips, and purple nails listening to music through giant headphones.

'What's the difference between them and comics?'

Abbey glared at me as if I was the stupidest person in the room.

'They are much longer and more complex. While a comic book will tell a story over many issues, graphic novels have their storylines wrapped up in only one or two books.'

It sounded like something she'd rehearsed after being taught the lines by one of her new friends. She continued to stare as if there was something wrong with me. I decided to try to get on her good side.

'Okay. Do you have a favourite out of these?'

I remembered the one she'd shown me the other day, the one about Jack the Ripper and its stark black and white illustrations. I hoped she hadn't become fascinated by that; one person in the family focusing on serial killers was bad enough.

My daughter's grumpiness vanished in an instant, her eyes sparkling with newfound enthusiasm. She grabbed one and held it up so I could see the cover.

'*Page by Paige* is great. It's in America, but I really feel it's about me and it's given me an idea for my new secret identity.'

I considered Abbey's words. Was this recent interest of hers something I should worry about? Was it connected to her session with the psychologist? And how would I find out what had happened between her and Felicia without making it too obvious?

A red-headed girl and her twin adorned the cover of the graphic novel. One girl used a pencil to write out the story's title as it twirled up to the twin, upside down at the top. The New York skyline lit up the background.

'What's it about, love?'

The stress seeped out of me as I allowed myself to be a mother again.

She clasped it to her chest.

'Paige Turner has just moved to New York with her family, and she's having trouble settling into the big city. In the pages of her sketchbook, she tries to make sense of her new life, including trying out her secret identity as an artist.' Her excitement shone across the table. 'I love this book, Mum. It's inspired me to be a writer or an artist.'

Seeing her happy like this, witnessing the contrast to what I'd viewed on that terrible video sent a wave of pride and joy through me.

'Or you could do both, Abs.'

Her eyes widened. 'Do you think so?'

'I don't see why not.' I'd never been one of those parents who believe telling their child they can do anything is the best option for installing self-belief and confidence. I'd seen enough examples of kids crashing and burning when they realised life wasn't as easy as some adults had implied. And some of those teenagers fell between the cracks and found themselves in criminal activity without even realising it. But encouraging Abbey to do something creative, to explore that side of her, would be beneficial, regardless of how far she took it. And I could see how happy it was making her.

She grinned at me. 'You must buy me this, then.'

'We can take it out of your first month's wages.'

Steven Morris had sneaked up on us like a ninja; thankfully, not dressed as one or carrying weapons, unless you counted two bottles of iced peach tea as detrimental to your health. He handed them to us and Abbey took hers. But I declined, peering at him instead.

'You want Abbey to work here?'

Before he replied, she ran around the table, clinging onto her latest treasure and talking fifty thousand words a minute.

'It'll be great, Mum. I'll earn some money, give you some for rent and food and bills and stuff, and be able to buy more comics and books. Then I can practise writing and telling stories, and even get some art materials so I can draw or paint or sketch or whatever.'

When she stopped, she took a swig from the bottle, an aroma of peach irritating my lungs. I expected to see random words scattered on the floor like alphabet soup.

'We need to talk about this at home, Abigail.' Abbey having a part-time job was something I'd already thought would be good for her, but I didn't mention it. 'Remember, you have to fit other things into your day, like your school schedule and homework.' Not that she was attending school right now.

And the potential threat of a stay in a juvenile detention centre hung over our heads. I understood why she hadn't broached the subject yet, but I continued to delay talking to her about it. Yes, I was busy, and work was stressful, but I couldn't deny any longer I was running away from this issue. I kept telling myself it was for Abbey's benefit, this constant silence between us about the attack, but I was only kidding myself. If I delayed finding out why Abbey had done it, it would prevent me from dealing with my guilt for her behaviour.

These things crammed themselves into my head alongside the images of four dead people and those irritating penguin stamps, but the excitement never left Abbey's face.

'Oh, don't worry, Mum. I'll still have plenty of time to see Dr Nelson.'

My eyes shrank at the mention of the psychologist's name, glancing at Steve for his reaction. I liked him and all, but I didn't want our family problems aired in public.

'Well, Abs...'

'I told Steve about the sessions, Mum. You needn't worry about that.'

Too much unexpected and unwanted information was assaulting me at once; I dreamed of vodka in that bottle of peach ice tea. I put my hand on her arm.

'We need to go, Abbey.' I looked at him. 'I'll get back to you about this, Steve.'

He nodded. 'No problem, Jen. It's only for a few hours on Saturdays, but you talk it over with Abigail and let me know what you decide.'

My mouth formed a resemblance of a smile.

'I will, as soon as possible.'

I pulled Abbey with me towards the exit, her expression returning to a single pallet of teenage angst. I was dragging Abbey past a group of customers so didn't hear his reply; I only let go of her when we got outside, her face telling me it was pointless to get into a conversation.

The journey home would have been more palatable if I'd told her I was okay with her taking a part-time job in the comic shop, but I preferred the silence; it gave me time to consider what I'd ask her about the session with Felicia Nelson. What was it I wanted to know? What if her violent act had its roots in Abbey's upbringing, in what I'd done, and hadn't done, as a mother? Did I want to hear that?

Abbey was halfway upstairs before I stepped inside the house, slamming her bedroom door hard enough to shake the blinds in the kitchen. I resisted the urge to drag a bottle of beer from the fridge and put the kettle on instead. After taking my jacket off and making myself a large coffee with extra sugar, I retired to the living room and processed my thoughts about the case; talking to Abbey would wait.

I got the phone and read through my notes: Edwin Blair strangled while on an early morning run; Clive Hamilton dismembered in his studio flat after meeting a man through a dating app; and now, Mags Evans and Billie Moore with their throats slit in an abandoned factory where they thought they'd become Instagram stars.

Three of the four victims had illustrations of penguins stamped into their palms. That was deliberate; a definite message. But was it communication to us, to the police, or perhaps a message to someone else? It might be, considering the murderer was already sending us direct messages with the letters: vague text sent as a game for the killer.

There must be a link between the penguins and the letters; unless it was all one big distraction. Until we discovered something about the penguins or the notes, it was best to focus on the only connection we had between the murders; between the first two at least: Carrie Spector. I sent a text to Sutton, asking her to check any link between Spector and the latest victims, Moore and Evans.

Spector had resources, so it would be easy for her to pretend to be some important bigwig on Instagram to lure those girls. But why would she do that? I could get why she'd kill Edwin Blair, as payback against his father, but why Hamilton? Was it something to do with that painting she'd bought from him? With his death and its notoriety, his art would be worth a lot more than she paid for it; but it wasn't money driving Spector. It made me wonder if there was any truth in her claim of being framed for the embezzlement. She didn't need to steal half a million pounds from the family firm with her family's wealth. If someone had set Spector up as a patsy, it might have driven her to revenge; but would it be this complicated? If there was a connection between her and the latest murders, then yes, I saw a possibility, but I didn't buy it yet. And there was one other thing to consider.

Even though we hadn't found Devon Grace, I'd discounted him as a suspect. As Sutton mentioned, the evidence of his flat and his disorganisation counted him out for any of these crimes. Then again, the mess in his place might have disguised someone ransacking it; or it might have been a carefully constructed facade. We didn't know where Grace was. If he had been working with a partner, the brains of the outfit, then maybe his disappearance was suspicious.

Upstairs, Abbey barged around in her bedroom and added to my growing headache. It would be impossible to get much sleep tonight since I'd be focusing on one thing.

What would be in the next letter?

27   INSIDE THE LINE

The letter was there when I got to the station at nine the next morning. Printed copies were on a table and a version of it was displayed on the big screen and a sense of *déjà vu* hit me. The team were in the main room; Jack sipped on his coffee as he peered at the text, while Grealish and Sutton spoke to each other in the far corner. No one approached as I gazed at the words writ large in front of me, standing tall as if passed down from Mount Olympus.

DEAR JENNIFER, *how lovely to see you working on my case. You don't know how good it makes me feel to see the nation's finest focusing so much time and effort on little old me.*

Chaos harbours anarchy passing through eternal rest. These hours require entropy's existence.

Ta-ta for now. See you on the other side.

'THE KILLER SPEAKS TO YOU.'

Chief Superintendent Cane's voice made me jump. I'd forgotten she sounded like broken glass dragged over an open wound.

'They're speeding up.'

I didn't remove my gaze from the screen, so she moved in front of me, her frame blocking everything in the room, so all I saw was her unsmiling face. When I was a kid, I remembered my father watching old videotapes he'd made of the Olympic Games from our tiny TV. Cassandra 'Prophet' Cane wouldn't have looked out-of-place in one of those grainy clips of an Eastern European woman chucking a javelin or hammer for the glory of the communist empire.

'And how do you know that, Detective Inspector Flowers?'

I stepped to the side, so I wasn't staring into her glassy eyes; everybody was watching us.

'The frequency of the murders, four in as many days, plus the personalisation and delivery of the letters. There's something our killer wants to tell us, but they can't come out and say it; that would be too easy, so they have to hide it in these messages.'

'Are you sure they're speaking to us, or is it just you, Inspector?'

I was unsure either way, but I wouldn't give her the satisfaction of saying it.

'The murders and the letters are two levels of communication. If we don't figure out what they mean, there'll be more bodies to deal with.'

'With dire consequences for some.'

It was a veiled threat of my career going in reverse. Since the conclusion of the Hashtag Killer case, my media-fuelled meteoritic rise into a near-celebrity had displeased a lot of my colleagues. I was aware several of them wanted me to fail.

I picked up a copy of the latest letter.

'Then I'd better make sure we solve this as soon as possible, ma'am.'

'Not so fast, Inspector.' When Cane didn't address you by your first name, she was displeased. 'I want an update on the Cathy Daniels incident ASAP.'

'Right away, ma'am.'

I turned and walked towards Jack, still aware of her presence behind me when I reached him. Jack pointed at my name at the top of the letter.

'At least someone likes you.'

I sucked air into my lungs.

'Has she gone?'

He removed the mug from his lips.

'The Prophet has left the room.'

'Do you think she's seen my future and is ready to dance on my grave?'

I glanced over at the boards filled with crime scene photos from the four victims and regretted my choice of words.

Jack dropped the plastic cup into the bin.

'We're all in this together, Jen. And we'll find the bastard doing this, don't you worry.'

I flopped into a chair, staring at the letter, wondering how right he'd be.

'Has anyone analysed the message yet?'

He attempted a grin. 'We waited for you.'

I picked up one of the paper copies.

'Perhaps we should try a forensic linguist to analyse the language, choice of vocabulary, sentence structure, level of spelling and grammar. Understanding these things might show certain character or personality traits of the writer, such as age, level of education, gender, social status, and others.' His stare told me he continued to be unconvinced. 'The text is shorter than the previous letters. There must be a reason for that.'

Jack nodded. 'Should we contact the university in Birmingham you mentioned?'

Desperate times called for drastic measures.

'Why not? With three letters, there's more text to analyse. Get Sutton or Grealish to call them and see what they say.'

'Okay.' He sat opposite and rubbed at his chin. 'I don't like how the murderer is homing in on you.'

'Perhaps they listened to the first of the Alice Voss podcasts last night.'

'The Vosscast? Did you listen to it?'

'Of course not, but I guarantee she mentioned my name more than once.'

'She did, but only at the end. They used it as a teaser for the second episode tonight.'

I switched my concentration from the letter to him. He wanted to talk about the podcast, but it was the last thing I was interested in. Perhaps he'd listened to it out of professional interest, out of concern for me; or was it because he needed to hear her voice again?

I returned to the latest letter and read the second paragraph aloud.

Chaos harbours anarchy passing through eternal rest. These hours require entropy's existence.

'It sounds like Greek philosophy,' Jack said.

'There's one thing we've learnt from this letter already.'

'What's that, Jen?'

'Our perpetrator views themselves as intelligent,

someone with style and culture. They'll perceive their victims as being below them; the police are something to be toyed with and not clever enough to decipher their grand plan. The more they kill, the more extravagant things will become, and that'll be their undoing because they'll get overconfident and sloppy.'

'And more people will die.'

His words stabbed at my heart.

'That's unless we solve this now.'

Jack looked at his copy of the letter.

'What do you make of it?'

I reread the paragraph.

Chaos harbours anarchy passing through eternal rest. These hours require entropy's existence.

'They've focused on time as if it's running out for them. It would explain why they're killing at such a rapid rate.'

'Maybe they're ill, or have something terminal.'

'Eternal rest and entropy's existence might suggest that. If it's true, then they'll want to kill even more while they can.'

I threw my copy onto the table. Jack picked it up.

'I'm more concerned about how this killer is making it more personal for you.'

I reached into my pocket and the space for my ghost cigarettes. How long before I'd fall off the nicotine wagon?

'How are they making it more personal for me?'

He ran his finger across the first paragraph of the letter.

'You've just said they're intelligent and playing games with us. Well I think they're playing games with you, and it's getting dangerous.'

He read the text out.

'Dear Jennifer, how lovely to see you working on my case. You don't know how good it makes me feel to see the

nation's finest focusing so much time and effort on little old me.'

I pushed my foot against the bottom of the table.

'So, they addressed it to me. We both realise that's only because I was in the media with our "famous" case. This isn't about me. I'm just an easy face and name for them to lay their obsessions on to.'

Jack shook his head, seemingly unconvinced by what I'd said.

'Twice in that paragraph, the killer mentions seeing you. That's as deliberate as anything they've written so far. What if they're watching you, possibly stalking you?'

I laughed at the absurdity of it. 'I'd know if someone followed me.'

'Would you? I'm unsure. And what if it's not only you they're spying on?'

Perhaps the stress was getting to him.

'You'll be all right, partner.'

'I'm not talking about me, Jen.'

I dismissed all of his concerns with a flick of my head.

'We won't get anywhere with this.' I turned to the computer screen. 'Is there anything from Forensics or Cybercrime?'

He glared at me for a good thirty seconds. I think he wanted to continue the previous conversation, but my scowl dissuaded him.

'There's been nothing worthwhile so far. We discovered plenty of fingerprints in the warehouse, but most were from our victims or too faint to be identifiable. They're still going through the blood and fibres they took, but I doubt our killer is so careless.'

I stared at the information on my computer screen.

'And Cybercrime couldn't trace the girls' contact on Instagram either.'

I closed the file and opened the folder containing the crime scene photographs, comparing them to those from the other murders: strangulation, dismemberment, and now two slit throats. Did the killer focus on the necks of the victims? Was Clive Hamilton's body chopped up to hide evidence?

A piece of software on the system found connections a human might not, and it allowed users to link information from different files. Shortened to CAP, the Collate and Analyse Program was new and shiny and bright, but not everyone loved it. It was an attitude I struggled to understand. Perhaps some wanted to return to writing on tiny cards and inserting them into an unwieldy and complicated system.

I created a new file and inserted images of the victims from the three crime scenes into it. While I set the software to examine the photographs, I opened a second piece of software: ViSOR, the Violent and Sex Offender Register. It's a database of records of those required to register with the police under the Sexual Offences Act 2003, those jailed for over twelve months for violent offences, and those thought to be at risk of offending. I searched for anyone on the database within five miles of each crime scene.

While the computer whirled through its gears, my thoughts returned to Abbey and her violent actions. I'd heard nothing from the officers investigating her case and was in no rush to seek them out: no news is good news was working for me at the moment. I hoped her sessions with Felicia Nelson would get to the heart of her troubles.

I was deciding there was no immediate solution to this when the computer finished its modern magic. ViSOR brought up a dozen names, some of which I recognised, and

I saved the search results as a separate file. I sent it to Constable Grealish with instructions to share the details with the team to find out where these people were during the murders.

Then I switched to CAP's analysis of the photos, but there wasn't much. The only interesting detail was the result of the wounds on Hamilton, Evans and Moore's heads. Jack leant over my shoulder and touched the screen.

'How did Clive Hamilton's autopsy miss that?'

There were three images of Hamilton's head, plus another four from the morgue showing each angle of the beheading. What Jack meant was the software analysis of the evidence of a cut across Clive Hamilton's throat underneath the blow which severed his head.

'Some things are tough to detect with the naked eye, Jack, even when it's right in front of you. I'm guessing Dr Cooper, or her staff, didn't see this wound below the one from the axe since they're virtually on top of each other; only the computer could pick that out.'

'And the killer.' Those lines which had increased under his eyes in the last few days vibrated in his skin. 'The bastard must have tortured Hamilton before killing him.'

I'd believed that from the start, the same with the Blair murder; but we'd found no signs of torture for Evans and Moore. Possibly the killer was disturbed before they could get that far.

'You're right, but I guess it's more to do with trying to cover up the original wound.'

Each of the young women had their throats slit from a different angle; Evans was from a right-handed person, Moore from a leftie. Some in the team speculated on two killers working together, but I didn't believe it. I assumed the killer used different hands for the murders so we wouldn't know which they favoured. With the analysis from CAP, and the discovery of the cut on Hamilton's throat, we had a good idea; before his beheading, a right-handed person cut his throat.

I saved the data, added my notes to it, and sent it attached as an urgent message to everyone in the team. Finally, after four murders, I had an impression of our killer: right-handed, cultured, well-read, a bit of a dilettante detective, and confident.

And when that confidence turned into arrogance, we'd get them.

28 CEREMONY

I was eating a sandwich when the Chief Super summoned me to her office. There were bits of cheese stuck between my teeth as I entered, my face warmed by the scowl I received from Detective Chief Inspector Merson standing in the corner. The Prophet ignored me, her head buried into the computer.

A whiff of gorgonzola escaped from my lips as I swallowed the last of my hasty lunch. I said nothing to either of them, having learnt a long time ago it was best to wait and let someone else provide you with information.

Chief Superintendent Cane leant away from the screen, pushed the glasses up her nose before they crashed onto her desk, and peered at me. The cheese dropped into my gut as she spoke.

'Lucy Smith's death is not a Penguin murder.'

My stomach rumbled, and I wondered how far out of date that cheese was.

'That's correct, Chief.'

'So why say it was?'

'I'm not sure I did.'

Merson slammed her fist into her leg, and I hoped it hurt.

'Yes you did, Flowers. You told the media scrum outside the house you'd caught her.'

'That's correct, Detective Chief Inspector Merson. I told them we'd caught the murderer of Lucy Smith. And we have.'

The Prophet glared at me.

'Stop playing semantics, Inspector. You implied to the media that Cathy Daniels is the serial killer known as The Penguin. Why did you do that?'

Why did I do that? Was it desperation or inspiration?

'I thought it was time we sent a message to the killer, Chief, instead of waiting on them.'

'And what was the message you wanted to send, Inspector?'

'To shout out how dumb we are?'

Merson appeared happy I was about to receive my long-overdue comeuppance. As stodgy bread and cheese partied inside my guts, I told my superior officers what I thought about our killer's personality based on the letters.

'Before they started this, our Penguin assumed they were smarter than the police. Now, with me claiming the Smith murder as one of their crimes, they've had confirmation of this assumption.'

Merson stopped grinding her teeth.

'And what will this achieve, Inspector Flowers, apart from motivating them to kill more people?'

At the top of my bowels, a tickling sensation told me I needed to finish this meeting sooner rather than later.

'They would always have killed again, Detective Chief Inspector, but now their feelings of superiority might make them more arrogant and hopefully prompt them into making mistakes leading to their capture.'

Merson snorted at me. 'Hopefully!'

The Prophet changed tack.

'I see you've had some success with the crime scene photos and discovered a hidden wound below the cut which decapitated Clive Hamilton. It looks like the killer is right-handed.'

'Yes, ma'am.'

She nodded at me. 'Is there any other progress?'

'The last murders, of Wilhelmina Moore and Mary Evans, differ from the previous two.'

Merson snorted again, a pig-like motion which unnerved me.

'We know all this, Inspector. They're different victim types and different methods.'

'That's true, Detective Chief Inspector, but there's something else.'

'And what's that, Jennifer?'

The Prophet using my proper name meant the threat of a reprimand for what I'd said to the media had passed; for now. Even though she knew I didn't like being called Jennifer.

'The only constant we've had for the methodology is the penguin tattoos, and only one of the young women had them. Wilhelmina Moore didn't have any penguins stamped on her palms.'

The Prophet leant back into her chair and clasped her hands together.

'Is it a different perpetrator?'

I shook my head. 'This killer enjoys inflicting as much pain as possible; then they leave the penguin as their calling card in this game of theirs. For these latest murders, I'm guessing they were interrupted in the warehouse, with no time to stamp both women.'

The Prophet nodded at me. 'Yes, Jennifer, you might be right. But you must consider something else.'

Relief swept through my guts, but I'd be visiting the little girls' room before I went back to my desk.

'And what's that, Chief?'

'I'm not sure if our Penguin is playing a game with us, or with you.'

I left the office with that final thought ringing in my head, the implication of it making me walk faster to the toilet than I'd intended.

TWENTY MINUTES LATER, I'd transcribed the letters' contents into a file and printed three copies; then I sought PC Grealish.

'It's time to down tools, Constable.'

She turned from her computer and peered at me through a fog of confusion.

'Ma'am?'

'We need a new environment to sharpen our brains.'

Jack grinned. 'Let me guess.' He slipped the paper into his jacket. 'We're going somewhere darker than this.'

He knew me too well.

It was a five-minute walk down to the river, past the Cenotaph, and then into the Red Lion pub. I needed to remove the taste of cheese from my mouth and erase the memory of that meeting with Cane and Merson. I handed Grealish a twenty-pound note.

'Get pints of cider for Jack and me, and whatever you want.'

She headed to the bar while Jack and I grabbed the last free table near the window. The afternoon trade was busy, milling around with tourists and maybe the odd local.

Jack slumped into a wonky chair. 'You know I've given up drinking during the day?'

'I thought you would've hit the sauce again after the split from Jean.'

His eyes narrowed at the mention of his estranged wife.

'It's only temporary, Jen. Once we solve this case, we'll be back together.' A waft of pie and peas drifted through the bar, and he grabbed a menu from the table. 'Since we're here, I might as well have something to eat.'

He removed his jacket and placed it on the chair. I noticed the stains near his shirt's pocket, dark red blobs that could have come from wine or tomato sauce. I switched my gaze to the bar, wondering why it was taking Grealish so long to get the drinks. Two smartly dressed men were supping on beer and talking to her as she collected the change from the barman. I returned my focus to Jack.

'You can't beat a traditional pub for a bit of inspiration.'

Grealish had wormed away from the attention of the blokes and returned, expertly carrying three pints in her hands as if born for it. Being the perfect gentleman, Jack rose and helped her. He handed me my cider, the aroma of fermented apples bubbling from the glass and into my nose. I took a sip as Grealish placed her pint of fruity hops onto the table.

I removed two copies of the combined letters from my jacket and gave one to Jack and the other to Grealish, who continued to attract glances and stares from men and women. She grabbed the paper from me and laughed nervously.

'I always thought coppers drinking while on duty was a

media myth created by lazy TV shows and bad crime fiction.' She gulped her beer.

I lifted my drink and gave her a nod of acceptance.

'If it's good enough for Chandler and Hammett, it's good enough for me.' Half a pint was gone when I put it back on the table. I pulled the letter from the glass and ignored the stain at the bottom. 'Let's crack our heads together and get something from these.'

Jack got up. 'Let me order some lunch first. Do you two want anything?'

It was not long after my cheese sandwich, and bits of it were still playing havoc with my guts, so I settled for a drink. Jack went for a traditional East End meat pie with posh mushy peas, whatever they were, and pie liquor. He took the staff's recommendation and added malt vinegar to get the real authentic London flavour. I assumed this to be smog mixed in with a sniff of the Thames. Grealish agonised over the calorie count before ordering flatbread and red pepper hummus, plus a mini roasted cauliflower and Lincolnshire Poacher pie.

I was about to send her back to the bar when Jack waved his copy of the letters at me.

'He, or she, has changed the style at the beginning of each letter.' He pointed to the first example. 'Dear Boss in this one, with no greeting in the second, and then calling you by your name in the third.'

Grealish drank more beer as she removed her jacket. Her top was as tight-fitting as the jeans and turned more heads her way. Jack did his best to ignore her as she spoke.

'It's as if they're trying to get to know you, to forge a connection somehow.'

I finished my cider.

'I'll connect with them when we catch them.' I thumped the glass onto the table. 'Go to the bar, Jack.'

He nodded and got up.

'No more for me, Inspector,' Grealish said.

Jack gave her his best smile and took our empties away. She looked at me, sheepishly.

'Don't worry, Constable, I won't be getting drunk. The first one always goes down fast and is essential in squeezing out the oil around my brain.'

'Is it working, ma'am?'

'I hope so. Have you reread the letters?'

'Too many times to mention, ma'am.'

Jack's voice rang through the room as he spoke to someone at the bar. I focused on the text.

'Do you recognise the patterns in the letters, Constable?'

She stopped looking at the portrait of Churchill on the wall.

'Death and time are repeated.'

'They are. Ever eternal with no more suffering, resurrection of the soul, eternal rest, and entropy's existence are examples in the text.'

'What does that mean?'

Jack returned with our drinks, an opened packet of chilli peanuts in his hands. He offered them to Grealish, who took a couple and smiled at him; the glint in his eye may have only been noticeable to me. He dropped the packet onto the table, brushing her fingers as he did so. Jean would never take him back, and I wondered if he realised this. I peered at him and saw Alice Voss's face.

'You'll ruin your appetite, partner.'

My stomach grumbled as I spoke. He ignored me and answered her question.

'Our killer may be running out of time, so rushing their plans.'

Grealish pondered this. 'They might be leaving the city?'

I pushed the packet of peanuts out of the way, the whiff of the chilli playing havoc with my nostrils.

'It could be they have little time left to complete whatever their depraved end goal is.' I looked at her. 'When we get back to the station, I want you to speak to Constable Sutton to see if she completed the check on Carrie Spector regarding any connection to Wilhelmina Moore or Mary Evans. I'll have a chat with Spector's doctor.'

Jack crunched on a peanut. 'They won't tell you anything about Spector's health.'

I reached into my mind and dug out the research I'd done.

'The General Medical Council says a doctor may justify a breach of confidentiality in the public interest where failure to do so might expose the patient or others to risk of death or serious harm. You need to balance the patient's interest against the public interest in reporting a crime. I should be able to motivate Spector's doctor to get the required result.'

Constable Grealish appeared to be enjoying her trip out.

'The perpetrator has this compulsion to kill. If they have a terminal illness, they're fulfilling this desire in the time they have left. Have I got that right?'

I wiped cider from my lips.

'It's as good a guess as we've come up with so far.' I stared at her. 'What about the use of language and vocabulary in these letters, Constable?'

She picked up her copy and brought it closer to her face as if proximity would unveil all its secrets.

'There are no spelling mistakes and text you'd only expect from someone with decent lexis: exquisite and entropy are not words you hear every day.' She rubbed at her chin. 'But then they sign off the third letter with "Ta-ta for now." That sounds like somebody from the 1930s or 40s.' Her eyes bore into mine. 'Could there be two people involved?'

'And one is right-handed and the other left-handed?'

Jack sighed loudly. 'I thought we'd used the photo analysis to agree the killer is right-handed?'

I drank the second pint a lot slower.

'We have. The point I'm trying to make is, as with the cuts to the throats of Hamilton, Evans, and Moore, the style and complexity of the text is deliberately varied to throw us off the trail.' I leant into my seat. 'Even though we have no trail.'

'You don't think there's a message in these letters, Jen?'

'Oh, there's something in them, but I can't help feeling we're missing the wood for the trees.'

As we continued to stare at the words on the paper, the food arrived.

I watched them eat and wondered what came first, the detective or the crime.

The next morning, I drove Abbey to see Felicia Nelson for the second session.

'We can decide on the Saturday job in the comic shop after you've seen Dr Nelson a few more times.'

She unpeeled her face from the window and glared at me.

'You only want to know what I've told Felicia, don't you?'

So it was Felicia already. I wanted to hear what my daughter spoke about, but it wasn't the real reason I was driving Abbey out of London again; the pub's conversation had given me an idea about the letters that involved the good doctor.

I parked the car outside her house, considering my reply.

'I only want to keep you out of a juvenile detention centre, Abbey.'

The words appeared to have a calming effect on her, the anger dissipating and replaced with trepidation.

'Do you think that might happen?'

We'd heard nothing yet, neither of us ready to rush towards those in authority. I assumed Abbey hoped the whole thing would go away; I know I was while understanding it wouldn't.

'Let's hope not, love.'

As we got out of the car, Nelson opened her front door, greeting me with wide-open eyes.

'How nice to see you two again.'

I smiled at her before turning to Abbey.

'Can you wait inside Abs while I have a word with Dr Nelson?'

She stomped past me, a grey cloud over her head threatening to crack thunder at any second.

'Is there a problem, Jen?'

I took her arm and led her from the door.

'No, of course not, Felicia. I think Abbey enjoyed her time with you.' I let go of her. 'I wondered if you might do something for me.'

Her surprise changed to curiosity. 'This sounds official.'

'It could be, at some point, but for now, I have to keep it between you and me if that's okay.'

'I'm intrigued.' Her eyes lit up like the stars.

We stood in the shadows like conspirators in a spy movie. I removed the paper from my pocket and handed it to her.

'These are copies of three letters a serial killer has sent to us over the last week. I'm trusting you with these, they need to be kept confidential, but I hoped you'd look at them and give me your professional opinion.'

'You want my professional opinion?'

'Your opinion on what these reveal regarding the killer's state of mind.'

She glanced at the text.

'Are you sure you haven't been watching too many American crime dramas, Jen?'

My heart sank with the sudden feeling I'd wasted my time, before I recalled why I was there and my daughter waiting inside. Here I was putting work before her again.

'I'm sorry, Felicia. I shouldn't have sprung this on you.'

I reached to retrieve the paper, but she pulled away and grinned.

'I'm only joking, Jen. Of course, I'll look at these.' She appeared excited. 'I've always wanted to be involved in a police investigation.' She checked her watch. 'Why don't you come back when I've finished with Abbey, say in two hours? She can eat here after the session, and I'll read these letters. How does that sound?'

It sounded great, but how would I occupy my time; there was no point driving to London and then returning.

'Thanks, Felicia. I'll do that.'

She moved inside while I returned to the car, phone in my hand as I checked what was nearby. The Harry Potter studio was fifteen minutes away; but I'd tried watching the first three movies to keep Abbey happy because she'd loved the books but fell asleep every time. I drove to St Albans instead.

Half an hour later, I'd parked the car and took the brief walk to the St Albans Museum and Gallery. Since I was there, I thought I'd get a bit of culture and history. Perhaps an influx of new and different information would make me think better.

It was an impressive building, spotlessly white and looking brand new with its restored Georgian pillars. The reception area and sweeping staircase caught the eye, but inside I struggled to find much which would attract children or teenagers. There was nothing interactive or eye-catching, no buttons to push, nothing to feel or smell, and little which resembled anything kids might see in a television show or movie. That was great with me since I was there to avoid noise and distractions.

I strode past a bored-looking member of staff holding out a donation tin. I dropped two pound coins inside it, hearing them rattle. I wondered how places like this competed with mobile phones, computer games, the internet, social media, and apps that let you do the stupidest things in the shortest amount of time.

The woman smiled as I considered how lucky I'd be if Abbey avoided a juvenile detention centre. She could focus on her new interest in art and start the job at the comic shop. Perhaps her violent attack would herald a fresh beginning for her; I tried not to think about the poor girl she'd attacked.

The rumble in my stomach took my mind from Abbey and reminded me I hadn't eaten. I followed the sign for the café down the stairs and into the basement. Disused Victorian prison cells lined the way to the courtroom housing the café. There was a book containing a list of cases in the St Albans Court from 1831 to 1967. I flicked through its pages, fascinated by what I read: 1835, Thomas Veal transported for larceny; 1838, Fredrick Cockle whipped and transported for larceny; 1841, Levi Green, a transported apprentice. What did that mean? What was he an apprentice of? Did he get to continue his apprenticeship when he arrived on the other side of the planet?

I went through the list of people likely whipped and beaten, then sent across the world; forced from their families, friends, neighbours and communities, and all because they did little more than a bit of petty thieving; stealing to stay alive. What Abbey did to Olivia Coates, causing facial damage which would remain with the poor girl for the rest of her life, was far worse than anything those 19th-century convicts did.

And what would happen to our penguin killer when we caught them? Maybe they'd become another celebrity like Alice Voss, now the darling of internet podcasts. As I'd driven Abbey to her counselling session, I'd wondered if she'd listened to the first episode the other night. Wouldn't I, if I'd been in her shoes? Surely she'd want to know what a convicted serial killer said about her mother. I had an image in my head of Abbey sitting in her bedroom wearing headphones, scrunched next to her laptop as Voss spouted lies about me. Nightingale had been quick to search me out and warn me about the podcasts; perhaps there was a legal reason she did so. If I listened to them, there may be something I could sue her for.

Only after leaving Abbey at Felicia's had I considered the podcast might mention Jack and his letters to Voss. We'd both be in trouble if his relationship with her became public knowledge. And what if Nightingale used his letters to get a mistrial? Perhaps I should find out what he wrote to her.

My hunger poked at me again, an echo through the ages to remind me how those less fortunate than me suffered; a reminder of how so many life stories remained unknown, of how many lives go unnoticed throughout history. And then people like Voss spread their lies all over the media, and her crimes would mean she'd be remembered for eternity. Too many things crammed inside my skull and my head hurt as much as my stomach did.

I scanned the menu and plumped for a Wiltshire ham, mature cheddar, and onion chutney sandwich, with a cup of peppermint tea. I passed my money over to a spotty youth who looked as if they should still be at school, got my order and took it to a table. I assumed somebody had created the seats from the benches of the courtroom; they were uncomfortable enough. I ruminated on my discomfort until I recalled the names of those transported to the colonies two hundred years ago.

I grabbed a bite from the sandwich, my teeth snatching tasty ham and delicious onion chutney, and returned to the four murders. My phone vibrated with an incoming text; it was from Detective Chief Inspector Sandra Merson.

The Home Secretary wants an update as soon as possible.

I didn't reply to her. Sandra Merson, a woman on the verge of retirement before she'd changed her mind. Who wouldn't want to retire at fifty-five, spending their days on extended holidays and uninterrupted wine tasting afternoons? I guessed she'd understood making other people's lives a misery was the only way she'd be happy; and if not happy, at least content. In a race between ambition and integrity, the ambition would always win with her. She'd never left the force, and already she was back like a rotten apple snatched from Snow White's fingers. And Sir Oswald Blair; how could I forget the Home Secretary? And what new information could I tell him?

Always start at the beginning, one of my instructors at the academy told me.

The first murder: Edwin Eric Blair, Eddy or Eddie to his friends; twenty-eight-year-old barman strangled while out on his regular morning jog. It never looked like a random attack, and subsequent events had proved that true.

Was he killed for the sizeable amount of cash missing from his bank account? Money given to him only a few days before his death by his estranged father; finances we still hadn't traced. We only had Oswald Blair's word he gave

Edwin the money because his son had asked for help, but what if it was for something else, possibly to keep Edwin Blair quiet? Perhaps somebody murdered him for the same reason.

Drug dealing was a theory, but we'd found no evidence of it. He was popular with the ladies, so what if it was a jealous girlfriend behind the attack, or a scorned husband or boyfriend? What was the link between Blair's murder and Clive Hamilton chopped to bits in his flat? The letters and the tattoos plus one person: Carrie Spector.

I deleted Merson's text and sent one to Constable Sutton.

Do we have anything from the surveillance on Carrie Spector? Is there a connection between her and Mary Evans and Wilhelmina Moore?

This should reveal if Spector had an alibi for the women's deaths, or if she had a motive to kill them.

I bit through the sandwich and sipped on the tea. A little kid scrambled past me with a chocolate biscuit unwrapped in his hand, bits of it smearing his lips. A young woman, his mother, I assumed, grabbed him and the wrapper floated to the floor. It appeared as if the Gods were playing a joke on me as I stared at the image of a McVitie's Penguin bar.

Early in the case, some wag on the Murder Investigation Team had suggested the killings might be chocolate related, but a glare from Jack sent the poor bloke scampering back to his computer screen.

What did those penguin tattoos on the victim's hands mean? Why didn't Wilhelmina Moore have one? Was the killer interrupted? Amongst all this information, what would I tell Oswald Blair about our progress or lack of it? I still wasn't sure.

The woman shouted at the kid for nicking the chocolate bar from the counter in the café. As she dragged him away, I wondered how long it'd be before he'd get sent to Australia if these were different times. He pushed his tongue out at me as I imagined Abbey stuck behind bars.

30 ICE AGE

I spent an hour in the café before heading into the town centre, which was so small I walked around it in forty-five minutes. I only stopped to investigate the charity shops, where I purchased two books: Andrew Loog Oldham's autobiography and *Choke* by Chuck Palahniuk. There were some evocative pictures of the Stones and Marianne Faithfull in the Oldham book, but I didn't feel like immersing myself in the 60s right then. My parents were children of the 60s, and my father always claimed he hated it; something which made me like the music and popular culture of the time even more. Instead, I read the first fifty pages of *Choke* while I waited outside Felicia Nelson's house.

It was a curious novel, equal parts genius and tedium, with a central character trying to come to terms with their dysfunctional childhood. As I read about a mother whose mental health problems led to her constantly kidnapping her son from foster homes, and including him in a range of dangerous and illogical schemes, it made me picture my parents. I'd always assumed most adults had decent relationships with their parents if they were still alive, or at least fond memories if they weren't, but I had neither of those things.

My mother entered a nursing home a decade ago. I hadn't visited her since, but I'd lost her a long time before that. She was a woman for whom emotion was a mythical creature, like elves and unicorns. Over the years, I'd made excuses for her lack of kindness and love, blaming it on the complications of my birth. I was born ill, underweight and puny, with a soft skull. It was difficult for her because of a tough pregnancy, and she never recovered from it.

According to my father, it affected him as badly as it did her. As I grew up, he never missed the opportunity to tell me how lucky I'd been he didn't drop me on my head that day in the hospital. He'd resisted the temptation, he told me not in jest, but he'd always wanted a son and heir, and I'd ruined it for him.

Because of my soft skull, I wore a specially made baby hard hat for the first year of my life. It would have been better for me if I'd worn it until I finally left my parents. It was a curious thing how she was a constant block of ice, while he was a fiery comet always crashing around me. They were opposites who'd attracted and then transformed into virtual mirror images of each other; two people not cut out for raising children but who ended up as parents.

The only time I witnessed a show of emotion from my mother was the day we came home from a trip to the shops and found her mother, my grandmother, with her head in the gas oven. The aroma was overpowering and made me sick as soon as I stepped into the kitchen, seeing her legs splayed across the floor as I bent my face to puke.

When I raised my head, my mother was standing there,

gazing at her mother; her cheeks wobbled and she wiped away a single tear from one eye. Then she left the room to phone my father, leaving me standing there fixed to the spot and gazing at the body in the oven. I was six years old, but even now, I still smell the gas and hear my mother's calm voice describing what she'd found.

My father was the opposite of her, bursting with emotions. Fire and brimstone and an obsession with ridding the world of sinners fuelled most of them. I never met my paternal grandparents, but I guess my father's outlook on life came from his upbringing.

But he was also a man of deep moral contradictions, quick to usher me into an abortion when he discovered his forty-year-old friend had impregnated his eighteen-year-old daughter. I pushed the thought of him back into the shadows of my mind as I received a text from Sutton.

We had a problem with the surveillance, ma'am. Spector gave the constable the slip when she left the house last night. She reappeared this morning when she put the cat out. She's still at home now. Should we speak to her about her movements?

Before I thought of a suitable reply, I got another message, this time from Felicia Nelson informing me Abbey's session had finished. I replied to Sutton.

No. Leave her as she is. Just make sure she doesn't give us the slip again.

She must have known we were watching her. Shaking the surveillance was deliberate. I put my phone away and stepped out of the car. Nelson's door was unlocked, so I entered in time to see my daughter striding into another part of the house. I didn't call out to her, content not to disturb her state of mind after finishing the session.

Felicia beckoned me into the room Abbey had just left.

'Did you keep yourself busy, Jen?'

I waved the paperback at her.

'I read about a man who pretends to choke himself to gain sympathy from others.' She peered at me through wide eyes. 'I assume it's all to do with a troubled childhood and a mother living on the edge of sanity.' Her look made me wonder if she thought I was speaking about my life, so I changed the subject. 'Is Abbey okay?'

Dr Nelson's smile gave nothing away.

'She's fine. I have some creative writing books which she's looking at since she told me she wants to be a writer or an artist.'

'Or both.'

She guided me to a seat in front of her desk.

'It's always better to aim high.'

'Like Icarus.'

Felicia laughed. 'Well, no, not to crash and burn. And anyway, the moral of the Icarus story isn't about aiming too high, but to listen to wise advice.' Her gaze cut deep into me. 'I'm sure having you in her life is a great comfort and benefit to her.'

'Is that what she told you?'

She ignored my ploy to wangle information from her and took the seat behind the desk. Felicia removed the paper from her pocket.

'These are fascinating letters.'

My spirits rose. 'Did you get something useful from them?'

Her eyes sparkled, her fingers pressed against her lips as if stopping herself from laughing.

'I don't want to disappoint you, Jen, but psychological profiling is worse than useless.'

My back arched into the chair as I removed the invisible dagger she'd thrust through my hopes.

'I'm surprised to hear you say that, Felicia. Police forces worldwide ask behavioural scientists to draw up profiles of killers still at large, based on knowledge of the victim and details recorded at the crime scene. Or from using clues like the letters I gave you.'

She sighed and tried to muster up a smile.

'I know that's the common perception, Jen, especially one advocated through the media and fiction. But there's been several recent studies by forensic psychologists which discovered offender profiles to be so vague as to be meaningless. At best, they have little impact on murder investigations; at worst, they risk misleading investigators and wasting police time.

'In the UK, the Home Office holds a register of psychologists, and other professionals qualified to give offender profiles to police forces. Yet behavioural profiling has never led to the direct apprehension of a serial killer, a murderer, or a spree killer, so it seems to have no real-world value. Modern forensic investigators are more interested in discovering the everyday aspects of a potential murderer's life. Where they live, who they know, where they work, what access they have to transport links, rather than trying to understand the dark recesses of their mind.'

'So why bother looking at the letters when I gave them to you?'

I did my best to stay calm, but the blood boiled beneath my skin.

'I'm sorry, Jen, but I wasn't misleading you. I'm fascinated by the criminal mind, and the opportunity to take a sneak peek inside it was too good to miss.'

'I'm glad to be of service.'

My words were heavy with sarcasm. She moved closer, her hand on my arm before I protested.

'I should have mentioned this earlier, but it's easier to show you instead.'

Nelson kept hold of me and led me towards the over-flowing bookcase at the back of the room. Sliding wooden doors covered the top two rows. She reached up and, one at a time, pulled them open: there must have been sixty plus volumes on those shelves, and a cursory glance at the titles told me they were all about serial killers.

'Is this a secret hobby, Felicia? Should I be worried about you?'

A nervous giggle slipped from her lips.

'I've always had an interest in the psychology of violence. I keep the books covered so as not to disturb my patients.' She held her right hand up to them. 'I've read all these and many others, but I'm not sure I could "profile" a killer still at large.'

My annoyance lessened somewhat.

'So why bother with them?'

'I find them fascinating.' She reached up for a book and removed it from the shelf: a hefty tome about Fred and Rose West. 'You can discover more from the lies they tell than the supposed truth. Did you know Fred West claimed to be a roadie with Lulu in the 1960s?'

'What does that tell you?'

If he'd claimed to be a roadie for Cilla Black, I might have believed that.

'It's the perception he had of himself, of someone close to fame, someone providing a valuable service to somebody important, which provides a little insight into how his mind worked. Whether that perception was a contributing factor to the horrific crimes he and his wife committed is another matter. I think your killer, the one the media have nicknamed The Penguin, at least from reading these letters, has a unique perception of themselves.'

'Doesn't everybody?'

'At some point, we all believe that to be true, but most of us don't act on that belief. Famous people - celebrities, politicians, sports stars and athletes - undoubtedly a belief of uniqueness drives some of them. Still, serial killers appear to combine this with a sociopathology, leading to their crimes.'

Maybe she would provide some use.

'What's your opinion of the letters?'

She handed them back to me.

'To me, they read like unrequited love letters.'

Something in my heart popped.

'Unrequited love letters to me?'

Felicia shrugged. 'I don't know about that, Jen. The killer only addresses you in the third one, when they must have realised, from the media, you're leading the investigation.'

'It's unrequited love for someone else, then?'

'It could be. But it might also be the manifestation of the frustration of not getting something they've wanted all their life.'

I considered her words as Abbey bounded through the door.

'I need to go to the comic shop, Mum. There's a games session in an hour.'

Before I replied, she ran from the building and towards the car. I returned my attention to the doctor, wondering again why there were no certificates or diplomas anywhere.

'Thanks for your help, Felicia. I'll be in touch about Abbey's next session.'

'I'll watch your progress in the media with interest, Jen.'

Abbey's eyes were bulging with anticipation as I left the psychologist's house, unsure if I was any further forward at all in either of my pursuits.

31 STILL

Abbey thrust her face into her phone as I drove to the comic shop, her fingers flicking across the screen as I focused on the road. The car bounced over a pothole and I jumped an inch into the air; she was unmoving like a victim of Medusa.

'How's it going with Dr Nelson, love?'

She stopped attacking her mobile.

'Do you want to hear what we talk about, Mum?' Abbey turned her head to stare at me, her eyes, rimmed in black pencil darkening in my direction. 'Are you worried we're talking about you?'

A motorcycle overtook me on the wrong side, forcing me to swerve to avoid hitting a cyclist.

'I just hope you're making progress, Abs.'

And of course, I was concerned about what she'd told Nelson; not specifically regarding her thoughts of me, but if there were things in her life, in her head, which made her unhappy. She returned to her phone and laughed at me.

'It's only been two sessions, Mum.'

I caught up with the motorcyclist at the traffic lights,

resisting the urge to wind down the window and chastise them.

'As long as you feel you're getting some benefit.'

Abbey put the mobile down and some tension seeped from the car. She peered out the window into a street littered with boarded-up shop windows and rough sleepers. Some of them appeared to be younger than Abbey, and my shoulders slumped as if stuck under lead weights.

'We talked about me doing something creative with my spare time.'

The enthusiasm in her voice lifted some pressure from my body.

'That's a great idea.'

She turned to me as I drove.

'Felicia thinks it would be good for me to be in an artistic environment whenever I can.'

I guessed where she was steering this conversation.

'You mean like working in a comic shop?'

Abbey twisted her body around and gazed at me, her eyes wide with anticipation.

'It makes sense, don't you think, Mum?' Nothing but sweetness and light flowed from her now. 'I'll be near art and writing, and there'll be loads of other people with similar interests. Steve said they sometimes have real artists and writers in the shop so I'll meet them and get advice and encouragement and all kinds of benefits.'

She spoke as if running out of words, but she was right. I wasn't sure why I was reluctant to let her take this part-time job. I'd worked at her age, so why shouldn't she? I was hesitating to decide in case I made the wrong decision.

In her excitement, Abbey jumped out of the car as soon as I parked. One perk of being a copper was the ability to park wherever I wanted, as long as I remembered to put the badge in the windscreen. The afternoon sun warmed my face as I followed her across the road, watching as she bumped into some other kids outside the shop and they clambered inside.

As Abbey disappeared out the back, I searched for Steve, finding him stacking books near the window. Even from a distance, he appeared tired, with shadows under his eyes which weren't there before. He glanced up as I approached, his grin appearing to lessen some of his weariness.

'It's lovely to see you, Jen.' He stepped over, seemingly unsure how to greet me, so I gave him a quick hug before we pulled away. 'Is Abbey with you?'

He smelt of expensive cologne, which seemed out of place for him and the shop. Had he made an effort for my benefit?

I nodded towards the back.

'She's down there with her friends.' I continued to smile at him. 'I want to talk to you about her working here, but I need more details.'

'Of course. What do you want to know?'

'What's the position and duties, how many hours and what's the wage?'

I didn't try to sound like an overbearing mother, but I'm sure I did. He switched to professional mode.

'It's a Saturday job, working nine till five with thirty minutes for lunch. Duties include serving, replenishing stock and dealing with customers. Hourly wage is the national rate for someone her age.' He leant into me. 'I'd like to give her more, but it wouldn't be fair to the rest of the staff.' His grin was warm and welcoming. 'I'll throw in some free books every month.'

The aroma of his aftershave crawled through my senses,

and my heart thumped against my ribs. It sent a vibration through my stomach and down my legs. I was unsure if it was a good feeling or not.

As he spoke, people entered the shop, attracting his attention as they moved. Acknowledging each one by name, he continued to unpack stock from the boxes at his side. I scrutinised the place for the umpteenth time, taking in the comics, books, toys, posters, memorabilia, trinkets, statues, and clothing, wondering how satisfactory it must be running a business which was also a hobby.

'Will working here help Abbey's creative instinct?'

He slit the top of a box open with a knife.

'Absolutely. We're always having visits from artists and writers who pass on tips and advice.' He glanced at the customers browsing through his stock. 'And she'll get to talk to like-minded people when she's here. It's a great environment for nurturing the imagination.' He placed the blade in his pocket, a glazed look in his eyes. 'I had all the creativity knocked out of me at Abbey's age, stuck in a school system which favoured maths and science over the imagination, and in a family who thought reading a waste of time.'

His voice dropped a level, his gaze drifting beyond my shoulder. I was surprised at how easy it was to talk to him, considering I'd known him less than a week.

'It wasn't too dissimilar for me, Steve, which is why I want to give Abbey as many opportunities as possible.' If only I could keep her out of custody. 'Working here would help her.'

He beamed at me. 'That's great, Jen. I'll sort a contract out for you to look at, and if you're both happy, she can start next Saturday.'

I thanked him, but there was something else on my mind.

'Steve, about the other night...'

He held up his hand, his head sagging to one side.

'It's okay, Jen. I had a brilliant time, but I'll understand if you don't want to do it again.'

I shook my head. 'Don't be silly. We should do it again, soon.'

I wanted to do it very soon. His eyes widened in surprise, his grin like a kid who'd found a mountain of free sweets.

'Well, that's... that's fantastic.'

'When work settles down, we'll arrange a date.' I glanced down at Abbey, who appeared to be having a grand time with her new friends. 'You're open late tonight until eight?' He nodded. 'Great. Will you tell Abbey I'll see her at home later?'

'It'll be my pleasure, Jen.'

I left the shop before the beam on his face blinded me. The drive back to work was a pleasant one, my mind in a settled place for once regarding Abbey's immediate future and my burgeoning romance with Steve Morris. And the job in the comic shop, along with Abbey's sessions with Felicia Nelson, would look good if things progressed with her assault on Olivia Coates.

Now I had to find The Penguin.

A HIVE of activity greeted me when I got to the Murder Rooms, busy for a Saturday, but there'd be no regular weekends for most of us until we caught this killer. Jack gazed at his computer. I strode up to him, shocked by what he was peering at. The display was full of reviews and comments about the second episode of Alice Voss's podcast. My reflection in the glass must have startled him. He reached over to turn the screen off, but not before I'd read some posts. To say they were less than flattering towards me was an understatement.

'Have you listened to it?'

He hesitated as he turned to me.

'It's not what you're thinking, Jen.'

'I don't know what you mean, Jack.' I narrowed my eyes. 'Unless you think I'm still worried about your fascination with Voss.'

He stood, scanning the whole of the room before returning to me, his voice a near whisper.

'It's not about her. I'm concerned with what she might say about you.'

'And maybe you're nervous she'll mention the letters the two of you shared.'

'That's not it.'

'I read the comments before you switched that off; they weren't complimentary.'

His hand touched my arm as he spoke.

'They're just a few idiots. You get them all over the internet. It's nothing to worry about.'

I slipped from him.

'I'm not worried, but since you've listened to both episodes, I'm curious about what Voss said. I'm guessing she didn't confess to what she's done, that she didn't tell the world how she manipulated people into committing her crimes.'

Jack shook his head. 'The first episode focused on her life in Australia and the trauma of her twin sister's unsolved disappearance. The second focused on her time in the UK and working for the police.'

Now I was more interested than irritated.

'No mention of the Hashtag crimes?'

'She's saving that for the last podcast. Alice is claiming to reveal the real truth of what happened.'

His use of her first name didn't go unnoticed.

'You mean compared to the unreal truth?'

'It's some new revelation she's promising.'

'And when will this podcast appear?'

'It should have been tonight, but they've delayed it until tomorrow.'

'I can't wait.'

I left him to check on the rest of the team. Sutton and Grealish stood on the far side, deep in conversation. Before I reached them, a tap on the window distracted me; a sound heralding nothing good. Turning my head towards it only confirmed that. The Prophet stood outside the door, next to Sir Oswald Blair. They didn't need to do anything for me to realise they were requesting my presence elsewhere.

Lead socks covered my feet as I trudged forward, opening the door and dredging a smile from somewhere. I didn't speak, waiting for the Chief to confirm how much trouble I was in. She moved away, and I followed behind like a lapdog. Only as we stepped inside her office did Cane speak.

'Do you have an update for the Home Secretary, Jennifer?'

I sucked in stale air and stuck out my shoulders. Then I rattled off what we'd discovered so far, their expressions unmoving as I added up the little we had. As I spoke, the only thing I thought about was those comments on Jack's screen from the Voss podcast.

The Prophet and Oswald Blair sat down. Blair gazed at me while I spouted on.

'You suspect Carrie Spector has something to do with this?'

I was glad to have such a simple question to answer.

'She's connected to your son and the second victim.'

Cane joined in. 'And those two women killed in the abandoned building?'

'We have nothing yet to link her to those, Chief. She slipped from our surveillance during the time of the murders. Her alibi needs checking for those.'

Blair shifted in his chair.

'Why would she kill them if her motivation is revenge on me?'

I told the truth. 'I don't know.'

'What progress is there with the letters?' Cane said.

I mentioned my conversation with Felicia Nelson.

'So, this letter writer, this killer, is doing this because they have an inferiority complex?'

Blair sounded doubtful.

'There could be many reasons, Home Secretary. The letters may be only to distract us from something else. Whatever this is, the murders and the one-sided communication, I'm convinced of one thing.'

Blair gazed at me. 'And what is that, Inspector?'

'This is a game for our killer.'

And I hated games.

Robby Riot nursed his warm drink while avoiding his reflection in the mirror behind the bar. After six pints, he hadn't decided on the more stupid thing a man of his age might have: a Sid Vicious hairstyle or a fake punk name.

Everyone had left the pub after the gig, some joining the rest of his band at a club. His band. Those words lingered in his mind as the tang of tepid lager curled his lips.

How many bands had he been in since his first at sixteen? It must be at least twenty, one for every year of his failed musical career. But this group would be the one to make him famous; they had great songs and three attractive women half his age at the front of the stage, while he drove the rhythm with the drums. With all his music business experience, he'd believed it was a combination guaranteed to provide success.

Still, after twelve months of playing the back rooms of dive bars and pubs, they'd got no further forward than entertaining audiences of fifty people. Now he found himself on a Saturday night sitting alone at the bar, wondering where all his ambitions had gone. Frustration squeezed his brain; so much he didn't notice the shadow slip into the seat next to him.

'That was a great gig tonight.' The voice sounded as if it had crawled through a lifetime of crushed cigarettes and barbed wire. 'I'm glad I got to see you before you became famous.'

Robby gazed at the stranger in the mirror, seeing nothing but dark glasses and an enormous hat covering long curly black hair. For one second he nearly choked on his pint as he thought it was legendary Queen guitarist Brian May until he realised they weren't old enough to be him; plus he was unsure if this person was male or female and he didn't want to make a fool of himself by getting their gender wrong. He played it safe and stuck to the music.

'Did you see all of the set?'

'I sure did.' They pushed a business card through the dregs on the bar towards Robby. 'I've been to all your gigs, and you're getting better and better each time. You just need a lucky break to go along with all the internet downloads of your songs.'

Robby swallowed his laughter.

'The last time I checked, we'd had over a hundred thousand plays on YouTube and about the same streams on Spotify.' He slapped his hand onto the bar hard enough for the empty bottles to rattle. 'Do you know how much we've earned from that as a four-piece?'

'Not enough to buy a decent meal, I'd guess. Streaming is a total scam, but there's a huge amount of money in it. Huge. Just none of it goes anywhere near the artist. You need to use it and the internet as a profile generator. The whole concept of buying music seems alien to this generation.'

Robby picked up his card.

Dee Clark. Music Journalist.

The booze tickled his throat as he laughed.

'You must earn less money than me, Dee.'

'The traditional music papers may have died out, but there are plenty of online sites crying out for content.'

Robby returned the card.

'Is that why you're here, to make your fortune from watching us?' The sour taste in his mouth lingered along with the booze. 'You must be drunker than me.'

'You're an old hand at this lark, Robby; you understand how things can change with a spot of luck. What was the name of that group you quit, and then they had a massive hit across Europe with their replacement drummer? I think you were just plain Bob Galbraith then.'

Robby reached for his sweaty drumsticks, resisting the urge to stick one into the so-called music journalist's eye. He didn't need reminding how successful one of his former bands had become after he left them; they supped champagne in penthouse apartments while he got stuck drinking cheap beer in rundown clubs.

'So, what are you here for? An interview with me, or were you hoping to hit on the girls from the group?'

The journalist laughed out loud.

'You should get some humble pie to go with your pint of bitter.'

Robby growled through gritted teeth.

'Or I could smash this glass over your head.'

Dee Clark scratched at their chin.

'Don't be like that, Robby; this is your chance to spill the beans on twenty years in the music biz. Admittedly, it's been at the shit end of the industry, but that will make it easy to sell to the blogosphere and social media nuts. I can see the headline now: Robby Riot's Rock-and-roll Nightmare!'

Robby slumped out of the bar stool.

'Fuck off, twat.'

'Now, now, Robby; this could be your final opportunity for cracking the big time. Surely it's better to be famous and ridiculed instead of unknown, but with your reputation intact? This is your legacy I'm talking about.'

He resisted another urge to slap the bastard and lurched from the empty bar and towards the toilets. Drinking six pints of warm piss hadn't done his shrinking bladder any good. Christ, if he was like this before he got to forty, the years after fifty promised to be a disaster.

Robby pushed open the door into the corridor. He faltered into the bathroom and peered into the cracked mirror; the damage didn't improve his reflection: there were more lines on his face than at a train station, with blood-red eyes, and skin stolen from an arthritic tortoise. The glass was sticky as he ran his fingers across it, trying to wipe away the years from his flesh and failing.

What was he doing with this group of young women? They could be successful without him, would have more opportunities minus some old duffer sitting at the back of the stage and scaring potential fans off. Maybe the music journalist was correct and this was his chance to tell his story for posterity.

'No, that's a shit idea; just like Robby Riot's a shit name.'

He admitted the stupidity of it to himself as a syringe pierced his neck.

33 LEADERS OF MEN

The Dog and Duck was one of those English pubs with a lengthy history and even older décor. Stuffed severed heads of bleary-eyed animals covered the walls, while the carpet stuck like glue to the feet. The stink of booze and stale sweat couldn't deflect the familiar aroma of death. A squelch of tortured guitars boomed from the jukebox before a uniformed officer turned it off and put us all out of our misery.

Jack stood at the bar, speaking to three women who appeared too young to be there. Sutton and Grealish interviewed other witnesses. I waited for my partner to realise I was there and scanned the rest of the room, taking in the ambience of dilapidated tables and chairs, broken glass, empty beer bottles and posters peeling off the walls.

Jack slipped away from the girls as they consoled each other amongst a deluge of tears which shed the glossy makeup from their faces. I guessed they were more than just casual customers of this dump.

'They're part of the band who played here tonight, the Starlight Razors. It was their drummer our killer attacked.'

He led me from the main room and towards the toilets. When we got there, the bouquet of piss and blood was overpowering. Athena Temple and Samantha Cooper stood deep in conversation as we approached, forensics and pathology coming together to tell me how the drummer had died.

I pointed at the half-open toilet door. 'Is he in there?'

Jack nodded. 'Robby Riot, thirty-six-year-old eternal punk rocker.'

'He's not so eternal now.' I pushed past Jack and into the gents' toilet. Temple and Cooper followed me. I delayed looking at the body. 'Did you fancy a trip out, Sam?'

Cooper had a unique ability to use her eyes to shrug.

'I was at Athena's when she got the call, so I thought I'd tag along since I'll be running my fingers through the victim at some point.'

She meant cutting open and scooping out the poor bloke's insides and popping them into dishes, before slicing off the top of his head and dropping his brain into a bowl.

Athena handed me a pair of disposable protective gloves. My knees cried as I bent to get a closer view of the victim's face pushed into the floor's dirty tiles, toilet paper sticking to the bottom of his boots. I checked his hands to see if the penguins were there, seeing the stamped birds peering at me.

I turned to Jack.

'Help me turn him over.'

Jack bent down and got his hands under Robby Riot's legs as I pondered the impossibility of that being his actual name. I placed my fingers on his shoulders and we moved him together, putting his back onto the transparent plastic sheet forensic officers had laid next to the victim.

For a man in his mid-thirties, Robby Riot was dressed

like a teenager in tight jeans, an ill-fitting shirt punctured by safety pins and holes, and a faded leather jacket. Temple and Cooper continued their conversation as I spoke to Jack.

'What did his band tell you?'

We stood together, letting the pathologist and forensic scientist inspect the body.

'They played a gig here. Then the girls popped to the nightclub across the road and left Riot on his own. He wasn't in a pleasant mood, and they didn't want to hang around him when he was like that. They said all he'd do was keep drinking and get worse. They only returned when they heard what happened. All of them are distraught.'

'I bet they are.' The memory of them in the bar triggered an idea. 'Which nightclub did they go to?'

Jack pursed his lips. 'The Blitz.'

'That's where Edwin Blair worked.'

'That's some coincidence, right?'

'Why don't you see if the girls knew Edwin Blair?'

I assumed it was a longshot. Jack trundled off while I turned to the Glimmer Twins. Temple spoke before I asked the question.

'There's no apparent cause of death, no visible marks, apart from his existing tattoos, one of a fetching naked lady on his arm and an unattractive bleeding skull on his chest, and those penguin stamps. There's a slight puncture mark on his neck which is fresh and doesn't match the other needle marks on his body, which are way older.'

'I'll know more when we get to the mortuary,' Cooper said.

I left them to their discussions and searched for Sutton or Grealish, finding them leaning on the bar making notes. They snapped up straight as I approached them.

'Do you have the victim's address?' I said.

'Yes, ma'am,' Sutton replied. 'I've also got a message for you from the station.'

'Go on then, Constable.'

'The surveillance we have on Carrie Spector has followed her to a restaurant in Islington, ma'am.'

'And this is relevant, why?'

'It's one of Tommy Cromwell's places, ma'am. She's having a meal with him now.'

It took me a split second to recognise the name: the Cromwell crime syndicate ran one of the largest organised gangs in London and controlled most of the East End crime.

'Where are the officers?'

'At the rear and the front of the restaurant. Spector hasn't left the building.'

'She's taunting us.'

Or maybe taunting me; just like our killer.

Sutton cleared her throat.

'And there's one other thing, ma'am.'

Her tone told me it wasn't good news.

'Go on.'

'Spector slipped the surveillance again tonight, between seven and eleven before she returned home.'

A long growl rumbled around inside my stomach; someone would be on traffic duty for a while because of this.

'How long has she been at Cromwell's restaurant?'

Grealish joined in. 'Twenty minutes, ma'am.'

'So she could have been here tonight.' Sutton and Grealish nodded in unison. 'Is there any CCTV footage from inside or outside the pub?'

The gloom consuming Sutton's face told me the answer before she spoke.

'I'm afraid not, ma'am.'

'Does Robby Riot have any family?'

Sutton shook her head. 'None we could find, ma'am. He was an only child, and both parents died in a car crash five years ago.'

The unluckiest of men. So, why did our killer select him?

Jack strode towards me.

'They'd never been to the Blitz before tonight, and none of them knew Edwin Blair.' My expression must have concerned him. 'Have we got other problems?' I told him about Spector. He scratched at his cheek. 'Now we need two alibis from her.'

'We should get them now, partner.' I turned to the constables. 'You two get everything you need from here and remind Dr Cooper to send us the autopsy report as soon as possible.'

'Whose turn is it to drive?' Jack said as we got outside.

The whiff of pizza and kebab drifted down the street and made my guts unhappy.

'Did you come in your car?'

He turned his collar up to the night air.

'Nope.'

'It's a simple choice, then.'

He slid in and strapped on the seatbelt.

'What shall we talk about?'

'How much do you know about Tommy Cromwell and his empire?'

'His father, Billy, started the syndicate with his brother Pete in the early 2000s. Once they saw off their rivals, they got involved in drug trafficking, money laundering, extortion and the hijacking of gold bullion shipments and security fraud. They have links to over two dozen gangland murders of informants and rival criminals. From the start, there have been rumours of their connections to Metropolitan Police officials, plus supposed links with several sitting Members of Parliament.'

I stopped at the traffic lights and considered his words.

'Connections to the Met and MPs might link him to the Home Secretary, but there was something else in your info which is more interesting.'

'What's that, Jen?'

'You mentioned money laundering.' The lights changed and I pulled away. 'And now he's having a cosy bite to eat with a woman convicted for embezzlement from her family firm.'

'You think that's why she did it, to pass the currency on to him?'

'That's what my gut tells me.'

That and I needed something to eat. At least we were heading to a restaurant.

'But why him?'

'We're about to discover that.'

Ten minutes later, we arrived at the restaurant. Jack walked in first, searching for Spector while I hunted for an empty table. A large man wearing an expensive Armani suit and smelling of Hugo Boss aftershave approached us. His clothes must have been custom-designed to fit into his impressive physique. Both Jack and I are over six feet tall, but this bloke towered over us. I assumed he was one of Cromwell's goons until he introduced himself.

'Good evening, Inspectors. I'm Thomas Cromwell.' He held out his hand between both of us. 'I expected you sooner.' My stomach rumbled as he spoke. He focused on me. 'Anything you want is on the house, Inspector Flowers.'

'Someone could perceive that as attempting to bribe a police officer, Mr Cromwell.'

He burst out laughing, his hoot as loud as a roaring train.

'Okay, tell me what you want, and I'll charge you double instead.'

'Is Carrie Spector here?'

'She is.' His laughter died as his eyes narrowed. 'This was the only way we could stop you from harassing her.'

Before I replied, he turned his back and strode across the restaurant. The other diners kept their heads down and concentrated on their meals. We followed him to the table where Spector sat sipping a glass of wine. He sat next to her and indicated for us to join them in the seats opposite.

Jack leant on a chair.

'Were you expecting us?'

Cromwell picked up his fork and poked at the raw steak on his plate. Blood slithered from it, and I pictured Robby Riot's body prone on the floor of the pub toilet.

'Those grunts you've got spying on Carrie would never come in here, would they? So we waited for the organ grinder.' He peered at Jack. 'And not the monkey.'

Spector put down her drink and stared at me.

'How nice to see you again, Inspector Flowers.'

'Where were you tonight, Ms Spector, before you came here?'

'And where were you last night?' Jack said.

Cromwell thrust the fork so hard into the steak, I thought he'd snap the table in half.

'You coppers are all the same, always trying to fit someone up when you can't do your job properly.'

Carrie Spector ran a finger around the top of the glass, its squeak irritating my ears. She smiled at me, a curious expression resembling a cat about to pounce on a bird.

'I was with my daughter both times.'

Jack and I exchanged a glance. There'd been nothing about a daughter in Spector's file.

Cromwell stood with the fork in his hand.

'She was with our child.' He turned to face one of his goons and nodded. Ten seconds later and a tall, willowy girl, no older than thirteen, stepped out of the shadows and walked towards us. 'Say hello to the police officers, Holly.'

Holly Cromwell inched forward, the light shining off the braces covering her teeth. She seemed as nervous as a mouse at a cat's convention. For one awkward second, I thought she might curtsey.

'Hello, Inspectors. How nice it is to meet you.'

Jack was about to say something, but I stopped it with my hand on his arm. I smiled at Holly Cromwell, but focused on her mother.

'We'll be in touch.'

Jack followed as I strode away. As we reached the exit, Tommy Cromwell's booming hyena laugh battered the back of my neck. We were in the car before I tried to scratch the itch on my skin.

Jack slapped at the dashboard.

'How come we didn't know she had a kid?'

I could have smoked a thousand cigarettes at that moment, before wondering how my daughter was getting on. I'd forgotten to text her to see if she'd got home from the comic shop. Not that I didn't trust her using the Tube on her own, more that I wasn't sure if she'd have another violent episode with the wrong provocation. I messaged her before replying to Jack.

The Cromwell restaurant lights glittered in the periphery of my vision. The illuminations played tricks on my brain as if they were signalling some secret message to me about this investigation; as if there was something I'd already seen, but I'd missed its significance.

'We need to find out at the station.'

I started the engine as Abbey replied to me.

It was fantastic at the shop. Steve dropped me off at home. I hope you're OK.

It had been a while since she'd shown any concern for me, so that was progress. I wasn't sure how comfortable I was with Steve taking Abbey home on her own until I told myself I was worrying for nothing. And anyway, didn't I want to invite Steve back with me sooner rather than later?

'So, Jen, what did you think of Tommy Cromwell?'

'He's the narcissist's narcissist, someone who can't imagine a world without him at its centre. That was all fake anger he displayed there. He enjoyed every minute.'

'Do we bring the kid in to check the mother's alibi?'

I snorted derision. 'I can see that going down well in the media No, we must hope we can find something which connects Robby Riot to the other killings. Or...'

'Or what?'

My legs felt like lead as I bundled the car down the road on the way to dropping him off at his cheap hotel.

'Or we wait until we get the next letter.'

34 THE ETERNAL

Choose harmony and percussion to erase reason from our unwaking realm.

The letter taunted me at the station on Monday. Sunday had been a relaxing day, surprising to the extent Abbey had spent most of it writing in a notebook Steven Morris had given her. In the manic periods at home when I fixated on the investigation, I'd glance over at her and wonder if she was turning her violent action into a piece of writing. And now I had more text from our killer to consider.

The sender had stamped my name and the small penguin symbol onto the front of the envelope. Jack and I read the text together. Lack of sleep had driven us both to the station before anyone else. The stubble on his chin was transforming to grey as the bags under his eyes grew larger and darker.

He handed me a coffee.

'At least they're getting shorter.'

I let the drink burn my lips.

'Perhaps our killer is running out of time, or patience.'

'The postmark is from Islington.'

Heat spread through my fingers from the plastic. Strange how, as a society, we have become obsessed with eradicating plastic straws, but plastic cups and glasses have appeared everywhere.

'That's some coincidence considering where we visited Saturday night. Is there a time on it?'

He nodded. 'Twelve-thirty Saturday afternoon. Way before Robby Riot's murder and before Carrie Spector arrived at the restaurant.'

'One of Cromwell's people could have posted it.'

'You think he's behind all this, him and the mother of his child?' Jack didn't sound convinced. 'Why would they do it?'

It was a good question.

'To get back at Oswald Blair for prosecuting Spector all those years ago and cutting off the lucrative cash flow she stole from her family. Gangsters like Tommy Cromwell pretend they live by a different code of honour than the rest of us; this might be a twisted part of his code.'

'I could see it for Blair's son, but what about the other murders; and why the penguins?'

'Perhaps there's a connection between them and Oswald Blair we haven't found yet, or the other victims were people Cromwell wanted out of the way. The deaths could all be a smokescreen to hide gangland murders.'

Including those two young women? Something about those deaths continued to irk me. Why did only one of them have their palms stamped?

'Everything is possible. We must examine the lives of each victim again for a connection to Cromwell or Spector.'

'Get Sutton and Grealish to pursue that.' The hot drink

awakened some of my brain cells. 'But there's another possibility we have to consider.'

'What's that?'

'That there's no link between the victims and the killer is doing this to mess with us. And these letters are an important part of that process.'

He stared at the paper on the table.

'*Choose harmony and percussion* looks like a direct mention of Robby Riot and his musical career.'

'Did he sing and play the drums?'

Jack sat at the computer and went online.

'According to the band's website, he sang backing vocals on several songs.' He flicked through a few more pages. 'He was the lead singer in some of his other groups.'

I reread the letter in my mind.

'Do we assume the unwaking realm is supposed to be death? It's not one of his former bands, is it? Robby Riot and the Unwaking Realm.'

Jack scrolled through the rest of the site.

'Not according to this.'

I checked the updated case files, flicking through the crime scene photos and settling on Dr Cooper's autopsy report, which wasn't helpful: Riot's murder was still undetermined.

'Has anyone been to his flat? I can't see any information about it on the computer.'

'Uniforms visited yesterday but left empty-handed. The key's at the front desk if you fancy a trip out there.'

I considered the option as the rest of the team arrived. Constable Sutton stepped through the door first. Jack nodded at her.

'I'll get her started on the victims again for links to Tommy Cromwell.'

'They taunted us last night, Cromwell and Spector.' It continued to burn at the back of my head. How brazen they were. 'Twice she dodged our surveillance at her flat, and then she let the officers follow her to the restaurant.'

'From what I've heard from a mate in the Organised Crime Squad, Cromwell is a right arrogant bastard, and a vicious one.'

Might they be responsible for these Penguin murders and letters? Perhaps they started it to get back at Oswald Blair, and then continued for their own twisted reasons.

I left Jack to give Sutton and Grealish their duties and returned to the latest letter, typing the text into the computer file with the other three. I printed the combined document so Jack could hand it to the rest of the team. Then I stared at the words for an hour until my eyes blurred. In between, there were many conversations with Jack, Sutton, Grealish and anyone else unwise enough to seek my opinion.

Lunchtime was approaching when I received the summons to Chief Superintendent Cane's office. Perhaps she was ready to replace me.

But it was worse than that.

'I need to inform you about Abigail's case, Jen.'

'Case?'

I'd hoped it wouldn't get this far. It was foolish of me to think that, but I'd been kidding myself. I guess ignoring it wasn't the best strategy. The time at the comic shop and the sessions with Felicia Nelson weren't to distract Abbey from the seriousness of what she'd done; they were to distract me. I slumped into the nearest chair before my legs gave way.

'Yes, Abbey's case.'

'What's happening?'

The words tumbled from my lips like climbers falling

down a mountain. She opened a folder and rifled through its contents.

'The Detective Constable in charge - I think you know him, Bullock - is preparing the case file. His team have interviewed students and staff from your daughter's school.' She shuffled the papers between her hands before placing them on top of the folder. 'Even though we have a statement from Abigail regarding the incident, he'd like to speak to her again.' Her gaze never left my face. 'To clarify a few issues, you understand.'

'Yes, Chief.'

'So we need your permission for the interview.' She pushed a new piece of paper towards me. 'And you must be with her.'

'With our solicitor?'

I hadn't even contacted one yet.

'That's your prerogative, Jen.'

Every part of me ached as I got out of the chair, the sound of drums beating inside my head. I took a pen from the desk, read through the text, and signed the paper. I'd stepped halfway out of her office when she asked me about the progress of The Penguin investigation. I closed the door behind me without replying. I must have had a face like thunder when Jack approached me.

'I'm guessing it wasn't good news?'

My fingernails tasted of soap and I craved a packet of cigarettes. Or a large glass of wine. Perhaps both.

'I'm popping home to speak to Abbey.' He didn't ask why. 'I'll meet you at Robby Riot's place in two hours.'

He didn't reply as I left. I slumped into the car before reflecting on how I'd known Jack all these years, and it was the first time I'd lied to him. I was in no rush to tell Abbey the news; I didn't want to worry her. My face collapsed onto the steering wheel as terrible images filled my head. The pain was too much; I needed to get rid of it quickly, or I'd be no use to Abbey or my colleagues.

I convinced myself I was doing the right thing during the ride to the comic shop. The clock slipped past midday, and I'd had nothing to eat since breakfast, but my hunger was for something else. Steve was sitting behind the till when I got there, his smile warm enough to start a fire. I didn't give him time to speak.

'Is there somewhere private we can talk?'

'Sure, Jen. My office is at the back.'

He snapped out of the chair, and I followed him past a stack of life-sized cardboard cut-outs of *Star Trek* characters. Inside, the room was a mess, with books and comics everywhere, piles of toys and promotional material piled against the walls. His smile hadn't left him.

'I lied to you, Steve.'

'What?'

The fear in his face made me laugh.

'I don't want to talk.'

His eyes widened as I pushed him against the wall, my fingers pulling at his shirt as my lips found his. He tasted of apple juice and smelt of pine trees. He appeared confused at first, with his arms in the air as if he didn't know where to put them. As my tongue sank into his mouth, his hands gripped my waist and grabbed at my clothes.

I drew away, searching for breath as I tore off my jacket. A rainbow sparkled in his eyes. I seized his trousers and undid the button, fumbling with the zip before pushing him onto the desk. He lay there and stared at me, our heart's beating in unison.

'Are you sure about this, Jen?'

I was. I had to wipe away everything rushing through

my skull. It didn't matter if this was right or wrong; I needed something to make me feel good, to help me forget all the bad stuff, if only for a short while.

'What did I say about talking?'

I straddled him as our clothes dropped into the surrounding junk.

———

HE APPEARED GLAZED when it was over. I gathered my discarded gear from the clutches of a Darth Vader statue. One of its arms had broken off in the frenzy.

'I'll see you tonight, Steve. Back here sometime.'

He nodded, seemingly lost for words. I turned and left the office. I'd lied and been impulsive all in one afternoon, and it felt great. My hair looked like a bird's nest when I saw my face in the shop window. A few members of staff and customers gave me startled looks as I went.

Back in the car, I did my best to return a semblance of respectability to my appearance. Seeing my reflection in the mirror shocked me; my face was a mess, but I was happy.

I wondered how long it would last as I drove to Robby Riot's house in Camden.

Jack was inside when I got there.

'Do I need my hands and shoes covered?'

He shook his head. 'I wouldn't think so.' He scrutinised me. 'There's something different about you, Jen.'

'I've just had sex.'

'Ah.' He seemed lost for words. 'Some afternoon delight, eh? Anyone I know?'

I ignored the question and checked the house.

The place stank of damp and mildew. The entrance was rotten and needed a lick of paint; the doors inside were

no better. The hallway was narrow, its carpet scuffed and discoloured. The first room contained two sofas, an armchair, coffee table and a bookshelf, plus a combined TV and sound system. A speaker was attached to the wall in each corner, patterned paper peeling from the walls.

Scattered over the floor were empty bottles, glasses, and cups, while a bucketful of stains added colour to the carpet. A bunch of CDs were stacked against a chair, the Doors reaching down to the Velvet Underground. Tubes of lipstick stood close to the music, alongside discarded cigarette packets and a suspicious-looking white powder.

We walked across the room and into the kitchen containing a fridge and a microwave. Empty tins of baked beans and spaghetti hoops were upturned on the sides, snuggled next to breakfast cereal boxes and a mouldy loaf of bread.

Upstairs were two bedrooms and a bathroom. The toilet was broken and used, but unflushed; the bathtub had more rings around it than Saturn. A cracked mirror was so dirty that I hardly saw my reflection.

The first bedroom was the bigger, including a large double bed, table with lamp, wardrobe, and shelves; records and tapes filled the other one. I rifled through some of them, discovering material Robby Riot had played on. Three VHS copies of *On The Waterfront* lay under the bed.

We stared at each other in frustration at finding nothing to show who had murdered him, with no apparent links to any of the other victims or Carrie Spector or Tommy Cromwell. I walked through a pile of another person's rubbish, strode through the remains of someone's life, and out of the house.

I spoke to one of Riot's neighbours as we exited, a tall man who, going by his physique, had more in common with a giraffe than a person. The rash of spots covering his face did nothing to discourage that. His name was Alan Bleater. Jack asked the question.

'What did you think of Robby Riot, Mr Bleater?'

His nostrils vibrated as he snorted derision.

'Robby Riot! That wasn't his real name, you know.' He waved a wrinkled hand in front of him. 'Robert was a used car salesman putting on Jagger's airs and graces, and as interesting as the small print on the back of a tube of Toilet Duck.'

He was twisting his head to one side to spit on the floor until he remembered who he was speaking to.

'Did you ever see any evidence of drug use here?' I said. 'Or any criminal activity?'

He shrugged. 'I keep myself to myself.'

I thanked him and we left. A drizzle of rain was hovering in the air when we got outside. Jack wiped a bit from his forehead.

'What next, partner?'

'I don't know about you, Jack, but I'm starving.' The water settled in my hair. 'Let's return to the station and order food. It'll be a long day.'

My stomach rumbled, my legs ached, and my mind swam with images of Abbey behind bars.

The time crawled towards eight o'clock. Everyone had left apart from Jack and me as he made coffee. The big screen in the centre of the room displayed a news channel with the sound muted. I stared at the information we'd gathered for five murders and wondered again what I'd missed.

My eyes drifted from the bundle of papers of Edwin Blair's unpublished novel and towards the screen where his father was speaking to a gaggle of reporters. His words ran across the bottom, but I wanted to hear what he said so increased the volume. Jack handed me the drink as the Home Secretary addressed the nation.

'It doesn't matter how long it takes, even if we have to stay up all night to get the final touches finished for this Bill, we will get it done.' He looked as tired as I felt. *'Never again will violent criminals leave prison after completing only half of their sentence.'*

'Poor bastard,' Jack said. 'This comes too late for his son.'

Blair continued, waving an imaginary piece of paper in

the air. '*There will be no more creative loopholes in the legal system exploited by the privileged and well educated.*

'He's got a cheek, saying that.'

I ignored Jack and peered at Blair's words rolling across the bottom of the screen.

'Fuck.'

I rarely swore, the last time being when I thought Abbey was about to meet a paedophile who'd groomed her online. Jack gazed at me in amazement. Then I dropped the mug onto the floor. It didn't break, but the dark liquid spread everywhere, forcing Jack to jump out of the way to keep his flash shoes dry.

'Jesus, Jen. Are you okay?'

I watched the coffee consume the wood as Oswald Blair's face disappeared from the screen. Then I barked instructions at my partner.

'Get the team back. And ring Cane.'

'Everyone's tired, Jen. Some haven't slept for days. Whatever this is, can't it wait until morning?'

My response was a glare; he sighed and started the calls. I grabbed my phone and dialled a number. A miserable bloke answered.

'The Office of the Home Secretary.'

'This is Detective Inspector Flowers. I need to talk to him immediately.'

The grumpy man spoke as if I was a child.

'Don't you watch the news, Inspector? He won't be free to talk to anyone until the morning. You can call back then.'

'This concerns the murder of his son. If he doesn't speak to me, the killer is likely to escape. Then I'll let you explain to him how it happened.'

The silence lasted for thirty seconds before I heard a heavy thump and then footsteps scampering from the room.

Jack looked at me as if I was crazed. Before I could say anything, Oswald Blair spoke to me.

'What's this about my son's killer, Inspector?'

I expected him to spit blood down the line.

'You said Edwin left school with no qualifications, but was there a chance he might have gone to Oxford or Cambridge?'

There was silence again, but I imagined him seething on the other side of London.

'Edwin could have attended any university in the world, Inspector, but he refused. He hated academia and the educational system. He put on a rebellious front as if throwing the opportunities back in my face because he knew how much it irritated me. Deep down, I knew he was hiding something from me.'

'Do you know what that was?'

I'd felt enough guilt about raising my child, and now, even though only a thin piece of cable connected us, I sensed it seeping from him.

'Edwin and I never talked about this, Inspector Flowers, so I hope you appreciate the sensitivity of what I'm about to tell you.' I said nothing and waited for him to continue. 'I'm unsure if it was due some learning disability, maybe dyslexia, but Edwin struggled to read. I never understood how difficult it was for him at school, always believing his difficulties were about rebelling against me.'

'I'll be back in touch soon, Minister.'

I hung up as the team shuffled back. They must have been in the building when Jack called them. He was mopping the drink from the floor when he spoke.

'Are you going to tell me what's happening?'

I grabbed the title page from *The Mage of Avalon. A*

Novel of High Fantasy by EE Blair and turned to Constable Sutton.

'Did you go through this?'

She appeared guilty. 'I only read the first couple of chapters. It's terrible. And once he started getting into sexual assault as a plot point, I needed a break from it. I'm sorry, ma'am.'

I waved away her apology and strode towards the boards covered with photos from Edwin Blair's apartment.

'What's missing in these images?'

Everyone gathered around, staring at them for the thousandth time.

Jack dropped the mop against the wall.

'My head hurts, Jen. Put me out of my misery.'

I pushed the manuscript's title page up against the big screen, static electricity making the hairs stand up on end on my arm.

'There are no books here. How do you write a novel if you don't read?'

Jack pointed to one photo.

'He had all those horror DVDs, but nothing else; no newspapers, no magazines or any reading material.' He turned to me. 'There was no computer, laptop, or printer in his place. So how did he complete that manuscript?'

'That's the whole point, Jack. He couldn't have.' I dumped the title page back with the rest of the manuscript. 'Our killer wrote *The Mage of Avalon* and left it there for us.'

'Shit!' Sutton said. 'And I didn't read it all.'

'We're all going to read it. Get copies for everyone.' I couldn't wipe away the guilt on her face since I felt the same for missing something so obvious. 'Did you digitise the four letters from the killer into text files?'

She nodded and pointed at the computer. 'They're on the desktop.'

I sat at the machine, found the documents, and made copies of them. Jack was at my side as I worked.

'How did we miss the significance of the manuscript?'

I finished the first file and sent a dozen copies to the printer before moving onto the next letter. I talked as I typed.

'You go to a person's home, and you assume everything there is theirs, don't you? We had no reason to believe the killer visited the flat, so why assume those papers came from them? We were searching in the wrong places from the start, including these letters.' The second was done and sent to the printer. 'Hand these to the team while I complete the others.'

He did that as I sprinted through letters three and four. When I'd finished, everyone had a copy of each letter where I'd separated the sentences into single paragraphs. I put the first one onto the screen and addressed the team.

'Forget the *Dear Boss* bit at the front. That was a distraction, so we'd focus on hoaxes and Jack the Ripper. It's the start of each sentence which is important.'

I read them out as separated paragraphs.

Choke the man in the woods.

Hung out to dry and die.

And watch him struggle and squirm.

Perhaps I'll let him live.

To dream he could have a better life.

Ever eternal with no more suffering.

Ready player gone.

Only to die every day.

Now send this out to the media so they'll know my message.

Exquisite corpse with no tongue for tales to tell.

'Ignore the words and stop trying to analyse what each part means.' Something we'd done from the start. 'Scrutinise the initial letter of each line.'

'CHAPTER ONE,' Jack said.

I changed the screen to show the second letter and read it out.

Catch the blood from his neck.
Harvest the organs into a fine pie.
A tasty morsel for the masses to feast upon.
Purse your lips before licking them.
To eat is to live.
Eager to dine on the divine.
Resurrection of the soul.
Two for the price of one.
When day changes into night.
Only the brave come out to play.

'CHAPTER TWO,' Sutton said.

'For the third and fourth letters, they either became frustrated with us for missing their message, or they got bored we were taking so long. So they shortened and simplified them.'

I switched the display over.

'The third letter is CHAPTER THREE: *Chaos harbours anarchy passing through eternal rest. These hours require entropy's existence.*'

'Damn, damn, damn,' Jack said.

'And the last letter is CHAPTER FOUR: *Choose harmony and percussion to erase reason from our unwaking realm.*'

I let that information sink in, and then highlighted what we'd all missed until now.

'Each murder is a chapter in a book he's writing; this is all about being a writer.'

'It's a serialisation,' Jack said, 'in chapters.'

'That's what makes him an original Serial Killer.' It was funny how things fell into place once you knocked down the first domino. 'He's a failed writer.'

Jack scanned the pages for the third and fourth letters, and then dropped them onto the table.

'This is about the Avalon book?'

'I'm guessing that isn't his only attempt at writing a novel. This may be his fifth or sixth go, the one he's most proud of, but he still couldn't get anywhere with it. Any normal person would have self-published it online, but his ego doesn't work that way. He got creative by trying to commit perfect crimes while playing with the police, playing with us.'

Jack picked the title page of the novel up.

'But this isn't his name on the front, it's Edwin Blair's.'

'No, it's EE Blair. What's Edwin's middle name, Sutton?'

She rifled through the files on the table instead of heading for the computer and found what I wanted.

'It was Eric.'

'Eric Blair,' I said, 'whose pen name was George Orwell.' I pointed at the murder boards. 'All our victims have the same name or pseudonym as famous authors.'

'Mary Evans, Clive Hamilton and Bob Galbraith,' Jack said. 'I'm no expert on books, so I don't know who they are.'

Grealish completed quick searches on the computer.

'Mary Ann Evans is George Eliot, Clive Hamilton is CS Lewis, and Robert Galbraith is JK Rowling.'

'The Harry Potter writer,' Jack said.

'That's the one.' It was like light bulbs exploding inside

my head. 'In his warped state, he started killing people with the same name, or pseudonym, as famous authors.'

'A failed author kills in chapters while playing cat and mouse with us.' Jack grabbed a chair and slumped into it.

'That's how it appears. So how do we use this information to find them before they strike again?' I spoke to all of them. 'We need to read this novel for anything identifying the author. We must contact every literary agency in the country and ask if they remember this book.'

Sutton looked at me.

'They get hundreds of unpublished books sent to them daily. It'll be a needle in a haystack expecting anyone to recollect this.'

'It doesn't matter; we must do it. And we have to consider where our killer got the names of his victims.'

Jack finished his coffee and placed the cup on the table.

'I'd guess it was the phonebook or the electoral register.'

I agreed with him. 'It's more likely to be the register. Many opt-out of the phonebook, but it's the law to be in the electoral register.'

He stood and led me to the side.

'This will take time, Jen. These people need some rest; so do we. We'll start again in the morning.'

'And if our killer strikes again tonight?'

'If they do, then our Penguin is way ahead in the planning stages. There's nothing we can do to stop it now.'

He was right, but my brain was operating at a thousand miles an hour, no matter how tired my body was. I told everyone to take a copy of the book home, and we'd return to work in the morning. As they left, I understood we'd be no closer to catching our killer until they struck again.

I was about to grab a copy for myself before realising I had to be somewhere else.

'I need a drink.'

'That's an excellent idea, Jen. Let's go to the pub.'

It wasn't about to happen. I wanted male company, but not his. And I couldn't tell him that, so I lied again.

'Thanks, but I'm going straight home.'

'Okay, but get some rest.'

The phone was in my hand before I'd left the building.

'Do you want to get together now?'

I wondered if Steve heard the desperation in my voice.

'Definitely. I'm still at the shop. Meet me here?'

'You're working late?'

'I had a flash mob sale tonight, and the last of the customers are just leaving.'

'Okay. I'll see you in fifteen minutes.'

My mind was a mess on the drive over, chastising myself for missing all the clues our Serial Killer had planted right from the beginning. When I pulled up outside Soapbox Comics, two young women dressed all in black were laughing as they left the shop. I recognised them as Steve's staff.

The place looked like a bomb had hit it when I walked inside, with shoe marks all over the floor and boxes and rubbish strewn everywhere. Steve came from behind the counter and stared at me. Then he strode over and gave me an enormous hug. He let go about a minute later.

'I think you needed that.'

'I need a drink more.'

He glanced around his emporium.

'No problem. I'll clean up tomorrow morning.'

'Were you attacked by a plague of locusts?'

He grinned as he ushered me towards the exit.

'Something like that. The customers on my mailing list get the first option of merchandise during a flash sale, and some of them are quite energetic. The regulars will have their chance tomorrow.' He set the alarm and locked the door behind us. 'Which bar first?'

'Do you have booze at your house?'

'Always.'

I grabbed hold of his hand and dragged him towards the car.

'Then I'll drive there.'

36 ATMOSPHERE

As we stumbled off the pavement, I pushed my mouth onto his. When I came up for air, there were no thoughts of failed writers or dead authors in my head. I forced him against the wall, my hand inside his shirt and pulling at his flesh. He returned the favour as heat rushed through me. We only stopped when bystanders gawped at us. I wiped the desire from my lips as he dragged me to the car. What I was doing was terrible, a dereliction of duty while forgetting about Abbey's current predicament. But it had to be done.

The drive took fewer than twenty minutes, the air tingling with anticipation between us. He drove erratically, his eyes barely on the road, and it didn't improve when I put my hand on his leg. Some loud dance music blared from the radio, but it only added to the noise in my head.

He drove into a parking garage.

We got out, and I stepped past the stack of boxes at the door, noticing the piles of comics and books. I was moving towards a table of toy figures when he grabbed my hand and pulled me into his grasp. His mouth was on mine, his fingers fumbling at the top of my trousers, his yearning all over me. I eased him away and caught my breath. His smile could have lit up the night sky.

'Welcome to my humble home, Jen.'

I followed him up the steps and into his house. There was nothing humble about it.

'How can you afford this?'

There were more comics everywhere, the walls adorned with framed artwork of characters I didn't recognise: a Nordic woman brandishing a broadsword, a vampire swooping to devour a victim, and a preacher wearing an eyepatch.

He slipped the lock on the door as I removed my jacket and hung it in the corridor.

'I bought it when I started teaching twenty years ago. This entire area was far less chic then than it is now, and I got it for a bargain price. Do you want a drink?'

He led me into a spacious living room transported from a Victorian mansion, with the walls covered by the heads of stuffed animals and shelves overflowing with books. Computer equipment and mobile phones lay on a table at the back. An expensive-looking sound system stood in front of me, with a stack of records either side of it. I scanned through his collection, most of which was from the 1960s.

'Pour me a rum and coke if you have it.' I glanced around the place. 'It seems rather large for one person.'

He headed for the drinks cabinet.

'It gives me enough space for storage.' He handed me the drink. 'There's a bedroom, kitchen and bathroom at the end, then this room and my study here.'

He pointed into a spot behind me. I picked up the second Kate Bush album from his pile of records, the cellophane wrapping wrinkling against my fingers. An alcove separated the living room and his study. I had the glass at my lips and peered into the other room, noticing a cabinet full of what must have been the first edition books he'd told me about.

I held the alcohol from me.

'This isn't Coke.'

'Sorry, but I only have Pepsi. Do you want something else?'

'That's okay. If I drink it quick enough, I won't taste it. I'll have the next one straight, but I need the bathroom now.'

He pointed back along the corridor.

'It's on your right through there.'

I smiled and left him. When I returned five minutes later, I handed him my empty glass.

'It's been a stressful day.'

'I bet it has.'

I moved towards the alcove and eyed the dozen novels on the wall in his study.

'When you told me about collecting first edition books, I assumed you meant hardbacks and not those.'

'I've always preferred paperbacks, ones with a history behind them. And these are the original ten novels published by the most famous of British publishers.'

I moved closer to his collection. They were thin volumes with white across the middle and three different colours around that: two green, two blue and four orange. They were a well-known design. I reached over, expecting him to tell me to stop, but he didn't. I removed Agatha Christie's *The Mysterious Affair at Styles*. The bird in the middle differed from the one I'd seen stamped on the palms of the victims, but the animal was unmistakable.

I held the book towards him.

'Penguins?'

He nodded. 'They are the best.'

He stood between me and the exit. Staring at his face, I noticed for the first time the pronounced gaps between his back teeth as if they were bars separating the guilty from the innocent. I let the edition slip from my hands, waiting for him to jump forward and catch it, but he only watched as it dived into the carpet.

'Oops,' I said.

There was no fire in his eyes, no flickering of eyebrows or twitching of those chiselled cheeks. I glanced down at the book and noticed the new dent along the spine.

'Don't worry about it, Jen. You're not yourself at the moment.'

His feet were frozen to the spot, arm rising like a flag at half-mast as he brought the drink to his mouth. He nibbled at the glass, his teeth making a grating noise which set my nerves on edge. I took one step forward and put my shoe over the image of the penguin on the book. My gaze fixed on him as I pressed down on the novel.

'Do you remember telling me about your failed efforts to create a comic book when you were a kid?'

His eyes darted around me, moving everywhere but towards that precious book of his under my foot.

'I couldn't forget that. I've told no one else about my creative failures.'

I stepped back from him.

'Did you try to write novels after that?'

'I did, many times.' He sipped at his drink. 'I've lost count of all the rejections I've had.'

'Life is one long revolving conveyor belt of rejections, Steve.' Sand stuck to the insides of my mouth, so I wriggled my tongue around while I spoke. I must have sounded like a tape recording played in slow motion, or a radio station drifting in and out of frequency; at least I did inside my head. 'It starts for us as children when we realise how imperfect our parents are. Then it continues at school with daggered words from the teachers and bullets of insults from our peers. As we grow up and enter the real world, expecting everything to improve once like-minded adults surround us, we find most of them don't have brains, never mind ones similar to ours. We're rejected by family and friends all the time; even the occasional stranger will discard us if we're dumb enough to fall for them. We're throwaway people, Steve, that's all life is.'

He shook with laughter, his shoulders undulating like a leaky waterbed.

'Jesus, Jen, who fucked up your life?'

I didn't bother to tell him the answer was me. Instead, I spoke to the heart of the matter.

'Is *The Mage of Avalon* your newest book?'

He placed his drink on the bookcase and clapped his hands. The sound echoed around the room, adding to the irritation nipping at the insides of my ears.

'Congratulations for figuring it out, though I'm surprised it took you so long.' He returned to his glass. 'It's the latest and last of my great works. Did you know it was me before you came here tonight?'

I ignored the question and kicked the Christie book towards him.

'Is that why you stamped the penguin image onto the hands of your victims, because of your collection?'

'I thought it a nice touch. I wanted to be a more intellectual criminal than you'd dealt with before.' He grinned at me. 'More well-read, you might say.'

'The letters were clever.' His ego didn't need a massage,

but I did it anyway. 'What triggered you on this splurge of murder?'

Stars sparkled in his eyes and in that instant I knew this was what Steve had been waiting for all along, why he'd killed five people, and scattered a trail of breadcrumbs for me or someone to find: he needed to tell his story in person. He drooled as he spoke, vast gobs of spit cascading over his lips.

'Do you recognise what everyone wants?' I recognised my urge to flatten him. 'We need to be larger than this life, to grace a pedestal and peer down at everyone else, to tower above the masses and decry how magnificent we are compared to the rest of them. There's a reason we stand in awe of great statues, and it's because of their height, because they reach up to the prominence that every one of us strives for, whether or not we realise it. Do you think people gaze in wonder at Nelson's Column because of who it represents or because of its size? My greatness is my writing, but nobody would acknowledge its existence, would acknowledge my existence.'

'You couldn't get your book published?'

'I sent *The Mage of Avalon* to more than a hundred literary agents and publishers and received nothing but silence and rejection.' Anger rose in his voice. 'It wasn't about the writing or the quality of the story. It was more insidious than that.'

He towered between me and the exit from the house. I'd thought dropping the Christie book might distract him, now I had to think of something else. First, I had to increase his rising emotional state.

'How was it insidious?'

'It's hard for people like me, older white men, to break into the publishing industry.' His knuckles cracked as he gripped onto the glass. 'Everything is about diversity today. I never had a chance, regardless of the quality of my writing.'

His cheeks turned red, his flesh a sickly shade of gammon. He stepped forward, and I moved further back, away from him and my only means of escape.

'I'm sure traditional publishing contains ninety-plus per cent white blokes, Steve. But even if it didn't, you could have self-published your book online.'

He slammed his glass onto the desk so hard, bits of rum leapt over the side.

'No self-respecting author would do that. Have you read some of the cheap novels which have flooded Amazon and other sites? Most are littered with mistakes and writing so terrible, a child could have written them.'

He was a human kettle ready to boil. I only had to keep turning up the heat, making sure I didn't get burnt.

'So you sent your book out again but under a different name?'

'I considered lying and pretending to be a female writer, but dismissed it. Orwell is my favourite author, and I loved the idea of taking his real name as my new identity. And then I thought agents would laugh at me for that, so I chose EE Blair as my *nom de plume*. Imagine my surprise when I went online and found there was already someone with that name living near to me.'

'Is that when you decided on your killing spree?'

He shook his head and his lips trembled as he spoke.

'No, that was never my intention. It was only when I gathered more information on Edwin Blair and discovered he'd had everything handed to him on a plate that things took shape. I visited that club once, such a terrible place, and watched him pick up women with no effort.'

'You staked out his house, knew when he'd go jogging and which way. But how did you strangle him without Blair putting up a fight?'

I had to keep him talking while I figured a way out.

'You're right about me memorising his route. Before he entered those woods, he always visited the convenience store on the corner for a bottle of flavoured water. All I had to do was get in there before him, making sure nobody saw me when I switched bottles for one I'd prepared earlier. I bought the two bottles in the shop and slipped in the one I'd brought with me.' He gazed into the air and grinned. 'Just imagine, Jen, you wouldn't be here now if it had all gone wrong at that point. Fate favoured me then and ever since.'

There were more cracks in him than a box of broken Ritz.

'What was in the bottle?'

'Rohypnol; enough so it would affect him within a few minutes of drinking, and I knew he never opened the water until he got into the woods. Then I dragged him from the path, dropped the rope around his neck, and looped the rest of it over the branch. It was harder than I expected to lift him, but it was over quickly. All I had to do then was get his key and let myself into his flat to leave my book there.'

'Rohypnol?'

The date rape drug.

'Yes. It was a larger dose than I put in your rum and Pepsi, but you should experience its kick right about now.'

My legs trembled and I stumbled into the wall of books behind me. His collection of Penguin first editions crashed to the floor.

'Don't worry, Jen, the dose wasn't large enough to knock you out yet. I need you awake for your special treat.'

I didn't ask him what that was.

'Let me guess: once you started killing, you couldn't stop. But why send those letters to me? You could have played cat and mouse with any police force in the city.'

'None of that was my choice. One of your friends wanted you involved.'

'What are you talking about?'

As I backed up against the far wall, he reached onto the table and pulled a box towards him. He removed a bunch of comics from it.

'When we first met, do you remember me telling you about the literacy work I did taking comics to schools, community centres and nursing homes?'

'Vaguely.' I didn't, but I guessed it must have been on that initial speed date, which now seemed so long ago. 'You're a real pillar of the community, Steve.'

I tried to forget what we'd done in his office; the memory of it made my flesh crawl.

'It was a helpful experience for getting me into other places where literacy was important. I have to admit, though, working with the inmates was daunting.'

'Inmates? You took comics into prisons?'

That didn't sound good.

'I only visited one prison. Guess who I met there?' I shrugged, hoping he was becoming too relaxed by this little story of his. 'Someone you betrayed and abandoned.'

He could only mean one person.

'Alice Voss?'

'Bingo. Can you believe they don't let her read newspapers or books? God knows what they think she'd do with them. I couldn't take any horror or crime comics into the prison, they were far too problematic, and they vetted everything I took. But they let Alice read them. They underestimated her intellect, but once I started leaving coded messages in the comics, she replied to me the same way. It wasn't long before we got together.'

'You're in love with her.'

Christ, not another one. What was it with blokes and deranged women? Perhaps that's what attracted him to me?

He beamed at me.

'I cannot tell a lie. It was love at first sight, but I'm sure it took longer for her.'

'You've spoken to each other, not just through coded comic book messages?'

'I told you, the prison authorities wanted me to teach the inmates some literacy skills. Do you know sixty per cent of prisoners have difficulty in basic reading and writing? Once I told the governor I'd help with that, he jumped at the opportunity. Only I couldn't teach so many by myself, so I requested support from the more well-educated convicts.'

'And Alice was one of them?'

'It surprised me how it fell into place. It wasn't long after that we had wonderful telephone conversations. You featured in most of them.'

'She has access to a phone?'

He removed one from his pocket.

'You can smuggle anything into a prison nowadays.'

I gripped the wall. 'I hope you stuck it somewhere painful.'

He laughed. 'You are a card, Jen. Are you ready for your special treat?' He pressed the screen and I heard a number dialling. Then it stopped as he spoke into the phone. 'Flowers is here and knows everything. Do you want to speak to her?'

He showed me the device; Alice Voss stared at me. She looked as if she was on holiday in Ibiza and not a guest of the prison service with her tan.

'You look tired, Jen. Are you drinking too much again?'

'Your mug would drive anyone to booze, Voss.'

Morris raised his hand to hit me, the phone shaking between his fingers.

'Don't talk to her like that.'

His eyes blazed wide for an eternity before shrinking again; then he dropped his arm, and Voss gazed at me from a cell somewhere in the city. I considered the likelihood I'd get past him without the use of violence, which was minimal, and be able to beat him down in my current state. I spoke to her while the wheels turned slowly inside my mind.

'Even locked up, you're still manipulating others.'

Her face took up the entire screen and I resisted the temptation to smash it against the wall.

'We're a match made in heaven.'

'This is all your doing, these Penguin murders?'

She moved her head from side to side. I think she was trying to control her enjoyment. Perhaps if I got her angry, one of her guards would see what she was doing.

'No. I can't take credit for this killing spree. Steven had most of it planned before he visited the prison the first time. But it was my idea to get you involved, though he wasn't too happy with that.'

I glanced at him. 'You're not that brave, are you, Steve?'

He continued to sneer at me.

'Count yourself lucky I abandoned my original plan, or it would be your daughter struggling to stay awake now.'

My legs turned to lead and I had to use the wall to stop myself from slipping to the floor and joining the discarded book.

'What?'

'I didn't want to get this close to the police. I had to leave my clues, write my chapters as letters, and have someone in authority find my manuscript. My plan was for four murders - it was unfortunate Mary Evans brought her friend with her - and then I'd be captured, and my story broadcast everywhere. The world would recognise my genius, and I'd be famous forever.'

'You'll only be remembered as a serial killer, in the archives next to Peter Sutcliffe or Fred West. No one will be interested in your books, Steve.'

I pinned my back to the wall, my body searching for strength.

'You're wrong, Jen. The public is fascinated by true crime and murderers and what makes them tick. The masses will devour *The Mage of Avalon* and my other books.' His anger had vanished, replaced by unbridled joy. 'Even fifty years after the Manson murders, people still talk about the terrible music he made. They'll go mad for my books once everyone knows what I've done.'

The sound of Voss's voice from the phone shook him out of his euphoria.

'Now remember, Steven, we talked about this, and we changed your strategy for a better one.' He was holding the mobile so close to his face, I thought he'd try to kiss her through the screen. I wanted him to so I could push it into his ugly mug. 'We have an alternative plan now, and once you complete it, we'll be together again.'

He calmed his breathing and switched the device around so I saw her while he spoke.

'I followed you from your house, wanting to ensure you weren't coming straight back so I could sneak in and do what I had to and deal with Abigail.' Her name on his lips made me sick. 'But then I watched you head to that bar for a speed dating session, and the plan changed.'

'I told him it would be easy to charm someone as desperate as you.' Voss grinned at me from the phone. 'All he had to do was go along the next time and trick you into thinking he liked you.'

'This is all for revenge, Alice? I gave you more credit than that.'

Her laugh made the mobile quiver in his hand.

'It's much more than that, Jen. My fortuitous meeting with Steven will lead to my freedom and your downfall.'

'What?'

'Have you been listening to my podcasts with Charlie Nightingale? They release the final one tomorrow night.'

'I'm waiting for you to confess to all your crimes as the Hashtag Killer.'

She continued with that annoying laugh.

'Then you'll be disappointed, Jen. That's if you're around to listen to it. You're about to disappear from the face of the earth, once Steven separates you into body parts and disposes of them. Then he'll go to work in your house.'

I glared at her. 'If he touches Abbey...'

She sneered at me. 'Oh, stop worrying, Jen. It's your computer and laptop he wants.'

'Why?'

'It's a shame you'll miss my last podcast. The revelations are worth waiting for.'

'What revelations?'

'When the world discovers how your hatred for me added to your inability to solve the crimes of the Hashtag Killer and led to you planting false evidence in my home. That's what I'll reveal in tomorrow's podcast. The media will want to speak to you, but, thanks to Steven, no one will see you again. And with what he's going to place on your computer, hidden files which won't escape my old colleagues in Cybercrime, my wonderful new lawyer will get my conviction quashed in record time. And then Steven and I will be together forever.'

'You're a lunatic, Alice.'

'Now, Jen. Don't be bitter because you've been outclassed and out thought. Steven perceives our meeting as being like one of his comic book villain team-ups, but I've never seen myself as the villain of this story.'

'Perhaps so, Alice, but never rely on others for your dirty work.'

I stepped towards Morris's grinning mug and kicked him in the knee with the bottom of my foot. He must have had brittle bones because it snapped like a twig and he crumpled to the carpet with a beautiful look of agony consuming his face. The phone crashed to his side.

'Fuck!'

His scream was music to my ears. I stamped on his hand for good measure; he cried again as his fingers broke.

'That was a possibility when I came here, Steve, but you blew it.' I grabbed the mobile from the floor. 'Did you know, Alice, your partner was recording this call? Maybe he recorded all the others.'

Her eyes bulged with fury.

'He should have given you the Rohypnol.'

'Oh, you mean the cringe-inducing Pepsi drink he handed me earlier? I threw that in the sink when I went to the bathroom.' I checked the clock in the top corner of the screen. 'Don't worry, Alice, there's still time to change the denouement of your last podcast.'

I ended the call before her puffy face burst through the device. I flicked through the video files, happy to see I was right and Morris had recorded the other calls between him and Voss; there were over thirty on the mobile, including tonight's.

He clutched at his damaged knee.

'This will only bring Alice and me closer together.'

I shook my head and removed my phone to call Jack.

'No, Steve, it won't. I'm sure once my colleagues go through this place with a fine toothcomb, we'll find enough evidence of your crimes to put you behind bars for a long time. That and the videos you made of your conversations with Voss will put her in solitary confinement. There'll be no more podcasts, no more writing terrible novels for you. I'm only disappointed Abbey doesn't have a job anymore.'

I stepped beyond him as he sobbed. The call to Jack

lasted less than a minute, my partner and colleagues arriving at the house within fifteen. He offered me a pair of plastic gloves as he entered, glancing at Morris on the floor.

'Shall we start with the books in the study?'

I waved his hand away.

'No, you can do this without me. I have to see Abbey.'

They were cuffing Morris as I left, my mind focused only on one thing: what would Abbey be more disappointed about. The thought of going to juvenile court or learning she wouldn't be working in the comic shop?

I WAS at the station the next morning when Cane called me into her office. DCI Merson passed me in the corridor, averting her eyes from the smile consuming my face. I wondered what platitudes the Chief Superintendent was about to lay on me, but all she did was hand me her mobile phone.

'Someone wants to speak to you, Jen.'

I grabbed it from her and listened as the Home Secretary thanked my team and me for finding his son's killer so quickly. I told him I was only doing my job and congratulated him on getting the government's new crime bill through Parliament. And then he gave me the best news I'd had all year.

I TOOK a cup of coffee and a bacon sandwich from the canteen over to Jack. He grabbed it with relish.

'You look like you've won the lottery, Jen.'

'It's better than that, partner. Sir Oswald Blair just told

me he's spoken to Olivia Coates's parents, the school, and the officers dealing with Abbey's case, and he's convinced everyone to drop the entire thing.'

The sun blazed inside me. Jack used his coffee to salute me.

'That's splendid news, Jen. Are you going to phone Abbey and tell her?'

I settled into my seat and turned on the computer.

'I'll leave it for a few days and make her sweat a little.'

And perhaps the guilt I felt might eventually go away. But what could I do? It was terrible what had happened to that girl, but what mother would willingly let their daughter go to a juvenile court?

He shook his head and laughed.

'You're a cruel woman when you want to be, Jennifer Flowers.'

I stared at the screen, looking at the headlines about the discovery of fresh evidence proving Alice Voss was the Hashtag Killer and her links with Steven Morris, the so-called Penguin. I guess he got to be a comic book villain after all. Yes, I would have a pleasant morning reading through the webpages.

All I had to do now was find Abbey a part-time job.

SIX MONTHS LATER, Abbey was fourteen, had forgotten about comics, about being a writer and was busy working in a small café near Felicia Nelson's office. She continued with her sessions, going to Felicia's after her shift, and I'd pick her up when she finished. We hadn't spoken about them or what had fuelled her violence in the school library, but I was content to let her tell me at her own pace.

Around the same time, *The Mage of Avalon* appeared online. Published only as a free eBook, it was downloaded in the thousands in a matter of hours. I guessed once Morris's crimes became public, some dodgy literary agent remembered the terrible manuscript loitering in their slush pile and unleashed it upon the rest of the world.

I had no interest in that, but I found it amusing they'd spelt the author's name as Steph Morrison.

THANK YOU!

Thank you, dear reader for purchasing this book.

If you enjoyed reading about Inspector Jen Flowers her story continues in these books:

The Detective Jen Flowers series
Book one: The Hashtag Killer
Book two: Serial Killer
Book three: Night Killer
Book four: The Killer Inside Them

Bette Davis Eyes: Detective Flowers Short Story

Many thanks to my wonderful wife for all her support and patience.

Serial Killer edited by Alison Jack.

Extra special thanks to Karina Gallagher for being a dedicated reader of my work.

Cover design by James, GoOnWrite.com

ABOUT THE AUTHOR

Andrew French lives amongst faded seaside glamour on the North East coast of England. He likes gin and cats but not together, new music and old movies, curry and ice cream. Slow bike rides and long walks to the pub are his usual exercise, as well as flicking through the pages of good books and the memoirs of bad people.

Find out more at www.andrewsfrench.com

Facebook:

https://www.facebook.com/A-S-French-Author-150145625006018

Twitter:

www.twitter.com/andrewfrench100

Instagram:

www.instagram.com/andrewfrench100

And replies to all his email at mail@andrewsfrench.com

If you have the time, please leave a review at Amazon or Goodreads

Thank you!